What people are saying about

Priceless

"*Priceless* is one of those books that grabs your heart, breaks it, then spurs you on toward justice. Though fiction, the book shows the stark reality of the sex trade on the well-wrought canvas of Russia. It's an important book, a needed one, penned by one of our generation's prophets. Tom Davis captured me from page one, but the story still lingers."

Mary E. DeMuth, author of
Daisy Chain, A Slow Burn, and *Thin Places*

"I applaud Tom's courage in tackling this subject matter. While this is a fictional account, the sex trade is a reality for millions of people. My prayer is that through this well-written story, many would learn the actuality of this most heinous evil and discover our responsibility in becoming modern-day abolitionists. Thank you, Tom, for not only shining a spotlight, but for the reminder that every life, no matter who they are, is valuable beyond compare."

Natalie Grant, singer, songwriter, and
founder of The Home Foundation

"Tom Davis   est corner of society,
exposing a re   ruth that strikes right
at the heart.   )eing both challenged
and changed."

D1114660

Matt Bronleewe, award-winning music
producer, songwriter, and author of *Illuminated*

"Tom Davis's *Priceless* opens your eyes to a chilling reality that will rip at your heart as you come face-to-face with evil. But the story doesn't end before offering a ray of hope that even in the darkest places God's light can still break through. A must read!"

Lisa Harris, author of *Blood Ransom*

"*Priceless* is a compelling reminder of the value of every life. Tom Davis courageously and passionately captures the struggle of a nation, and gives a voice to children trapped in the horrors of sex trafficking. This novel will break your heart in the best possible way."

Anne Jackson, speaker and author
of *Permission to Speak Freely*

"If you are looking for a story that makes the harm of human trafficking visible, then *Priceless* is it. As one who has studied this modern form of slavery—traveled to over fifty countries to hear from victims and worked with hundreds of brave nongovernmental organizations who are fighting to eradicate it—I can say that Tom Davis has it right. This is a thriller that gets every detail right, down to the tattoos on the girls for sale and the soulless scum making money off these priceless children. Read it and weep. *And then take action.*"

Laura J. Lederer, former senior advisor
on Human Trafficking, Office for Global
Affairs, U.S. Department of State

What people are saying about …

Scared

"Tom Davis weaves his heart for orphans onto every page. The journey of *Scared* might lead you on a journey of your own—helping the orphans among us."

Karen Kingsbury, New York Times best-selling author of *Every Now and Then* and *Take One*

"With unflinching detail, Tom Davis uncovers the atrocity of the African AIDS epidemic and God's impossible triumph in its midst. Both sweeping in scope and intimate in expression, *Scared* leaves the reader with one burning question: How can I help?"

Matt Bronleewe, author of *Illuminated* and *House of Wolves*

"Tom Davis's first novel, *Scared*, is a startling beauty-for-ashes tale that takes readers on a journey to Swaziland and introduces them to the least of these Jesus speaks about in Matthew 25. You can't help but be changed by this heartbreaking, hope-fueling, oh-so-real story."

Claudia Mair Burney, author of *Zora and Nicky: A Novel in Black and White*

"Evocative and intense, *Scared* cuts deep into your heart as you read along. Healing fills the pages, yet there are no easy answers given, and it shows how each day is a struggle for the people of Swaziland to even survive. That's why the orphans and the widows need people who care. I loved how *Scared* showed that many of the sick and dying were truly victims of AIDS through no wrongdoing of their own. I've rarely experienced this level of realism in a novel, especially in the CBA. It's so realistic, it's downright edgy. Like the Holocaust, there are some awful things that happen in this book. Unspeakable things. But it also shows how God holds those who suffer close to His heart. You see that in this book in a way that is rarely portrayed in Christian fiction. All of the ugly stuff is not smoothed over, nor is the God-given compassion. It's graphic and harsh in some places, but so worth reading. I highly recommend it."

Michelle Sutton, editor-in-chief of
Christian Fiction Online Magazine

Priceless

Priceless

A NOVEL ON THE EDGE OF THE WORLD

TOM DAVIS

David C Cook®

transforming lives together

PRICELESS
Published by David C. Cook
4050 Lee Vance View
Colorado Springs, CO 80918 U.S.A.

David C. Cook Distribution Canada
55 Woodslee Avenue, Paris, Ontario, Canada N3L 3E5

David C. Cook U.K., Kingsway Communications
Eastbourne, East Sussex BN23 6NT, England

The graphic circle C logo is a registered trademark of David C Cook.

The Web site addresses recommended throughout this book are offered as a
resource to you. These Web sites are not intended in any way to be or imply an
endorsement on the part of David C. Cook, nor do we vouch for their content.

This story is a work of fiction. All characters and events are the product of the
author's imagination. Any resemblance to any person, living or dead, is coincidental.

Scripture quote in the Note from the Publisher section is taken from the HOLY
BIBLE, NEW INTERNATIONAL READER'S VERSION®. Copyright ©
1996, 1998 International Bible Society. All rights reserved throughout the
world. Used by permission of International Bible Society. Scripture quotes in
the AfterWords section are taken from the *New American Standard Bible,* ©
Copyright 1960, 1995 by The Lockman Foundation. Used by permission.

LCCN 2010923350
ISBN 978-1-58919-103-7
eISBN 978-0-7814-0444-0

© 2010 Tom Davis
Published in association with the literary agency of
Alive Communications, Inc, 7680 Goddard St., Suite 200,
Colorado Springs, CO 80920. www.alivecommunications.com

The Team: Don Pape, Steve Parolini, Amy Kiechlin,
Sarah Schultz, Jack Campbell, and Karen Athen
Cover Design: DogEared Design, Kirk DouPonce
Cover Photos: iStockphoto; 123RF

Printed in the United States of America
First Edition 2010

2 3 4 5 6 7 8 9 10

071813

FOR KATYA AND MASHA.

*May God bless you for your courage and
dedication to defend the defenseless.*

Acknowledgments

A very special thank you to Moira Allaby who helped this book come to life. My publisher, Don Pape, for always believing. Rick Christian and Andrea Christian (now Heineke!), my wonderful friends and agents. The entire staff at Children's HopeChest who I care for and love so much: Bob Mudd, Vince Giordano, Ginia Hairston, Hannah Chynoweth, Nicole Irwin, Greg and Brandi McElheny, Hannah Lehman, Mindy Stewart, Sarah Byrd, Leah Wade, Becky Kennedy, Teresa Hanson, and Matthew Monberg.

Thanks to my incredible wife, Emily.

A special thank you to those who helped me choose the title of this book: Angela Castillo, Susan Wimmer, Teresa Cupit, Alicia Ahlers, Ben Scholten, Deb Gangemi (and the rest of the Gangemi clan), Sarah Battle, Doug Hering, Robby from Utah, Marie Jennings, Bess Ross, Laura Allen, Kevin Bowman, Dawna Larsson, D. J. Payne, and Wes Roberts.

Prologue

"Whenever you're ready," I say, then press the On button to film.

The small woman, a nun in a traditional Orthodox black habit who has been talking to a girl in a quiet voice, looks at the camera. She straightens her habit, flashes a broad smile, and gives me a nod, as if to say, "Okay, proceed." Like Mother Teresa making a cameo. I laugh in spite of the context and the reason I've come back to this monastery in the dense Kostroma woods.

The young woman seated on a spare, sturdy chair before me is dressed in black jeans and a white blouse, ironed and crisp. Her hair, once long and light, is dark and cropped short. Behind her stands a marble-topped table, an altar, and a broad white wall covered with a large intricate tapestry decorated with icons, saints revered by the Russian faithful for centuries. She looks out of place in the frame, like a sleek modern figure painted into a baroque scene.

"How did you get here?" I ask. I measure my words and tone, like I would if I were trying to talk a woman down from the top ledge of a high-rise.

Her eyes seem to flash with light, but her face is hard, like pale stone. "I was tricked by people who considered me the trash of society. I was lied to by men and women who thought only of their own gain. Once, I thought I was free...."

"When was that?" I'm used to standing behind the lens, not asking the questions.

"When I met a priest, an Orthodox priest from my own country." She pauses and looks off into the distance, as if paralyzed by the memory.

I let her think for a moment, then ask, "What happened?"

Still looking off into the distance, she says, "Instead of showing me freedom, this priest took me to hell." Her slender hand, red and scarred, shakes as she pulls her arm to smooth her hair. The only sounds are the low hum of the camera and her breathing.

She closes her eyes, drinks in a deep breath, and then slowly pivots toward me, her steel blue eyes square with the lens.

"My name is Marina. Marina Smolchenko. And this is my story."

Chapter One

Pacing in this shoebox is nearly impossible. Four steps along the cracked plaster wall and four steps back. Every third pass, my knee smashes on the headboard when I turn around. The beds, lined up like military cots, are covered with matching brown terry cloth bedspreads. A spare wooden chair with a seat the size of my laptop has been wedged into one corner. In the other, a thirteen-inch television and a murky drinking glass sit on an old wooden dresser that leans precariously to the right. This Russian hotel room is a replica of the ones I stayed in over fifteen years ago, like cold war movie sets no one thought to update. The entire room couldn't be more than ten by ten. Not even space on the floor to do my push-ups.

On the bed an arm's length away are two young girls. Twins. They look like Bratz dolls. I'd guess they're about fifteen. Worn, dirty jeans hug their tiny frames. I'd bet the clothes on their back are all they own. Under their small jean jackets are snug tank tops, short to reveal flat stomachs and barely developed bodies. One of the girls wears stiletto boots that add a good four inches to her height. The other has tall red heels that come to long points at the toes.

They look identical with big blue eyes, except the girl with the boots has one green eye. I can make out dark rings under their eyes in spite of the heavy makeup. Watching me study them, the one with the green eye stands up, as if on command, and starts to unbutton her pants.

"*Da?*" she says and flashes a plastic smile.

"No, no! *Nyet,*" I say in a panic. "*Ostavaites na meste.* [Sit down.]" I motion my hands downward like I'm begging her to take cover from a shooter.

The girls look confused and sit shoulder to shoulder like statues.

My head hums with thoughts of the last hours' events.

I had been talking to Katya on my cell phone, making plans to meet for dinner and discuss my project. She said she wanted me to visit the orphanage where she was the director.

"To cover the rise of AIDS in Russia?" I asked. Katya always seemed to have an ulterior agenda, and the ability to get people to follow it.

"Oh, Stuart," she said in her excellent but heavily accented English, "you have no idea how much of that story is happening around me. You know, I'm meeting more orphans who are infected with HIV every single day—"

My hotel phone rang.

"Hold on a minute," I interrupted Katya midsentence. She could talk faster than any human I'd ever met, like a late-night TV pitchman on speed. "Someone's calling me on the hotel phone. Let me get it."

I picked up the heavy black handset. "Hello."

On the other line, in broken English, a woman's voice said, "You vant pretty girl come to your room?"

I was fairly certain she was the heavyset house-frau type I saw when I walked off the elevator, the key lady. Obviously, the crazy old lady had me pinned as someone else.

"No," I replied in Russian. "I don't want a girl." I put the receiver back on the '60s model rotary phone. I felt annoyance and a strange shame. It brought to mind the times when I traveled here years ago. Stepping into or out of the hotel doors, I was met by girls on the street who would ask outright if I wanted sex. Did I ever say yes? That was something I didn't want to think about.

I put my cell phone back up to my ear. "Katya, I'm back."

"Stuart, was that someone asking if you wanted a girl to come to your room?" She sounded irritated. Irritated and panicked.

"Katya, yes. But of course I said no."

"A man will call back," Katya hissed. "Tell him yes, you changed your mind and you want her all night. Have the girl come, and then wait for me to call."

"Are you crazy?" I looked around the room to see if there was a hidden video camera somewhere. Maybe I was on some new Russian candid camera TV show.

"Do it. It's important."

I opened my mouth to protest, but she hung up. Like clockwork, a man called within a minute with the same question, this time speaking to me in Russian.

"*Dobry vecher!* [Good evening!]" he said. "You are traveling alone, no? I have beautiful Russian girls to keep you company." There was nothing discreet in his manner. His voice was loud, even jovial.

My mouth wouldn't work. Shock froze my jaws together.

"Look, I will send you the best and make good price. Two pretty girls for cost of one," he said. "*Samaya vigodnaya tsena.*"

"What did you say? *Ya ne ponimayu.* [I don't understand.]"

"I'm sorry." He gave a loud, feigned laugh. "I will give you the best price for two girls, one thousand rubles. They will make you very happy, you will see."

"How much for the night? I want them for the whole night." Were these words really coming out of my mouth?

He laughed again, like we were old friends sharing an inside joke. "I see. Now you are very eager. Not expensive. Two thousand rubles. Cash. Or we can bill to your room?"

I heard my voice crack and say, against all rational judgment, "Cash is fine." I could just see my agency expense report with a "late-night entertainment" charge. Entertainment of this kind was treated with raised eyebrows from the guy who would review my expense report and nothing more, unless it was over the top. But I didn't even want the association, much less the reality. Especially since I'm married.

"Okay, then. They will come and knock on your door three times. They leave at six a.m. No later. They have other customers."

A half hour later came the small *knock, knock, knock* on the door and the appearance of the Russian Olsen twins. They stepped through the door and into the room in one move, arm in arm. I had expected women, not children. The heavyset key lady was with them, hand outstretched. "Sixty dollars," she commanded like a brigadier general. I put the money in her hand, and she walked back down the hall.

I closed the door and looked at what my money just purchased. The girl with the blue eyes looked down; the other followed me with her eyes. She put her right hand around my waist and let her fingers move down my chest like a waterfall. I moved her hand and stepped away.

My best friend has teenage girls this age. They're just children.

"I'm expecting a phone call, so please sit and wait," I said to them, trying to convey calmness. I paced, waiting for my next move.

I noticed, as they sat and their short tops rose, that both girls had what looked like the same depiction of an ancient dragon, all in black, tattooed on the small of their backs. They looked more like a brand than a fashion statement. Maybe this was a teenage rebellion carried out in solidarity. You'd think by this point they'd want to have different tattoos. I didn't know this was a big thing in Russia, like in the United States. Seemed risky in this country. Then I remembered why they were here. The words *tramp stamp* came to mind, words I would never again use with my buddies as we walked along the beach or street when we spotted a girl with a lower-back tattoo.

The cell phone finally rings, a blast of Russian techno music in line with my trip, and all three us turn to look like it was the fourth man in the furnace.

"Okay, Katya, what now?" I say quietly.

Katya's voice fires like a machine gun. "Stuart, the trunk you brought with all the equipment, empty it and put everything under the bed."

"What?"

"Just listen to me, there's no time to waste. You'll get it back. That I promise."

"Then what?"

"Then put the girl inside the trunk."

"Katya, there are two girls, twins." I look at my trunk. I'm not sure they'd be able to breathe in there.

Without hesitation, she asks, "Will they both fit inside?" I look at the girls on the bed. Minus shoes, I think yes. It is a big trunk. The girls look at me with growing terror in their eyes.

"It's okay," I say to them. "*Ya vas ne obizhu. Ya khochu vam pomotch.* [I'm not going to hurt you. I'm trying to help you.]"

Katya says, "Give the phone to one of the girls, Stuart." I hand it to the bewildered twin with the green eye and nod.

Her Russian is so fast and broken, and she uses so much slang, I can't understand what she's saying. Then, at Katya's words, she begins to slow her own.

"Da," she says quietly. Her voice sounds breathy. "Da. Da." In an instant, her boots are off, and she instructs her sister to take off her shoes. I stuff the clunky boots and high heels under the bed, feeling like a husband trying to stash evidence of a lover.

Whatever Katya said, it worked.

I have never been so thankful that a Russian girl—typical tall, blond, the kind you see in Bond movies—was in line with me twenty years ago at NYU when we were signing up for classes my freshman year. My mother spoke Russian, but I knew only enough to be insulting. And to ask for a date. So I signed up for what turned out to be one date and four intense years of language study.

My Russian minor made my mother proud and landed me photo shoots in Russia with *Pravda*, a Russian newspaper, soon after the fall of communism.

At that time, I bet I was in Russia at least three times a year doing photo shoots. Everyone in the West wanted to know what Russia looked like; they wanted pictures of the people and famous places. America was enchanted with the idea of Russia. That's how I fell in love with this country, its people, and one little girl named Marina.

My gut tightens as I begin to stash fifty grand worth of camera equipment under the bed, like putting my baby in a basket and setting it afloat on a river. I turn after stowing the last of it to see both girls slip into the trunk and fold together. I look down at them, curved into each other, looking like they did in their mother's womb. I know I don't have to tell them to stay quiet. The one with the blue eyes has them closed tight.

I summon a smile. "It will be okay," I say, trying to believe it myself. I lift strands of brunette hair hanging out over the edge and carefully place them inside as if they will break. I prop open the lid and put the key in the lock, ready to shut and turn on command. This feels wrong, like I'm burying them alive, but I trust Katya. I have to.

I sit on the bed and pat the trunk a few times, like you'd pat a dog if you were watching TV. Jet lag, hunger, and the reality of twin prostitutes enclosed in my camera trunk hit my brain with the force of a buffalo stampede.

My stomach starts to twist. Instead of hurling, which is my typical response to extreme stress, I begin to laugh. What would happen if the police stormed in? What would these poor girls think if they heard me laughing? I bring my arm up to muffle the sound.

Bozhe, pomogi mne, I pray. *Bozhe, pomogi etim devochkam.*

God, help me. God, help these girls.

Chapter Two

Looking out the small, fogged window of the Boeing 767, I see the familiar Sheremetyevo Airport.

I make my way into the airport down a long narrow hallway with the rest of the passengers toward passport control. The crowd puts one foot in front of the other, and we follow each other like silent sheep to a pasture. There are no advertisements, no elevator music, just pale, peeling white walls and the shuffling feet of the passengers. Outside the hall we spill into a larger room that has the same oppressive dark and gray ceilings. Thousands of metal cylinders close in like a looming constrictor overhead. Before this was an airport I'd bet it was a communist military prison.

Men and women in olive uniforms seem slightly out of sync with time, especially with their circa World War II military hats. These men and women are the equivalent of our TSA officials at the airports in the States. They're all olive drab and business, except the women who sport bright red lipstick that smears around their lips, like a four-year-old who's pilfered her mom's brightest tube. Maybe it's their way of thumbing their noses at the lingering communist suppression.

This place is cold, icy cold. Nothing's changed in ten years, except for one addition: flat-screen televisions. Western ingenuity with an

Eastern application. Now people standing in line to get into the country can be brainwashed with advertisements and anti-Western propaganda at the same time.

There is one symbol of hope standing in the corner to the right of the passport lanes. A twelve-foot-tall Christmas tree neatly decorated with colored lights and huge glass ornaments in a range of colors—azure blue, emerald, red, and white—with a gold star on top. Now that I've seen it, I can smell the pine emanating from the branches of this gorgeous Douglas fir.

When my turn finally arrives, I step up to the counter to greet a hardened young bleach-blond woman behind thick glass. Unlike the rest of the women, she's wearing pale red lipstick on her expressionless face. Her eyelashes are fake and caked in black mascara. I muster up a charming smile.

"Hello," I say, looking directly at her eyes as I slide my passport under the glass. Inside, I feel nervous as a cat. Maybe it's knowing that I'll see Katya in a matter of minutes. It's been a long time.

The woman glares at me. Not even a smirk or bat of her heavily makeupped eyes. It would appear the women of former USSR haven't changed. Warm as a Siberian morning.

My passport is scanned, and she looks at the archaic computer in front of her, then back at me, comparing my face with the picture on the passport. I smile again. Not a chance of reaction. She's granite.

She hands my passport back to me without a word, stamps the page with a metal pushdown gadget, and nods while looking at the exit. It was nice to meet you, too.

I shuffle through the metal gate to safety, take a deep breath, and head for baggage claim. The carousel grinds and lurches forward in its attempt to deliver our luggage. Every bag made it, thank goodness. Grabbing a pushcart, I load my bags, careful to place my carry-on equipment bag on top, and head toward the green line. Nothing to declare. If you can pass through without incident, it saves half a day of explaining your luggage contents. It's hit or miss.

God, give me grace. I just invested in new video equipment for this job off some speaking engagements I had over the past year, and I'd be mad as a hornet if something happened to it. So would Whitney. These days, she sees every extra lump sum as college tuition for our daughter, Adanna.

"She's stinkin' one year old!" I told her when we discussed it. "Think of all the money I can make with this equipment." She finally relented. We don't argue as much now, probably because I'm working steadily, but money's still a tough subject with us.

The guards look up at me, give a cursory look inside my bags, and wave me on. They must have wanted a smoke break. Sometimes you just get lucky.

The narrow hall ends as the double glass doors swing open to a corridor of people waiting for guests to arrive. Hundreds of anxious faces mix with an equal number of frozen faces, people waiting for business contacts, I suspect. I scan the crowd and wonder if I'll recognize her after so long.

"Stuart!" I hear a loud voice. "Over here."

I turn and spot Katya waving enthusiastically. She stands out in her tall leather boots, red hat, and matching red scarf. One bright spot in a sea of gray. She glides between the masses with ease, like a seasoned band groupie.

I rush to hug her, and she gives me a quick, strong hug back.

"You haven't changed a bit," I say, trying to sound sincere. I mean it, but she's got a nose for all things false. We stand for a second at arm's length, and I look at her beautiful almond-shaped brown eyes, her blond shoulder-length hair, and her soft, clear olive complexion. She smells great, the same as before. I had caught a whiff of that familiar perfume in New York not long ago when I was standing to cross at 8th and Columbus Circle. I'm only slightly embarrassed to admit I changed my course to keep up with the scent for a few blocks. It transported me right back to the last time I was here and put Katya on my mind. Soon after, I was offered this job.

"It's so good to see you, Stuart. It's been too long." She turns and grabs one side of my luggage cart and starts us moving. Never an idle second with her.

She says over her shoulder, "I wasn't sure if you would recognize me, so I wanted to wear something that would stand out."

I laugh. "*Kak ti mozhesh ne videlyatsya?* [How could you not stand out, Katya?] Love that red." Katya's lipstick is red, but firmly in the lines of her lips.

"I'm glad. It's been a few years."

I met Katya in the early '90s in the Ukraine when I was doing a story on the Chernobyl nuclear power disaster. Was that ever a catastrophe. People inside Russia, Ukraine, and Belarus were dropping like acid rain from disease normally attributed to radiation. Of course, the government adamantly denied any such thing. But that's what the communist government always did well: lie. It's not us killing you, it's the Americans, they said.

In the midst of such death and devastation, my relationship with Katya was a warm embrace in a Soviet chill. She literally kept me alive and safe from corrupt officials, and she was an amazing companion. We had a thing in those days, but nothing serious. None of my relationships back then ever were. I always had a thing for Eastern European women. Their long, muscular legs, beautiful bodies, and chiseled features are something to behold.

I think about Katya's body and then stop myself. Better get that image out of my head. I turn the thoughts away, replacing them with the lingering good-bye kiss I gave Whitney.

"This way. Nick is waiting in the van." Her accent is liquid velvet.

The first step outside reminds me of what I didn't miss about Russia: the cold. An icy blast of arctic air hits me square in the face. It's the kind of cold that makes your knees buckle. You can't get cold like this anywhere else in the world.

We push through the crowd and out the door. Cars are stacked on top of each other like Legos. Some of the drivers are standing outside their vehicles smoking cigarettes while others are quickly throwing luggage into the cars. Those still in the driver's seats are honking at the others to get out of their way. Shouts of "Taxi? Taxi?" echo in the corridor by the hundreds. She waves them off.

"Nick is still with you? You've got to be kidding. What is he now, sixty?"

She laughs loudly. "You'll see him in a minute. You can ask him yourself."

One thing that impresses me about Russians is their loyalty. Nick was Katya's driver ten years ago, and at least ten before that. Amazing.

A green Mercedes van waits just beyond the arrival terminal where the service vehicles pick up passengers. Nick looks just like he did years ago, balding brown hair, blue eyes, about five foot ten, and a smile as big as Texas. I remember him as the nicest guy in all of Russia.

"Nick!"

"Stuart, *zdravstvuite, moy horoshy droog!* [Hello, my good friend!]"

We embrace like long-lost brothers.

"*Kak dela?* [How are you?]"

"I'm fine, my friend. Much has changed since we last saw each other, but I am well."

He holds me at arm's length and gives me a good stare, like an old woman surveying a grandson's growth progress between visits. This would never fly back in the States. I resist the urge to pull away.

"You look well. Very good I might say," he says.

"And you haven't changed a bit! What's new in your life, Nick?"

"Well, I'm a grandfather. Two wonderful grandchildren."

"*Molodiyets!* [Good job!] I bet they're as beautiful as their mother." I had the privilege of eating with Nick, his wife, and his extended family when I was here last. It was one of my favorite memories of Russia. Luda, his wife, knew I loved Borscht soup, so she made a gigantic pot of it for me. There's nothing in the world like those red Russian beets and potatoes. When my spoon hit the bottom of the bowl, she was right there to fill it back up again. A little Russian potato salad, some cucumbers and tomatoes, and some chicken, and I was the happiest American in Russia. Especially after we toasted three times to family, country, and friends with a bottle of Nick's homemade lemon vodka.

"Even more beautiful. I'm glad they don't look like me. I have the brains in the family, not the looks. Let me take your bags and let's get going. *Segodnya holodno, osobenno dlya vas amerikansev.* [It's cold today, especially for you thin-blooded Americans.]"

As we speed down the highway toward the outskirts of Moscow, I observe that fifteen years haven't changed anything. The apartment blocks are the same Soviet style I remember. The old paint seems to peel before my eyes. Apartments stand side by side like soldiers in an army. There are no parking lots; the entire city practically functions on public transportation of buses and the Metro system that runs under most of the city.

The sky swirls in gray and black and seems close, as if it exists to subdue. I'm convinced the enormous amount of vodka consumption in the country is the common man's attempt to deal with the sky and the endless harsh weather.

"This is what I love about Russia. Not much has changed. It's just like I remember." Katya and I sit in the two backseats of the van. My backpack lays on the seat next to me, and I face backward so I can look at her while we talk.

"Our country is thousands of years old, Stuart. It takes a long time for change to have its way here," Katya says without a hint of nostalgia in her voice.

"That's why Lenin is still in his tomb at the Kremlin." I grin.

She gives me the evil eye.

"So, tell me, Katya, what's been keeping you occupied in post-Soviet Russia?"

We zip through traffic like we're late for a funeral. Cars honk at one another, and everyone drives like they're sixteen and drunk on a Friday night. Here, the most aggressive driver wins.

"My work hasn't changed. You know that my life recently has

been all about helping the poorest of the poor. Especially orphans. That's what I do."

Finally, she smiles. Get her to talk about her passion, and she lights up like a thousand suns.

"Still? I didn't know that's what you were doing. I thought you would have a position in the government as the head of humanitarian rights by now."

"Actually, I was offered a government job over all the orphans in the country."

"Really? Katya the politician. I like the sound of that. Why didn't you take it?"

"Too much bureaucracy. I'm much more effective doing things my way. There are so many children aging out of the orphanage. Most simply disappear. The boys become drunks, the girls prostitutes. They need help they aren't receiving from the government or anyone else."

"So you're overseeing orphanages?"

"Yes, and other quieter operations." She turns to look out her window, as if I might decipher the secret on her face.

"Is this top secret, or are you going to spill the beans?"

"Spill the what?"

I laugh. "Sorry, American saying. Are you going to tell me what this is about?"

"Oh, of course, I plan to tell you all about it. In due time."

The van comes to a sudden halt in front of the same hotel I stayed at years ago, The Hotel Izmailovo. It was built in 1979 on the site of the historic Izmailovo village and Royal Estate, owned by the Romanov boyars since the sixteenth century. When the Olympics arrived in Moscow in 1980, many athletes used this hotel. But visitors shouldn't be fooled; it's not that nice.

"Stuart, let's get you checked in, and I will meet you for dinner later. I have a new favorite place to show you."

"Sounds fantastic. Do they have good Borscht?"

"I haven't forgotten what you like, that's why I picked it. *Daitea mne vash passport.* [Now give me your passport.]"

Chapter Three

My watch says it's only been fifteen minutes, but I think it's lying.

Like a burglar peering into a window, I lift the lid of the trunk to check on the girls. Two sets of wide eyes stare up at me. They make no attempt to move. I shudder as I wonder if they've been shuffled around like this before.

"*Vsyo v poryadke.* [It's *ok-ay.*]" I speak deliberately to them, trying to sound calm, but the words come out as a stutter.

"*Ya pomogu vam.* [I am *go-ing to help* you.]"

I force a reassuring smile. It doesn't help any of us.

I hear three sharp raps on the door, and I lunge forward. My stomach feels as if I've just bungee jumped from fifteen stories. I close the lid quietly and turn the key in the lock.

There is no peephole. I open the door quickly.

"Thank God, what took you so—"

It's not Katya.

I immediately feel beads of sweat on my brow. The large woman from the front desk stands at my door with two towels and three condoms placed neatly on top. She hands them to me and walks off.

"*Spasibo tebye* [Thank you]," I say, then close the door and try to get my heart rate under control.

"God, this would be a good time for you to show up. I could

33

really use some help here." Praying is never my first response, but I've learned that it helps. Especially in difficult situations.

I'm convinced prayer was what got me out of Africa alive. I'd been stabbed in the back by a crazy man who had attacked a little girl. A little girl my daughter is named after. He barely missed my kidney. The doctors said it was a miracle. A centimeter off, and I would have been dead.

It *was* a miracle. An unexpected but welcome answer to the mystery that is prayer.

I sit on the floor with my arm draped over the trunk, listening to air that seems charged with fear. I hear another knock. And another. And one more. Three light taps.

I stand over the box that used to hold my camera equipment, pray a silent prayer, and make the sign of the cross, a gesture from my childhood. Then I open the door.

Katya pushes past me quietly and swiftly. Following her are two Russians carrying large suitcases. One looks like a Chechen rebel. He's short with pockmarks in his face and a thick dark beard. The other is an older female, maybe midforties, fairly heavy, with welcoming blue eyes and graying hair.

They move past me like a secret-ops force.

"Are the girls ready?" Katya asks. Cool and calm, like she does this every day.

"Katya, *kakogo chyorta? Vo chto ti menya vtyanula?* [What's going on? What have you gotten me into?]"

Katya stops her perpetual action and takes a deliberate step toward me, her face inches from mine. She says, as if trying to calm a frightened child, "Stuart, *pover mne. Yesli eto srabotaet, to ti spas zhizni etikh dvoikh devochek.* [Trust me. If this works, you've saved the lives of these two little girls.]"

"And if not?"

She steps away and starts moving again. "Then we all have big trouble. But don't worry, we know what we're doing."

"Easy for you to say."

"There's no time to waste. Where's your camera equipment?"

"Under the bed."

"Vadim, *polozhi vsyo oborudovaniye v chemodani.* [Put all of the equipment in the suitcases. Carefully.]"

On cue, the Chechen opens both large suitcases and places my camera and video equipment inside.

Instinctively, I go to help him. He gives me the stiff-arm and shakes his head no.

"*Ei, akkuratneye tam. Eto ochen vazhniye veshi* [Then go easy, man. That stuff's important]—" I stop myself, thinking about the current contents of my equipment trunk.

"Time is not our friend, Stuart," Katya says. Then she turns toward the trunk. "Give me the key."

The girls are as still as statues until they see Katya. Their heads pop up like jack-in-the-boxes. Katya leans in and puts her arms around their shoulders. Though I can only make out a few of her words, she speaks to them like a mother. I can tell they trust her. She closes the lid, locks it, and puts the key in her purse.

"So, Katya, what's my next instruction, comrade?" I fall back into my old tone with her, in spite of the situation.

She gives me a dirty look. I turn to look at the other two who have stormed my hotel room. Vadim is finishing up with my equipment, and the woman is wiping down all the furniture with a black cloth, obviously trying to remove fingerprints.

"First, relax. Everything's going to be okay. We've done this before. Many times."

"Katya, I feel like I'm caught up in some kind of crime. If the magazine finds out I've been involved in something like this ... If *Whitney* finds out about this ..." She hasn't been on me as much now that we have a baby and I'm working regularly, but she did manage to sneak in a not-so-subtle "Keep your nose clean" remark before I left.

"You're saving lives here. These two little girls are worth it; believe me. Now take a deep breath and trust your old friend."

In a matter of minutes my equipment is packed, the girls have been carted off, and I'm left standing shell-shocked in a small Russian hotel room. Just yesterday I was surrounded by the comforts of my home in New York and the affections of my baby girl and my loving wife. Now I have little more than the shirt and coat on my back, and I'm caught up in something that I just know isn't going to end well.

"Stuart, listen carefully. We don't know if anyone is watching your room. In our experience probably not until about two hours before the girls are supposed to leave. There are so many girls to watch, they can't keep up a twenty-four-hour vigil."

"So what does that mean?"

"It means you have to get out now."

"But they have records of me staying in this room. They'll find me, Katya. What am I supposed to do about that?"

"We have people working on the inside. They'll purge your records. It will be like you never checked in. You were never here, Stuart Daniels."

"This is totally crazy."

Loud noises come from outside of the room as a group of men yell in Russian, "*Da, detka, mi segodnya porazvlechyomsya.* [Yeah, baby, we're going to have a good time tonight.] *Vot uvidish. Bruno sdelaet tebya schastlivoy.* [You're going to see how Bruno will make you very happy.]" They laugh hysterically.

"It's the only way. Now listen carefully: We are going around to the right with the girls, the luggage containing your equipment, and your suitcase. There's a separate elevator where the key lady can't see us leave."

The older woman picks up my black High Sierra backpack as if on cue.

"And what am I supposed to do?" I take a deep breath, focus.

"You go to the left by the key lady. Act as if nothing is wrong. If she asks, you're going out to get cigarettes or beer for your late-night party."

Though my heart's pounding like an African drum, I can feel my senses heighten with the plan.

"Okay. Where do I find you?"

"Here's a cell phone. Don't use yours. My number is programmed in case of an emergency. Get out of here as quickly as you can. Go to Red Square and act like a tourist. We'll call you as soon as possible."

"How long?"

"I can't be sure but likely within the hour. We have to get the girls to a safe house first. I'm sure you understand that time is of the essence."

"So, I'm supposed to wander around the Kremlin until I get a phone call?"

"Exactly. In the name of the Father, the Son, and the Holy Spirit, God's protection be over you." She makes the sign of the cross and is off.

With precision and speed the entire party is gone, and the door closes behind them. I'm left alone in my tiny room. I take a few deep breaths. I can't stop shaking my head. How did all of this happen?

I sweep the room to make sure nothing is left behind. Then I open the door with my shirt and make a left toward the key lady and the elevator. She looks up at me, the wretched babushka who is nothing more than a pimp. She glances up from her magazine and stands up, all three hundred pounds of her.

She leans out with her thick eyebrows raised, then looks down the hall to see who's with me. I nod and walk toward the elevator, then hit the black triangle to summon the lift.

She starts to say something, but I cut her off. "*Tolko sbegayu za sigaretami. Skoro vernus.* [Just going down for cigarettes. Be right back.]" I try to give a reassuring smile. Thank God, the elevator doors open and I step on as she's saying, "My friend, I have those here …"

The elevator stops on the next floor to let some guests on. They are dressed for a night on the town in tuxes and gowns. My sensible side kicks in, and I decide it's best to make a run for it.

"*Izvenitye* [Excuse me]," I say and make my way through the small crowd and into the hallway. I spot a sign indicating stairs and quicken my pace. I've never seen anyone use the stairs in Russia. It's got to be safe.

A few moments later, I'm out the front door of the hotel and hit with the familiar icy air. I've never been so happy to step into the frigid night air of Moscow.

Chapter Four

I zip up my jacket as far as it will go and tuck my chin inside as I make a beeline for the Metro, which is straight ahead and across the street about a half mile away. My legs have walked this journey so many times they're on autopilot. I take a discreet glance over my shoulder to see if anyone is following and pick up the pace. It's good to be outside and moving, especially in the glow of a Moscow that's lit up and decked out for the nativity season.

In minutes, I step out of the cold and through the double-glass doors leading to the Metro. It's crowded. I calculate how long it might take me to buy a pass. Too long. I scan the place. No guards or police around, so with one arm on the turnstile, I leap over and bolt down the escalator to the train. My rap sheet is growing by the minute.

The door to the subway closes with a loud thud, and for the first time since that phone call at the hotel, I feel out of harm's way. Nobody seems to take notice of me, and for the next thirty minutes, no one can find me. I haven't been here in years, but I know exactly where I'm going. Another thing that hasn't changed in this country, thank God.

I put my head back but don't dare to close my eyes. Sleep has been a default mechanism when I'm under stress. I've slept in war zones. When I'm stressed, I always seem to have the same dream. I'm on a train just like this Russian Metro, but no one speaks a language I can understand. All the signs are gibberish, and no one can tell me how to get to my destination. However, I'm not dreaming now. I know the language, but I still feel detached and uncertain.

At Sergei Pasad, I exit the green line and emerge from underground just north of Red Square. In truth, there's nothing red about it. In Russian, *red* means "beautiful," and tonight, that's a pale description.

To my left stand two Russian Orthodox churches, sentinels guarding the city. The moonlight reflects off their multicolored onion-shaped domes that glisten like sparkling gemstones. The colors then travel down the hill and bounce off the Moscow River, making it look like a liquid rainbow. I blink, and it's like waking up in fairyland.

The sidewalks are lined with dozens of people, mostly lovers walking slowly along the cobblestone, holding hands, and looking into each other's eyes. The rest are tourists, obvious with cameras, fake mink hats, and indiscreet comments about the smell of the city and the unfriendly nature of the Muscovites.

Moscow, like New York, is a city that never sleeps. Amid the crowd, a couple moves toward me with both arms wrapped around each other, completely lip-locked and walking in a perfect straight line. I wonder how they can breathe. When I round the corner, I'm struck, as always, by the majesty of the square. It never changes. I have a photo book of Red Square from the 1950s, and it looks exactly the same today. Except the trees are bigger.

The Kremlin stands directly in front of me, a symbol of power protected by high looming yellow walls and a massive clock tower on the corner reminiscent of London's Big Ben. An intimidating guard, like a queen on a chessboard, stands in front of Lenin's Tomb. During the day you can actually go inside and view the body. I've always wanted to do it out of curiosity. What's a guy look like who's been dead for eighty-five years? Probably like the figure of him I saw in a wax museum somewhere. Today, he would be one hundred and thirty years old.

Gold and silver church domes appear majestically behind the walls of the Kremlin as if holding true control of the country, like the wizard behind the curtain in Oz. There are seven churches including the Cathedral of the Annunciation, the church of Moscow's princes and tsars over the centuries. I step out onto the cobblestone road leading down the middle of the square, bracing myself against a cold that's harsh and exhilarating.

Every time I walk in this square, I think the same thing: *I'm walking on centuries-old blood.* If the stones under my feet could talk, they would tell violent stories of riots, assassinations, and war—of all the blood that's been spilled here over the centuries. The *Lobnoye Mesto*, a platform where the tsar would address the people, sits directly ahead. It's also a place where many men and women lost their heads. Literally.

One of my favorite sites in all of Russia stands solitary at the entrance of the square, likely the most recognized icon for people when they think of Russia, St. Basil's Cathedral. It has stood for over four hundred years as a beacon of Russia's strength and fortitude. Its nine multicolored domes represent nine individual chapels, each one commemorating a victorious assault against the Mongols in the 1500s. More symbols of blood and war.

Russia's history fascinates me. The stalwart tower of religion has always been the backbone of the country. But it's also been the reason for so much bloodshed. People were even killed for how they made the sign of the Trinity. Was it two fingers pressed to your thumb or three?

Every building in the perimeter is lined in brilliant white lights, like a brightly colored Dickens' village on a grand scale. Ancient, beautiful displays of architecture enclose the square, with only the sky to keep people on the ground from feeling claustrophobic. I have a nagging sense I'm forgetting something, and I realize I'm reaching for a ghost camera that's not strapped over my shoulder.

"So what am I supposed to do now?" I say out loud. I take a sweeping look around me for a sign of Katya or her two friends. I don't like waiting. I don't like not knowing. I begin to feel the full wrath of the bitter cold and stuff my hands in my pockets. My legs start shaking like jiggled Jell-O.

Two men behind me catch my eye. One elbows the other and makes a slight gesture in my direction. I turn as if I haven't noticed and begin to walk. I don't know if they're really looking at me or if my lifelong paranoia about being chased by the KGB is coming to fruition.

I head for the opposite side of the square by the more populated GUM, the largest mall area on the square, and try to disappear in the crowd. I don't want to think about what might happen if they catch me.

"*Izvenitye* [Excuse me]," I say as I bump into a woman wearing a full-length red trench coat. It makes me think of my own coat, which I immediately pull off in the crowd and bunch up in front of me.

Not a smart idea in this weather, but perhaps a way to make myself more invisible.

"God, help me disappear," I say under my breath.

I'm certain they're still following me. Through the crowd I see a large group entering a rustic-looking pink Orthodox church. With my head down, I push through the crowd, as if boring my way toward the church, stepping on toes and shoving shoulders in the process. People yell insults at me in Russian. Reminds me of my teenage years. I'm running on adrenaline, and I don't care.

I burst through the doors like a diver breaking the surface of the water. Sprinkled throughout the quiet sanctuary, I see old women in headscarves. They turn in one motion and fix their eyes on me in an expression I recognize from my childhood, or from Whitney when I've gotten out of hand at a party; one that says, "Quiet, or else!" They don't look happy to see me. I'm relieved as a few others mill in around me, genuflect, and take their places in the pews.

I follow suit and make the sign of the cross beginning on my forehead, then to the right of my chest, and the left, whispering, "Father, Son, and Holy Spirit." It makes me feel cheap and stupid.

But it seems to tame the faithful, who turn from me and go about their worship. Walking down the right aisle, I slide into a pew toward the front and try to hide in a corner behind a large icon of Jesus with a golden aura over His head. Can't be a safer place than under the face of the Messiah.

A door at the front of the church, to the right of the altar, opens, and I expect to see the priest or altar boys. Instead, a line of eight girls pours out and files into the second row. Like the other women, their heads are covered, but each wears a large black lace scarf—a mantilla, my mom used to call the black lace scarf passed to her from her own mother. She didn't wear it, but it seemed to have sacred value to her.

I wonder if they're part of a confirmation class for teenage girls or maybe nuns in training until I notice their faces. The ones I can see are caked in makeup, their bright lips out of character with the austere black robes and head coverings. They kneel together and face the front of the church in one movement, then sit like choreographed puppets. I can't take my eyes off them. One girl turns and meets my gaze. Something about her blue eyes looks familiar. Striking deep blue, but empty, like the light behind them had been extinguished. She jerks her head back around toward the front as if lured by some invisible force at the sound of a man's loud singsong voice. A strange shiver runs down my neck.

A priest in a gold robe and red hat, a silver cross in the middle, comes down from the altar, chanting. He must be speaking an old Slavic dialect because I can't make out the words. Smoke pours from the holes in the censer he's swinging, forming crosses that float through the air and transform to amorphous clouds as they rise. The distinct sweet smell of incense hangs in the air: cinnamon, matches, and baby powder. These smells are reminiscent of my childhood. There was one aunt in my family, Aunt Beth, who was Catholic. I spent summers with her in Chicago, and she was determined to make me a good Catholic. She didn't succeed, but I'll never forget the sweet smell of the church.

The smoke rises as thin vapors, as if they were ascending prayers. God Himself is painted majestically at the top of the dome. He looks like the archetype: rolling waves of curled gray hair, a flowing silver beard, powerful biceps, and billowing white garments. Horses and the communion of saints in the form of the twelve apostles surround Him. Christ is seated at His right hand.

My eyes water. Bells ring with enthusiasm, and each row of congregants bows as the priest waves the silver ball toward and away from them. I am reminded of a toy I had when I was a kid—a crane with a miniature wrecking ball hanging from a string.

As he approaches me, he pauses. His eyes seem to linger on my face. I bow, and when I do, I hear a noise barely subdued by the priest's chant. It takes me a second to decipher it.

The cell phone in my pocket.

Chapter Five

I grab for the phone, try to silence it, and start to scoot down the pew, away from the priest and the musky billows of smoke. At first I think the priest doesn't notice the offensive ringing coming from my pocket. I know I'm dead wrong when I catch his eyes. They remind me of the picture of a hooded cobra I used to stare at in a book when I was a kid. His lip curls in a barely perceptible, but unmistakable sneer.

No time for penance. I make a quick pass around an icon of Saint George the Dragonslayer, a picture of a man on a horse shoving a spear down the throat of a dragon, and head for the heavy side door. Thank God it's unlocked.

"Hello?" I say quietly, as if I'm still in the sanctuary. I walk around toward the front of the church, staying close to the building.

"Stuart, it's Katya. Where are you?"

"I was hiding in a church off of Red Square."

My eyes scan the area around the church, then out beyond the Historical Museum where the thugs first started to follow me. People still occupy the streets in small crowds. Many of them are coming in and out of the stores that line the street, carrying large bags, doing their last-minute shopping for Christmas. Looks like Russians and Americans have similar holiday-shopping habits.

"Why are you hiding?"

"Because some guys that look like Russian mafia were chasing me. What have you gotten me into, Katya?"

"Calm down. I doubt you were being followed. Not that quickly anyway."

"Katya, I'm a lot of things, but I'm not paranoid. I know when I'm being followed."

"Okay, so you were being followed. Don't worry. We have everything under control. All of your information has disappeared from the hotel. Nobody will ever know you were there." She pauses and I can picture her expression, biting on her lower lip. Whitney does the same thing when she's mulling something over.

"What did they look like?" Katya talks in a brisk, matter-of-fact tone that would sound condescending to someone who didn't know better.

"They looked like two bad Russian men in black with cigarettes hanging out of their mouths. What do you think they looked like?"

"Okay, okay. We can talk later. Where are you, what church is it?"

"I hid in the first building I saw. How would I know?" I look at the imposing building beside me. "Well, it's pink."

"*A, ti imeyesh v vidu takogo persikogo* [Oh, you mean peach]," she says. "The Church of the Lady of Kazan." Katya is talking to me as if we're discussing where to meet for lunch. "Stuart, get away from there as quickly as your feet will take you. This is not a good place for you to be." Then she adds, almost as if she's talking to herself, "What a coincidence that you would end up *hiding* there, of all places."

"What is that supposed to mean?" I take another look around. "It seems nowhere in Russia short of Siberia would be a good place for me right now, Katya. So, get me to a place that is safe."

"Yes. Okay, go around to the back of the church. On the other side you will see the entrance to the GUM. Go inside and wait there."

The more cheerful she sounds, the more irritated I feel. It's that way with Whitney when we're discussing things. I never realized how much these two women are alike. This is probably why I feel so comfortable being antagonistic in the friendliest sort of way with Katya now, after so many years. Physically, they're as different as day and night, but both are driven, certain, and powerful.

I need to send Whitney a text. She's not a worrier, but ever since we had Adanna, she's more uptight about my survival on the planet. I am too, which is why I've been taking on local speaking engagements and safer international assignments. Like one to Russia. Or so I thought.

"Go to the Sbarro's. My associate Vladimir will be there in a few minutes; he's close by. You can't miss him. He's tall and has a large scar on the right side of his face."

"You have a Sbarro's here?" The fear-infested chambers of my heart are momentarily filled with light. I haven't eaten in hours.

"This isn't Russia. It's Moscow, a totally different country." She sounds exasperated. "Now, hurry up. But, Stuart, there's something I want to talk with you about...."

I laugh. "I hope so, Katya."

"Do you remember Marina?"

"Of course I do." How could I forget her?

I'm already around the back of the church and moving toward

the GUM, a colossal building three stories high. It looks surreal with every single window circled by huge white Christmas lights. There must be a hundred windows. I can see the displays of clothes and toys inside.

"Uh, okay, I need to go. We will talk when I see you," I say. I'm running for my life and don't have time to talk about Marina at the moment.

I walk toward the center of the building, where the food area would likely be. Different music tracks blare from each storefront I pass, all ambient sounds. Christian Dior. Hugo Boss. Armani. The mall is crowded with Russians wearing full-length fur coats, gloves, and hats. Except for the fur and sea of flawless Slavic faces, you could be in the Galleria in Dallas or the Mall of America in Minneapolis. Some people in this country have serious money.

It doesn't take long to find the food court. My nose catches a waft of pizza, garlic, and fried hamburgers. Right outside the doors of Sbarro, I see a behemoth of a man sitting on a bench, reading a Russian newspaper. Katya said he was big, not three hundred pounds enormous. He brings the paper down, revealing a six-inch scar on his face, curved in the shape of the sickle on the Russian flag. He gives a slight nod in my direction, rises two heads above the crowded tables, and begins to walk toward me. I'm either completely safe or dead.

I follow him through the swinging double doors. Parked outside is a black Russian car I immediately recognize as a Volga, a square-shaped ride that's a cross between a Mercedes and a Buick Roadmaster. On the roof is a blue light typically reserved for the police and FSB, the former KGB, officials. It's running. Someone inside slides from the driver's seat to shotgun. The giant hasn't said a word to me. Every movie that involves kidnapping and abduction flashes before my eyes.

After Vlad opens the door, I take a deep breath and get in.

Before I can close the door, we are moving.

"Hello, Stuart Daniels," he says to me as his bulky frame turns around from the front seat. "My name is Vladimir and this is my colleague, Sasha."

"*Zdratsye*," Sasha responds and flashes me a picket fence of gold teeth. He's more my size, the wiry type, and his gray eyes remind me of a young kid's, bright and full of mischief.

"You can call me Vlad." The hulk smiles at me in the rearview mirror. When he does, his scar bunches together, turning the sickle into a long caterpillar.

"*Zdravstvuitea. Priyatno poznakomitsya s vami.* [Gentlemen. Nice to meet you.]" I swallow hard.

"It was a good thing for you to help those girls, Mr. Daniels. A very good thing," Sasha says to me with an accent so thick I can hardly understand his English. His long arm stretches back across the seat, and he hands me a bag from Sbarro. I open the bag and steam pours out. Thank God, a calzone and a bowl of soup. It's not the best Borscht in town, but it tastes like heaven.

"Hope you like the pepperoni," Vlad says.

I nod. "Thanks, man. I haven't eaten since breakfast."

We weave in and out of traffic like we're in a race on the Charlotte speedway. I still feel uneasy, like I'll end up in a ditch, frozen, identifiable only by dental records, like victims on the CSI shows Whitney loves. She's always ten steps ahead of the investigator. I look at my phone and see a full-strength signal. I remember the last time I was in Russia traveling from Moscow to St. Petersburg. I had a full signal in the middle of nowhere on a train. Guess there's something to say for Russian cell technology. I whip off a quick text letting Whit know I'm okay:

> Hey babe! All is well. Busy
> but will call soon. Miss
> U and Adanna. xx oo.

I read it three times before I hit Send. Short and sweet. Nothing that will cause alarm.

Vlad says, "We are going to Nadezhda Home. Katya waits for us there."

Hope Home. A good name for an orphanage. Restoring hope—one of the noblest causes in the world.

Everything I know about Katya is about her efforts to return hope to those who've lost it. I think of the orphans I've met over the years, so many of them left behind because of war or AIDS, without any resources to pull themselves up—dead poor.

But there's poor, and then there's Africa-orphan poor. I'm still sorting through my experience with orphans in Swaziland, even though I've spoken about it now around the country more times than I can count. The pictures I took captured despair most people can't fathom, but I also saw hope in the most unlikely places. God in the most unlikely places. I know that to be true. Or maybe in the darkest places is where we can see His light. Africa is certainly where He got a hold of me.

I went to Swaziland, Africa, two years ago to do another story. A story I didn't want to do but had to for the money. That's all I cared about at the time, trying to make a buck. And I wasn't doing it very well.

What happened to me in Swaziland changed me forever, and it was completely unexpected. I met a little orphan girl who was the head of a household. One of those kids who had to be the parent to her younger siblings. When I heard her story, I knew it would be a hit in the newspapers at home. The more I got to know her, and love her, the more I realized that I needed what this girl had to offer me more than almost anything else in my life. She was so beautiful, so brilliant, such a light in a dark world.

Her name was Adanna, and her legacy lives on in my very own home. I named my beautiful baby daughter after her.

The idea of being orphaned, looking into the eyes of children who don't have parents, is tough to reconcile when it comes to cosmic justice. Like those girls in the hotel room, like one little girl I met years ago the first time I stepped foot in Russia.

I was sent by the *Washington Post* to shoot pictures for a cover story about Russia after the fall of communism. It was 1994, just after the wall came down. Americans were still scared of their cold war enemy, and a skeptical public wanted some questions answered. News agencies were dying to get in, to report on a giant just awakened. Even though I was green as a photographer, my boss knew I was good … and more importantly, willing to risk everything to get the right shots. Plus, I knew the language. So, along with one seasoned

writer, a guy who got the name "Mac" because he was a dead ringer
for singer Michael McDonald, I got my chance. Fortunately, in a
group where everyone seemed to have an ascribed nickname, I was
just "Stu." Story of my life.

When it came to questions from the Western world, Russians
didn't have the luxury of answers. Nobody was sure who ran the
government or what would become of them as citizens. Lines to the
food markets stretched for a half mile into the brutal Russia winter.
People would wait for hours, wrapped in blankets, trying to stay
warm. You could watch the snow accumulate faster than those lines
moved, but nobody left. Food was too important. Opportunists were
selling American jeans in the street for the equivalent of one hundred
dollars, which was big money to Russians.

I would move through the streets, milling through crowds with
kids, mostly teenagers, following behind, and ask people if I could
take their pictures while acting as unofficial interpreter for Mac.
Everyone was enthusiastic about posing for an American reporter
while holding up peace signs, waving, and saying, "Hello, America."

The hard part was getting them to act natural, especially the
kids, who would pose like Ice-T, with a crazy gang hand symbol.
I remember Mac saying, "Good God, of everything they could get
from Western culture, they end up with gangsta rap?"

Knowing Russian helped build quick friendships. A Yank was
intriguing enough. A Yank who spoke Russian, irresistible, especially
to the women, but mostly babushkas, old Russian grandmothers,
who wanted to pinch my cheek.

I felt sad for the Russian people. I shot innumerable photos that
captured the calamity of a people who had no real sense of personal

destiny and no system in place even to access basic needs. Those pictures, and the entire trip, became the envy of my colleagues. We were all tooth-and-nail competitive at that time, so it's just what I wanted.

My assignment was twofold. One, I needed to catch the heart and soul of the Russian people in post-Soviet Russia. The *Post* wanted to bridge the cold war gap that existed not between governments, but between the American and Russian publics.

Two, I was working in partnership with a writer from the *Times* on a story of the death of John Plotnik, a Russian American who grew up in New York. He came back to his homeland with fire and vigor to help expose the corruption ruining the country. He started *Forbes* magazine in Russia, and the first few editions focused on exposing the oligarchs who were raping and pillaging the country of resources and finances. After only a few short months of being in Russia, John was gunned down after work on a Moscow street. In many ways life in this country was a lot like the wild American West used to be.

But the greatest tragedy was one neither Mac nor I expected. It hit me in a small, sleepy forest town called Neya. We drove five hours out of the city of Vladimir to "catch the Russian soul." Neya used to be a thriving village with a prosperous lumber mill and a number of successful farms. But no more. The town had been practically deserted. Crumbling factories lined the main street and sat vacant. Buildings were boarded up, glass windows were broken out, taverns closed; only a few shops and kiosks remained open.

You could see the poverty etched in the deep crevasses on people's faces. Those wrinkles said something to us. Desperation and hunger have a certain look. These people had that look. When they saw the nice car we were riding in and that we were foreign tourists, they flocked to us and begged. Mothers with babies in their arms, old men and kids—everyone asking for something, anything we could offer. There was no pride in the way of their pleading. That's what poverty does to you. Turns a human being into something they were never meant to be.

We pulled up to what looked like an abandoned three-story factory. It had been painted white, but the gray cement seemed to seep out in splotches through peeling paint. When I stepped outside of the car, I felt immobilized by the thickness of the air. I looked up at the building. Through the window I saw children's faces, three sets of hollow eyes staring out at us.

The cold had numbed me, but a bold, animated woman brought life to the desolate scene. Katya. She was working as a translator but was also in school for social work. Her head was crammed full of stats on orphans. She told Mac, "There are more than one million orphans in Russia. Most of them are social orphans, children who have been abandoned because their parents cannot take care of them or have lost their rights. A good many have been abused by alcoholic parents. You can imagine the psychological and social damage this does, knowing a parent has left them and is still alive out there...."

I don't remember everything she said, but I know we were silenced when we stepped from statistics into reality. When we arrived, the director of the orphanage came outside with two children dressed in traditional Russian attire. One girl wore a full-length white dress, the other red. The dresses were yellowed, stained with dirt, and torn but beautifully embroidered with fake pearls and lace. Both wore round fur hats that fit snugly around their heads and had the same pearls draped like a rope around the rim. They shouted, "*Khleb da sol!* [Bread and salt!]" Then they served us bread and salt, a customary welcome greeting to guests.

Inside, we saw kids standing in the corners, leaning over the rickety rail of the stairs, congregating in small groups of three or four in the foyer. The rotten smell of sewage crawled up my nose and elicited a gag, which I tried to quell. I looked over at Mac, who had the same reaction. I had to breathe out of my mouth to deal with the stench. The outhouses were located inside the building because it was too cold outside.

Of course it was inevitable that I really had to use the bathroom moments later. I was shown to a room just inside the entryway. The acrid aroma of ammonia, mixed with the sewage smell, burned my nasal passages. It was still extremely cold, and I could feel the chilled air pouring in from outside. A small stack of used notebook paper sat on the floor. Their version of toilet paper. And there was an icy ring about an inch thick surrounding the hole that had been cut out of the wooden seat.

All the children wore jackets. Holey, thin, moth-eaten jackets. When I exhaled, I could see my breath, like wispy smoke.

"Apparently, heat is a luxury here," I had said to Katya. From the way the kids appeared, food was too. Their faces were pallid. Skin was drooping from their bones like wax from a candle. Most clasped their hands in front of them and with heads partly bowed looked up at me with empty, faraway eyes. Eyes that asked many questions. Questions like *Why do my parents hate me? When will my misery end?* and *If there is a God, why has He forgotten about me?*

I remember exactly what I said to myself on that day, "So this is what hopelessness looks like."

I was young in my career, but I had already seen atrocity in my first assignments. Genocide in the Congo, starvation in China. In college I went on mission trips to Guatemala, Thailand, and the Dominican Republic. Every face of poverty looked the same. Didn't matter the color of their skin, or what part of the world they were in.

Without thinking, I lifted my camera and prepared to take a picture. "Be professionals first. Tell the story. Get the shot." That was what we were told in school, in our training. That's what I lived for back then. But something about this dirty orphanage, these kids, gnawed at me. Maybe because they were just little children, a preschool filled with some of the most beautiful kids I had ever seen, children who were suffering like neglected animals. It wasn't right, and for the first time since I'd been a photographer, I let the scene get to me. My anger boiled over at the injustice. I lowered my camera.

We followed the director back to her office. Her name was Tatiana. She told us how difficult it was being the director of this orphanage. There was little food and no coal for heat. The little boys and girls would come to her every night and say, "Mama, won't you please feed us dinner this time? We're so hungry our bellies are burning." She wept in front of us.

Katya comforted her, telling her she was a good woman doing the best she could. She vowed to Tatiana that she would help her get what she needed for this little orphanage out in the country. At the time, I thought Katya was just trying to make the poor woman feel better. Little did I know that Katya was a woman who meant exactly what she said.

After our meeting, we stepped out of the office and into the hallway. At the end of the corridor, I noticed a little girl sitting alone on the floor with her back against the wall. As we moved around the room, I could see her eyes following. Haunting deep blue eyes that kept asking me the same question by their penetrating gaze: *Are you friend or foe?*

"Is it okay for me to go and talk to her?" I asked Tatiana.

"If you would like." The director wrinkled her nose at me, as if I had asked to rummage through her trash. "She does not talk." What a strange person, I thought, to be so compassionate one moment and dismissive the next.

I shuffled in the girl's direction, clueless about what to say. She was clutching an old torn teddy bear that was missing an arm. She looked up at me with dull hollow eyes, less a child's eyes and more like the eyes of a man who'd seen war.

I crouched down beside her. No smile, not even an acknowledgment that I was there.

"*Priviet*," I said quietly. "*Kak dyela?* [How are you?]" Still no response. Katya came over to sit down next to her for what must have been an hour. I remember she stroked the teddy bear's head.

"What a handsome bear."

The girl shook her head no and pointed to the stuffing where the arm should have been.

"We all get broken from time to time. I will fix him for you. Handsome Bear will have a brand-new arm." I didn't know it at the time, but this was the first of many promises Katya would make to orphans. And keep.

Mac and I stayed at that orphanage all day, playing and talking with the kids, and returned the next with anything we could get our hands on to help them: soap, toothbrushes, even a few hundred-kilogram bags of coal. Mac asked the kids questions about how they ended up there. Tatiana didn't seem happy about it, but she didn't tell us to leave. She was a good woman doing a monumental task for pennies. An orphanage director was at the bottom of the food chain in Russia. If she didn't have the heart for those children, she wouldn't have been there. I don't think she even knew how to ask for help, and I felt sorry for her.

To my surprise, most of the kids loved posing for pictures. I brought a Polaroid camera and about ten packages of film with me. You would have thought I brought gold bullion bars. After each shot, the kids would take the picture gratefully and watch it materialize before their eyes.

By this time we were off assignment, but we didn't care. The little girl with the teddy bear barely spoke, but she stayed by my or Katya's side wherever we were for two days.

Katya fixed the broken bear. I gave the blue-eyed girl a heavy knit sweater I had picked up at a shop in Moscow and a pair of socks, black with little white flowers. We blew the rest of our cash buying warm clean clothes, fruits, vegetables, and shoes. I was selfish and pompous back then, but something about those kids shook me and led me to do something I knew was right.

The kids begged us to stay. We said good-bye ten times but kept lingering, not wanting to leave. There was something about this experience that was more real than anything I had ever known. They pleaded with us to return soon. "When will you come back, Daddy? Daddy, you won't forget me, will you? Do you promise?"

We arranged with Tatiana to send letters to the kids. It seemed like such an insignificant way to express our care for them. But it was all we could do.

"Don't make any promises," Katya told me. She didn't qualify that statement with textbook bullet points or statistics. That's when I started to like her. At that orphanage, our friendship was forged in fire and ash.

Before we left, I bent down in front of the little girl and asked, "*Kak tibya zavoot?* [What is your name, sweet girl?] I want to write you a letter from America, and I need to know who to send it to."

She lifted her sad, cherubic face and looked right into my eyes. With a hoarse but fierce voice she said, "My name is Marina. Marina Smolchenko."

Chapter Six

I check my watch and wipe off a smudge from the lens of the video camera. Marina comes back in the room and takes her seat in the creaking wooden chair. She takes a deep breath, composing herself, and continues her story.

Sanctuary. This word trails through my mind like smoke as I kneel and face an altar in a church that is no longer a sanctuary for me. When I was a young girl, I took comfort in going to the old church near my orphanage with the other kids. Even though the people in the town looked down on us because we were of bad blood, it was a day I felt most like I had a family. Sitting in the quiet, listening to the priest sing a liturgy I could say by heart, I would let my eyes study the stages of the cross depicted on the church wall and pray the prayers of the religion I learned when I was five. Back then, I thought the priest was God Himself. I felt close to God. Now the sight of the black smock, the smell of incense makes me sick. I rest my eyes instead on the icon of Mary, the Madonna with her Child. Even that is more than I can hold sometimes, so I mostly look down at my hands, raw and red from the number of times I wash them each day. It's never enough.

When I was fifteen years old, I was forced to leave the orphanage that had been my home for almost a dozen years. Except for one or two memories from before, it's the only home I can remember. That day came upon me like a bad omen at the end of May. One day I was two years old and the next I was standing outside the rusty orphanage doors with one small bag in my right hand—it was everything I possessed.

The director was cold to me that day. She wouldn't even look me in the eye. This woman was the only mother I had ever known, but she pretended like she didn't even know me. She grabbed a stamp, banged it on a small stack of papers three times, signed her name, and handed them to me.

"You will be fine, Marina," she said. "There's no need to cry. Many girls who have left our orphanage have happy lives. Soon you will see. There's one last gift your orphanage will give you. A ride to the capital city where you can check into technical school."

Outside, a group of my closest friends stood wishing me well. Some waved, some cried, and some handed me notes and gave me kisses. They had become my brothers and sisters. I wondered if I would ever see them again.

There weren't any jobs in Neya, so I chose to go to the main city of Kostroma. At least I would have a place to sleep until school started in the fall.

The city was bustling with activity. There were people everywhere, walking in the streets, driving in cars, hanging out in the parks. Big buildings were lined up like soldiers at roll call. There were shops and restaurants everywhere. I had never seen anything like this.

The car stopped in front of a six-story building. I grabbed my bag and got out. Birch trees lined the streets on both sides. It was a very beautiful place. The sign on the front said Lubodovev Technical College. Here, I would learn carpentry and how to lay brick. I could hardly wait.

I stepped through the gate and knocked on the door, but there was no answer. I knocked again and again, but no one came. I didn't know what else to do so I sat on the steps and fell asleep.

I was startled awake when a short plump woman with dark curly hair appeared and spoke to me.

"What are you doing here?" she asked.

"My name is Marina and I'm from Neya orphanage and I'm here to check in for school."

"School doesn't start until September," she said. Then she walked past me and put the key in the lock. "Come back in September."

I told her I didn't have anywhere to go, that I didn't know anyone in the city. I asked if she could find me a room, a place to stay. But she just laughed. I pleaded with her, but she said it wasn't her job. Then she went inside and slammed the door.

I had no family, no money, no way to survive.

I tried to look for a job, hoping someone would feel for my condition and provide work and a room, but because of the orphan stamp I had on my papers, nobody would hire me. I felt like a bird that kept trying to fly through a glass window.

Those nights I lived on the streets. I begged for food, I rummaged through trash bins behind restaurants just to stay alive. I tried to stay away from people because I was afraid. But thugs would always find me and tell me to give them money … and other things. They would grab me and hit me. Most of the time, I got away. I would run into the arms of a stranger and they would chase them away. Every day I was under the threat of being raped or beaten up. There was no one for me to turn to, no one to protect me, no one who cared whether I lived or died.

One evening, I was sitting in the Metro station to stay warm. My coat was pulled up around my neck, so only my eyes and the top of my *head showed, and my hands were cupped in front of me. I was begging. A woman came up to me, put a few coins in my hand. I looked up at her and said, "Thank you." She put her hand on my back and started to talk to me.*

"This is no place for a beautiful girl like you," she said. "Would you like a job so you don't have to live on the street? I can help you."

She seemed so nice. She was clean and had white straight teeth. I felt disgusting in her presence, with my dirty hair and clothes that hadn't been washed for weeks. She wore expensive clothes. Her breath smelled like peppermint.

I nodded. Of course I wanted a job.

"That's a good girl," she said. Then she gave me her card and told me to meet her at a certain address at a certain time to fill out paperwork. She promised to find me a nice job as a nanny somewhere like England or America. The pay was two thousand dollars a month.

My eyes got as big as two five-ruble coins. Two thousand dollars? If I had a job making two hundred dollars, I would be rich.

She assured me it was all true. She said, "People pay more in foreign countries than here in Russia where everyone is poor. Be there tomorrow. We'll even buy your airline ticket."

Then she told me her name. Alexandra. She put ten rubles in my hand and walked away.

Chapter Seven

I step out of the car through blinding snow and into a bright room that is more reminiscent of Disneyland than a Russian orphanage.

"Well done, Stuart. I'm glad you made it out of the hotel safely!" Katya reaches around my wet coat and gives me a tight squeeze before I can even get through the door.

Once inside, I am overwhelmed by color. Scenes from Russian fairy tales have been painted onto the walls with remarkable skill, icons of ancient tales in painstaking detail. I can't believe what I see around me.

Katya moves quickly, but I lag behind to take in the art. I recognize images from "The Fire Bird and the Gray Wolf" along the main hallway. One is a depiction of the tsar's son catching the tail of the Fire Bird. I recall the story as I pass.

The tsar has a tree that bears golden apples, and one of them is stolen every night. He tells his two oldest sons that whoever catches the perpetrator will inherit half of his entire kingdom. Both fall asleep and the youngest son, the character in the painting, has an opportunity to catch the thief. The painting is a dazzling display of bright greens and golds colliding as the son reaches for the bird. He is a handsome blond-headed young man of about fifteen, clothed in royal gold garments and wearing a red cape. He has the complexion of a porcelain doll and the determined look of a man on a mission. As the story goes, he reaches up and grabs one of the bird's fiery tail feathers at the last second. This leads him to finding the bird and capturing it to please his father and win him half of the throne.

As I continue on down the hall, I discover a depiction of my favorite fairy tale, "Snegurochka," or "The Snow Maiden." I see the Christmas-themed Snow Girl, the daughter of Fairy Spring and Father Frost. She's depicted in the painting as a young girl with a perfect white complexion. It's the dead of winter, the trees are covered in snow, the night is clear, and the crescent moon is hanging in the background. On her head she wears the traditional blue hat that looks like a crown made of cloth. A squirrel rests on her right hand, and two rabbits snuggle against her feet.

As the story goes, the immortal Snow Girl falls in love with a shepherd named Lel because she wants to know what it's like to fall in love like humans do. But her heart is unable to know love. Her mother takes pity on her and gives her this ability, but as soon as she falls in love, her heart warms up and she melts. Every time I see the Snow Girl, I am reminded of the first time I was in Moscow when I saw a play based on the story, set to the music of Tchaikovsky.

"I never could have imagined a Russian orphanage looking like this," I say to the walls. Katya is ten steps ahead. I walk into the auditorium to see a group of girls working on a set for a Christmas play. About twenty of them are milling around the theatre stage with paints, butcher paper, and material. They're divided into three groups, and each is busy working on different parts of the play: costumes, design, and props. It's got to be close to their bedtime.

"Stuart," Katya says, marching back down the hall toward me. She waves to one of the girls and motions for her to come. "Let's have tea. I'll introduce you to everyone later."

She leads me to a door sporting a large gold plate emblazoned with the word Director. We join Vlad, who is already in the office.

"Stuart, I have placed your camera equipment in the room where you will stay tonight," Vlad says. "It's all in perfect condition."

"Thank you. That gear is important to me."

There's a knock on the door and a young blond woman, the one Katya waved to in the auditorium, enters with a tray in her hands. On it are warm Russian biscuits and pastries.

"Stuart, this is Alyona." Katya smiles at her.

I stand up. "Nice to meet you."

Alyona is wearing a long dark skirt and an embroidered white blouse. Slight, with a small nose and rosebud lips, she could have jumped straight from the orphanage wall. Vlad takes the tray from her and, with a slight bow, pours steaming water into three cups.

"She's also a girl who's been rescued," Katya says. "Like the ones you've just helped." Alyona doesn't seem to mind the comment. "And she is the artist who made those beautiful paintings you were admiring."

I smile at her and nod in approval of her masterpieces. "You are an incredible artist. I truly mean that."

"*Spasibo.* [Thank you.]"

Katya turns to the girl and says, "You should show Stuart more of your paintings. He knows a little bit about art."

"Sure, I'd love that."

"Alyona is a great help to me."

"To us," Vlad interrupts and makes a deferential gesture, a slight bow in her direction. The whole scene is a little odd. Not sure what he's referring to. Maybe she's like a daughter to Vlad.

A bit of color rises in Alyona's cheeks, but she says nothing else. She seems to be the opposite of Katya, calm and slow but deliberate in her movements.

"Stuart, have a biscuit. You can't find these in America." Vlad hands me a plate with his beefy hands.

"*Spasibo*. [Thank you.]" I turn to Katya. "I've been in Russia less than twenty-four hours, and I've been chased by a couple thugs and likely made criminally negligent as an accomplice for the kidnapping of two—"

"Strawberry jam in your chai?" Vlad asks.

"Yeah, sure. Thank you." He places the crystal jelly bowl in front of me.

"Relax, Stuart," Vlad says in a calm voice.

Katya adds, "This is Russia. It's not *what* you know, it's *who* you know. We've covered your tracks well." Their blasé response ignites my frustration.

"It's illegal," I say. As soon as I say it, I know my complaint sounds lame. Katya smirks at me. She knows that's never been a concern of mine. And she's right. That's Whitney's voice coming out of my mouth.

"Okay, Katya. The bottom line is, I'm still not doing the job I came here to do." I take a bite of a sweet roll. It's warm, the taste familiar. At home, I'm a coffee guy. In Russia, it's chai or tea. You don't really have much of a choice here because the coffee tastes like the dirt from the bottom of your shoe. Although I've heard they just opened a Starbucks somewhere in Moscow. I made a mental note to find it before I leave. I could buy Whit a Moscow Starbucks mug for her collection.

"We have friends in high places," Katya says. Vlad and Alyona nod in agreement.

I finish my roll in three bites. Vlad serves me another. Alyona says nothing as she sips the tea Vlad has poured for her, but her eyes, bright blue and slightly wide set, don't miss a thing.

"How are those girls, the twins? Are they here?" I ask Katya. I hold my steaming tea like I'm waiting for a cue to drink.

"No, the girls are not here. But they are safe," Vlad says.

"Nick and the others, the lady and man you saw at the hotel, have taken them to one of the safe houses, one that is secure. I'd like you to see it while you are here. This is step one for the girls: safe, cared for in all ways, and most important, out of sight."

"Makes sense."

"We've been trying to find those girls for three months. They were literally stolen from the grandmother's home near St. Petersburg right after their mother died. A group of men walked in and took them at gunpoint."

"How can they do that?"

"There's nobody to stop them, certainly not an elderly grand-mother. Stuart, this is the biggest business in the entire world. Billions of dollars are trading hands in this industry. When you steal two beautiful girls, no matter where you find them, it means big money."

Alyona picks up the tray. Vlad opens the door for her, and she slips out silently.

I sit back on the narrow, comfortable brown velour couch. The rough fabric is patterned with rows of tan fleurs-de-lis. Katya has always liked this symbol. A single fleur-de-lis hangs behind her desk, along with an ornate Orthodox cross carved out of dark wood that looks like it weighs a ton. Each point on the cross is shaped like the onion dome of the Russian church. I can tell this is an Orthodox cross by the addition of a slanted line at the bottom. Looks like the place where Jesus would have put His feet.

Katya's desk is like mine at home, barely ordered chaos. The walls are burnt yellow, and Katya's credentials hang above her desk: master's of social work and doctorate in psychology from the University of Moscow.

The wall opposite her desk is filled by two huge bulletin boards. One is covered with faces of girls who look to be young teenagers, some perhaps in their early twenties. The other holds pictures organized with deliberate intent. It looks like something from a CSI show: black and white shots of girls on the streets in front of cars, girls in airplane terminals, groups of girls being loaded onto buses.

I walk toward it and run my finger along the photos, as if I can see better by touching them. I should be surprised at the boards, but I take them in with detached interest, looking for clues or connections. I notice a screen above the boards that could easily be pulled down to cover them.

I hear a light bell ringtone, and Vlad answers his phone with a gruff "Da" while moving out the door before I can even spin around to look.

"Who took these pictures?" I spot the Lady of Kazan Church in one of the photos. Tacked around it are pictures of girls. Each picture has a number assigned to it. My eye is drawn to a girl leaning against a building. She's dressed like she's going to a Russian disco, but her pallor has a gray aspect to it, like she's sick. Or maybe on drugs. Another is of a man walking with three girls, all young Russian beauties. I pull the picture off to get a closer look. As I do, I feel Katya at my shoulder.

"Hey, that's the priest from that pink church...."

Katya exhales. "Yes, the peach one," she says with an edge of certainty. I can feel her breath on my hair. She never did have much sense of personal space.

"Man, did he give me the stink eye when my cell phone went off. When you called during the service. He doesn't look like any man of the cloth I've ever met. Eyes like a snake."

"That's why I wanted you to get out of there. He is not a good man. In fact, *on bolnoy chelovek* [he is a very sick person]."

Katya points to one of the girls in the picture with the priest. "Do you recognize that girl, Stuart?" She's as tall as the priest, with long blond hair loose, hiding half her face. Her skirt is micro, barely there.

I take it from the wall to look more closely.

"Is that? Oh, God." I look at Katya's face, and I know. It's Marina.

"This is what I wanted to talk to you about, Stuart."

I can tell she is trying not to show emotion, so I keep my face turned away. She loves Marina, the first orphaned child that squeezed Katya's heart. Katya would give me reports about her over the years as if she were a proud aunt. She even forwarded me a couple of letters Marina had written to me after my first visit to the orphanage.

"Katya, how did this happen? The last I heard from you, Marina was doing great." I can't stop looking at the picture.

Katya's eyes are brimming with tears.

She grabs a tissue and talks as she dabs the water from her eyes and catches the clear liquid crawling below her nose. "Because the trafficking of young girls has received no attention in Russia, it has become much worse." Katya is pulling herself into teacher mode. "I told you the story of how the twins were abducted, but this is not the exception. It happens in home after home. There was even a rumor at one point that someone in the government was profiting from the mafia bosses in this industry."

"That has to be one of the sickest things I have ever heard in my life, and I've heard plenty."

"It is appalling. When girls like Marina leave the orphanage, they are prime targets for kidnapping. Nobody misses them—and there's no family to report them missing. Of course I blame myself for her disappearance because I was out of the country when she left the orphanage...."

A wave of emotion chokes the rest of her words away.

"So they don't exist. They're nameless." I scan the board again. "Is it mostly by force?"

"Sometimes. Other times, and this is what I think happened in Marina's case, the girls think they are applying for legitimate jobs in Russia or abroad. These traffickers are very clever at how they trap them."

"So you started helping the girls and started this center?"

"Da and nyet. I'm an orphanage director, and that's what this is. I'm considered some kind of expert on postadaptation of orphans into society. So I speak about this around the country. This is one way I've met people. You know, made connections and learned about this sex trade. It's how I met Vlad and Sister Irina—you will meet her, Stuart. An incredible woman. But anyway, once I started getting word of girls that I cared about disappearing, I had to do something. I couldn't stand by and just watch."

My mind is again drawn back to Adanna, my daughter's namesake. She was a young orphan who couldn't catch a break, even to the end. It wasn't her fault. But fate had decided whether she lived or died because of where she was born. Now Marina. I try to keep my mind from following the logical path to what she is experiencing, the detail of what's being done to her, maybe even at this very moment. I can't help but think of my daughter, and I feel a wave of disgust and a panic to protect her, though I know she's safe at home.

I remember just before it was time for us to leave her orphanage, I was taking pictures of the kids. Marina took my hand and led me back to the room she shared with six other girls. For some reason, she wanted me to know where she lived, the bed she slept in, and the things she owned.

I remember them clearly: her teddy bear, a note from her mother explaining why she left her kids, two shirts, one pair of pants, a hand towel, and a rubber ball. She wanted me to take a picture of her with those things. I can see the picture now. What did I ever do with that?

I place my thumb on her forehead in the picture on the bulletin board. "God in heaven, please help Marina," I say under my breath.

"Be with her; protect her from evil." If Katya saw me do this, she didn't utter a word.

"Why can't these kids catch a break?" I say. "What can a person do to help?" The sick feeling I had in my gut is turning to fear. Some voice is telling me I'm about to get an answer.

"You have helped, getting those girls out of the hotel." Katya's mind is somewhere else, her face pale.

"When was the picture of Marina taken?"

"See the date on the back—it's been several months, but we've been trying to track her."

I don't want to ask the next question, fearing the answer.

"Is she still alive?"

"As far as we know, she is."

The door flies open, and Alyona steps in, her face flushed.

"Katya, *Vladimir govorit, chto yemu nado pogovorit s toboy pryamo seichas.* [Vladimir says he needs to talk to you right away.]"

"I'll be right back," Katya barks, then disappears out the door.

She comes roaring back in seconds.

"Stuart, I have to go immediately. One of our girls has just been spotted at the Kropotkinskaya subway stop."

"But, wait a second—"

"*Nyet vremeni jdat.* [No time to wait.]" I follow her out the office door and watch her fly down the hall, throwing on her coat and giving orders to Alyona, who keeps up with her to the door. In the middle of her quickly spoken Russian, I hear "*Da, i ubedis, chto u Stuarta yest vsyo neobhodimoye dlya horoshego otdikha. On yemu ponadobitsya.* [Yes, see to it Stuart has what he needs for a good night's rest. He will need it.]"

Of course I'll need it. I've needed it for two days, but who can sleep in the middle of all this chaos?

I walk to the door and stand next to this willow of a girl, my new artist friend, surrounded by fairy tales. Vlad's already behind the wheel. Katya hops in, the tires screech, and they're gone.

The Russian night is crisp. The snow has stopped, and it's breathtakingly cold.

Chapter Eight

I thought that lady luck may have finally turned her face in my direction. Two thousand dollars? What I could do with that kind of money. I could buy an apartment and take care of some of my brothers and sisters from the orphanage. This was an answer to my prayers. And to travel the world and see America or some exotic place like that? I'd never been out of the Kostroma region.

The next day I found a church, and they let me take a shower and clean up. They gave me clothes for my interview so I would look really professional. These people were very nice and made me feel good.

I showed up at the right address fifteen minutes early. I was so nervous I broke out in a cold sweat. It was the first time I'd ever applied for a job like this. If they hired me, my problems would be over. But what if they didn't like me? What if I answered the questions wrong? I was so nervous.

A very tall, very big man answered the door when I rang the bell. He looked at me in a very uncomfortable way. Up and down his eyes went.

"Come in, golubushka, sweetheart," he said.

I followed him in the door. He didn't ask what I wanted or what I was doing there. We just kept walking down the hall.

"I'm here to apply for a job as a nanny in America. Alexandra sent me," I told him.

"Of course you are," he answered. "Yes, we have some very nice jobs for you in America. Cities like Atlanta, Dallas, and Seattle. You will love it."

We came to another door that was locked with a gold keypad. He punched in some numbers, each one beeping on command, then the door lock released. There was an elevator, and we went to the tenth floor. When the door opened, there was a very nice reception area with chairs and a couch and a large wooden desk and a sign that hung overhead and read "Bezperevoda, Welcome the World."

The place was busy with activity. Many people were running around, carrying papers, and conducting meetings. There was a conference room to the right with glass doors, and I could see a priest standing in front of the group. I figured, if there's a priest, this must be a good place.

And yet, the entire time, I had an uneasy feeling in the pit of my stomach. But I ignored it. The chance for a real job and real money was too good to pass up. Plus, this all seemed legitimate. A real office, professional people, an Orthodox priest? I knew I must be the luckiest girl alive.

This was the beginning of my new life.

Chapter Nine

"Where in the name of all the saints is Dr. Kudratseva?" It's Katya, her voice tight and frantic.

I step into the hall from the little room adjacent to Katya's office where I've been sleeping and see three-hundred-pound Vlad carrying a young girl toward Katya's office. She looks like a sleeping toddler in his arms, even more so with Vlad's long black jacket draped over her limp body. There's a dusting of snow on his jacket and on everyone's hats and shoulders.

When Vlad lays the girl down onto the couch, I see her hair is matted and wet under a makeshift tourniquet. Her white shirt is dotted with specks of dried blood, like red paint flung from a paintbrush onto a canvas. I can't tell if she's breathing.

Alyona appears behind them, a pale ghost. "Katya, he's on the way. I spoke with him minutes ago—he should be here any second." Alyona kneels down beside the girl, her mouth twisted in an empathetic twinge. "*O, Bozhe. Bednaya devochka.* [Oh, my God. Poor girl.]" This is the most expressive I've heard Alyona.

Katya kneels beside her, places her hand, her short, perfectly manicured red nails, onto the girl's forehead and begins to pray.

"*O Gospod moy, Sozdatel moy, proshu pomoshi Tvoey, darui istseleniye rabea bozhey tvoey, Natalie....* [Christ, who alone art

81

our Defender: Visit and heal Thy suffering servant, Natalia....]"

I remember this prayer from Sunday school, and I pray silently along with her, looking between Vlad and the girl slumped on Katya's couch. Vlad moves away and takes a position at the door. He slides his hand over his coat and clasps it on an object hidden inside, then crosses his arms, standing guard like a KGB agent. For all I know, he is a KGB agent. Katya continues to pray.

We all turn with a faint rap on the door. Vlad moves down the hall and returns with a short bald man in a short heavy coat with a fur collar. He's wearing small, round spectacles, which sit low on his wide nose, and he's carrying a large brown leather satchel. In spite of the cold, small beads of perspiration wobble on his thick head.

"Dr. Kudratseva." Katya stands and moves to give him room.

He takes off his coat and places it neatly on a chair and then rolls up his sleeves as if he has time to spare. He moves to the girl's side.

"How long ago was she shot?" He looks at a wristwatch that looks like it was made in the '60s.

"About thirty minutes."

"Tell me what happened, Katya." His voice has a calm, melodic quality to it, like a Russian Garrison Keillor. He reaches inside the case and pulls out a syringe filled with clear liquid. Two thumps on her vein with his forefinger, then he inserts the needle.

"She was shot in the head—right here, I think. That's where the blood was coming from." She points to the tourniquet, white except for one dot of blood.

"Hold her head," he says and begins to remove a torn undershirt.

He lifts her hair with surprisingly delicate hands. "Does this appear to be her only injury?"

"From tonight, yes."

The doctor turns to Alyona. "Darling, please get hot water and clean cloths to clean her up." She nods, and Vlad follows behind her.

I find Vlad and Alyona in the large rustic kitchen that reminds me of the Young Life camp I went to as a kid up in the mountains. An old electric industrial stove with six burners, two massive white stand-up refrigerators, and a stainless-steel sink so big you could take a bath in it. Vlad already has a large pot filled. Alyona has gathered up a pile of white cloths and towels.

"Can I do anything to help?"

Vlad looks back over his shoulder. "Yes, Stuart. Take a look out front to make sure no one has followed us, and make sure the door is locked behind you. Let me know the second you see anyone pull up."

I walk out and down the hall toward the front door, feeling like I'm walking in a strange dream. I see the Snow Fairy and the Fire Bird as glimmering silhouettes in the first light of day. It's still gray outside, but the snow has stopped. There are a few horns honking as the city comes to life in the early-morning hours.

I walk back into Katya's office just as the doctor raises forceps holding a small object, covered in blood. I can't really believe what I'm seeing, and yet there it is on the table: a small copper bullet.

"It was just at the top." Katya places a clean, wet cloth on the girl's head, and the girl's eyes shoot open. She sees me and the doctor in her field of vision, and she immediately begins to plead, "*Nyet! Nyet! Pozhaluista, ne delaite mne bolno.* [No! No! Please don't hurt me.]"

Katya swings around to face her. "Natalia, it's okay, sweetheart. You're with friends. Don't you recognize me, Natalia?" The girl works to study her face.

"Da. I know you." I can see her body relax. "*Vi director iz moyego detskogo doma*, Katya. [You're my former orphanage director, Katya.] Katya, my Katya. I've been praying to God I would find you again."

Chapter Ten

"We found her standing outside the Metro station and called her over to the car to ask her price. Someone must have been watching her." Katya is back to her jovial self. Her red lipstick has been reapplied with precision, her face smooth. Her eyes are bright, but like the rest of us, I can see she's still tired. We've had only a few hours of sleep.

She, Vlad, and I sit around the end of the long dark wood table in the empty kitchen. Natalia is in a deep sleep, with Alyona watching over her, keeping a vigil of solidarity.

Before us on the table is a late lunch of steaming, pungent *shchi*, a tomato-based soup. There's also a pile of *purea* (mashed potatoes), with *kotleti* (meatballs), and *chyorniy khleb* (black bread).

"You get your second-favorite soup, Stuart," Katya says. She is sitting across from me, Vlad at the head.

I reply, "*Shchi ta kasha peesha nasha*," and she busts out in a full laugh. It's an old joke, a phrase I used to say in jest years ago: Shchi and kasha are our staples. But the laugh is welcome.

"It tastes great. Just like my mother used to make," I say. It's actually better than anything my mother ever made. She would rather read a novel or paint than chop cabbage for Borscht. We were more likely to eat from cardboard takeout boxes, unless my grandmother Meema came to visit. When she was in the kitchen, pieces of vegetables would fly into pots and pans to become elaborate soups and casseroles. I remember Meema chasing my skinny self around with a bowl of soup, begging, "*Yesh, Stuart-vnuchok. Yesh!* [Eat, Stuart, my dear grandson. Eat!]" She took the same approach with her religion.

When it came to Meema's food and religion, my mother would just laugh, which infuriated Meema. Mom never worried about my physical or spiritual well-being; she thought it would all work out in the end no matter what happened. I suppose she was right. Meema would come twice a year for two weeks and leave us with a freezer stocked with avocado and orange Tupperware filled with Borscht that tasted just like the Russian soup in front of me.

Vlad skewers three meatballs on his fork, pops them into his mouth, and says, "I cracked open the door and told Natalia to get in. Katya was hiding in the backseat of the car and called to her—called her by name. But Natalia was paralyzed." He puts the fork onto his plate, like he needs his hand at rest to remember the details.

"I grabbed her arm, but before I could pull her in, I heard a shot. She was hit and fell *toward* the car, thank God. I got her inside, and we sped off." The scar on his face becomes red as he talks. "But it must have come from inside a building, since no one followed us in the car."

"At least that we could tell," Katya says.

"Do you have any idea who did it?" I say.

"I tried to see where the shot came from, but I couldn't tell." Katya sits back with her cup of tea. In the corner of the office, lights from a Christmas tree twinkle and reflect off silver tinsel. I can hear children singing Christmas songs from the auditorium, practicing for their show. Two days till Orthodox Christmas.

Vlad pours more hot water into cups around the table. Poor guy looks like he's sitting in a hospital waiting room waiting for bad news.

Katya says, "We think it's tied into a ring that's connected to the Lady of Kazan Church—the one where you were hiding."

"Connected … to a church?"

This is the world's worst nightmare. The church, the beacon of light and hope to the world, as the place of ultimate abomination.

"I wish it were just a story in a book, but sadly it's true. Girls have been trafficked in and out of that church for at least two years now. We have proof."

"That explains the young girls I saw on the front row of that church."

"You saw them?"

"Yes, they were caked in makeup. They didn't seem right. And the look in their eyes, it was so empty."

"Hmph," she says, then folds her arms across her chest, squints, and takes a deep breath.

"So the priest in that picture with Marina, he's involved."

Katya flinches at Marina's name, and I see that the guilt she's feeling is as heavy as her desire to get to her, to take her out of the hell she's fallen into.

"We are certain of it," Vlad says. "He's not your typical Orthodox priest."

I had recently started going to an Episcopal church in Manhattan with Whitney after years of wondering whether or not God even existed. Maybe it was an attempt to relive my childhood; maybe it was something more. I was still unsure about the whole idea of church—I walked in the door every week like I was testing a frozen lake for thin ice. Whitney liked the church because it was completely different from her pew-jumping upbringing, though she wouldn't trade the salt-of-the-earth people from her family church back home for anything. I continue to find it ironic that God used one of the smallest, weakest things in the world to reveal the strength of His love to me: that little girl on the African plain.

Adanna may not have meant much to many in this world. But meeting her was the beginning of life for me. It changed the way I saw God. It changed the direction of my life. She taught me that the small things I do matter. My decisions today can save a life tomorrow. That's why I'm here now.

"I've seen a lot of terrible things," I say. "I've even taken pictures of them. You know that, Katya. The whole reason I'm here on this assignment—well, the assignment I'm supposed to be on anyway—is because of my experience in Africa. I have seen what happens to a country—to kids—whose parents have died from AIDS and whose government is too screwed up to address the problem. It's ugly." I'm not sure why I'm telling them this, but I can't seem to stop.

"I met a little girl, Adanna. Her dad ran off God knows where, and then her mom died. This little girl was special, one of the most amazing people I've ever met. Then *she* died. She died while I was there in Swaziland." My eyes begin to water up, so I blink fast to stop the tears.

"Ah, now this is making sense. That's why you're so different. It's also where you got the name for your little girl, isn't it?" Katya says in a quiet voice.

I nod. Katya and Vlad look at me with intent, as if they're searching for other secrets in my words.

"What I saw there changed me. And what's even crazier is that, in that place where children are abused—raped by horrible people in their own family—where they can't dig graves fast enough to bury their dead, I found God. Or He found me. While I was there, I faced things where there wasn't any script. I brought food to a starving man in a hut whom I knew had raped his own daughter because he thought sex with a virgin would cure his AIDS."

Katya and Vlad sit and listen. Their faces are tense and their eyes are wide, but they're fully engaged in my words. I can't think of a time Katya was this quiet.

"Being there made me want to be better. I took on a mission, or was given a mission or something, to tell the world about AIDS and these kids. And now, what you're telling me, I don't know, maybe it's now that I'm a father—but I can hardly think of anything more evil than what's happening to these girls. And through a church? It's so, uh …"

"Sick. Inhuman," Katya finishes my thought. "And all for money."

Vlad rises, leans in toward me, and snatches my bowl. Startled, I jerk my head back. "It's the worst kind of slavery. Like living in hell," he says.

"At least you're doing something about it." I say this in an effort to make myself feel better. My life in the United States, even my work, seems remote, like I've stepped beyond it into another dimension. I am sitting here in this strange realm, this building filled with fairy-tale murals and happy Christmas songs sung by orphans and former sex slaves, eating biscuits that taste like shortbread placed before me by a giant with a scar the size of a banana on his face.

What are You saying to me through this, God? What does this mean for me? For my family?

As if sensing my thoughts, Katya asks, "Were you able to get in touch with your wife?" She won't call her by name. I think it's because Whitney is a tough name for a Russian tongue, more than anything else.

"Whitney, yeah. I sent her a vague text message to let her know I'm alive. I also checked in with my boss, to let him know I'm 'on assignment.' That's a joke."

But we are out of laughter. Vlad has stepped outside to have a smoke. I can see his profile, the wisps billowing in front of the kitchen window.

"There's one other thing." Katya looks directly at me, her blue eyes bright. "We saw Marina."

I swallow hard. Not sure if I want to hear what comes next.

"Katya! Why did you take so long to tell me?"

Vlad returns smelling like Prima cigarettes. They smell like wet pig hair.

"I am sorry. This is not so easy, Stuart." Katya pushes her shiny blond hair onto her head, holding her elbows out. It's a posture I remember from years ago, the way she sat for an hour in the car after we left the orphanage the day we met Marina. "Marina does not look well."

I'm immediately sorry I jumped on her.

Vlad sits and says, "You know, Stuart, we've been monitoring the logistics of how young girls are lured into the sex-slave industry. You may have noticed that our operation is much bigger than what you see here."

"I can only imagine."

"We have ten facilities spread across Russia including twenty-two others we partner with in different places around the world."

Katya lowers her arms and says, "We've been quite successful keeping girls from entering, and rescuing them once they're in. Planning and timing are essential." She looks down at the table. "Like in the case of Marina."

"I see." I'm not sure how to respond. I suddenly feel like Vlad and Katya are trying to sell me the Anti-Trafficking Multi-Level Marketing Business Plan. "Actually, I don't see. What do you mean?"

Vlad's eyes meet mine, and he says, "Stuart, Marina is in serious trouble. When we saw her, she had strange red rings under her eyes. Her color was white, like a ghost. We are not sure if she is sick or if they are keeping her drugged. I am guessing both. And we are sure she has been beaten."

"And much worse," Katya says.

Vlad folds his hands on the table in front of him and sits back, like a beefed-up Don Corleone.

"You have strong feelings about helping these girls, these children. I see that. And we realize you have already been put into a difficult position. But we are grateful for all you have done."

I feel like saying "You're welcome" and bolting to collect my belongings.

"It would be most helpful to us—" Vlad says.

"To Marina," Katya says.

"Da, to Marina," Vlad says, nodding, "if you would work with us one last time."

"Stuart." Katya puts her hand on my arm and tightens her grip. "It is very serious to get Marina out of there. And some of the other girls in that group. We have come to see that it is especially horrible." She spits this out like rapid-fire.

"What we are asking …" Vlad says with an exaggerated pause, "is for you to go undercover."

And there's the other shoe.

"Listen," I say, "I have to complete my assignment. I've got a job, a boss—not to mention a family to think about. I'm already at risk here." I sputter like a whiny child.

Katya holds her hand in the air, palm out like she's swearing on a Bible in court. "I know. I know it, Stuart. And we could never hold blame on you for saying no."

I can feel Vlad staring at me, testing my substance with his eyes.

"You know, Katya, I can't. It's not just me here anymore—the lone, single photographer."

How can I talk myself out of this one?

"I have Whitney to think of. And Adanna. Sweet, innocent little Adanna. I can't keep putting myself in harm's way. I have to think of them. I can't …" But as the words leave my mouth, I know I am going to do this.

Katya and Vlad know this too. That the reason I might refuse to do this is exactly the reason I will: *Moya doch.* My daughter.

Chapter Eleven

The man told me to sit down and then disappeared. A few minutes later the lady I met the day before came back. I clearly remember the conversation. I have thought about it many nights since.

"Hello, my sweet girl," she said with a big smile. A smile that reminded me of pictures I used to have of my mother.

"Hi."

"So you've come to apply for the job, have you? I knew you would come. This is going to change your life forever. You're going to be so happy. You'll bless the day you met me," she said.

There was nothing for me to say. I simply nodded and waited.

She told me to follow her. I did as I was instructed. We walked down the hall, past all the people. I remember walking by the glass conference room. The priest looked at me and smiled, and the queasy feeling went away. When I was younger, the director of the orphanage used to take us to the Orthodox church. The priest there was so kind to us.

When we got to her office, she asked me my name. I told her.

"Well, Marina," she said, "I have the perfect job for you. It just came open."

My heart was beating fast from the excitement. I asked if it was a job in the United States.

"No, it's not in the United States," she answered. "Although we may

have something open there one day soon. This one is in the beautiful country of Israel."

"Israel, the land of the Jews?" I asked.

She showed me pictures of Israel. They were beautiful pictures. Especially the ones of the sea. I had dreamed about the sea almost every night in the orphanage. The girls had a magazine with pictures from the Black Sea in the Ukraine. In those days I could imagine the smell of the salty water, feel the heat of the sun and the grains of the sand as they fell through my hands. All in the midst of that dark, wintry orphanage.

She told me that the nanny position was with a very wealthy English couple who live in Ashdod. On the beach. Their house was right on the beach.

Just when I believed my luck couldn't get any better, she added one more thing.

"I almost forgot to tell you," she said. "This position pays differently than what I told you. It pays more. Two thousand five hundred dollars."

My mouth hit the floor. I didn't know what to say.

"This is normal money for this kind of position," she said. "You've just been on the wrong side of the fence for too long dear. Auntie Alex is going to change your life."

I believed her.

Every ... single ... word.

How could I not? My only other option was to go back to the street. This had to be real. The office, the people, the priest.

"I'll take the job."

She asked for my passport papers and told me to be ready to leave Friday. That was in only three days. Could I leave that soon? What did I have to lose?

Then she reminded me that they would take care of my airplane ticket. And my expenses. She said they would put me up in a really fancy hotel until the job started. I was stunned. I asked her why she would do all this for me.

"We get paid a good sum of money for finding the best girls to nanny," she began. "And you, my love, are one of the best. Look at this opportunity as something God has given you. It's His will, you know," she continued. "He gives and He takes away. This is certainly a gift."

I was so hungry to be loved, to be seen as someone who mattered, and so afraid I'd end up living on the streets if I said no that I completely missed the lies in her words.

"Thank you," I said. And for the first time in a long time, I felt safe.

Chapter Twelve

I sit in my small room at the orphanage wearing a perfectly tailored dark gray Valentino suit and Italian-made shoes that probably cost as much as my entire wardrobe at home. My photo equipment hasn't seen the light of day, short as the day is in Russia this time of year, since I've arrived at Nadezhda Home.

"Let's review this one more time," I say to Katya. "You and Vlad want me to waltz right into the middle of the Russian mafia, pretend to be someone I'm not, and buy their girls for cash so we can rescue them? Hmm, sounds like a death sentence in the making to me.... Sure, why not? I'd be insane to refuse." I smile nervously at Katya. "At least I'll be wearing a nice suit for my burial."

"Stuart," Katya says on the verge of sounding bored, "we have worked on this plan for years. We have cells set up in different places in the world: Tel Aviv, Rome, Seattle. This is the final move, a checkmate, if you will, for us to free a number of girls at one time." She doesn't sound convincing. "Look, we can protect you. That I can say positively."

"Okay, why me? Why can't you just send in one of your old mafia friends like Vlad?"

She sighs loudly, as if explaining the rules of a simple game to a child who just isn't getting it.

"It can't be someone Russian. That's not clever enough to fool them. You're American. We have a completely new identity created for you. You have a past, bank accounts, homes, businesses. It's the perfect plan."

I'm tormented by the last letter I wrote Marina. The words on that page have been burned into my retinas since I discovered her plight a few hours ago.

> Marina,
>
> You have become so dear to me. There are so many things I want to say to you. "Do not fear, you are not alone, I will always be here," are just a few.
>
> I want you to remember in good times and bad that you have someone in the United States who is on your side, who is here for you. I want you to know you have someone who loves you and cares for you just like a father.
>
> That someone is me.
>
> Your friend,
> Stuart

"And what if I screw up, Katya? It's not like I'm trained for this."

Katya raises her eyebrows. "Now that is a good question. But Vlad thinks you will not screw up. If he didn't think you could do this, you would not know anything about our operation. He is a very good judge of these things. It's what he was trained to do."

"And when it's done, I suppose the mafia will thank me for stealing all their girls and let me live?"

"Oh, no, of course not. We'll stage your death, or we'll make you disappear just like we did in the hotel. Remember, we Russians are good at that." She laughs loudly. "Or maybe we'll just put you in Russian ice boots and drop you at the bottom of the Volga?"

"Oh, you're funny, Katya. This is totally crazy."

"What if you could save Marina from the torture she's had to go through? What if you could save thousands of girls just like her from such a hellish existence? It could be the difference in her living. Or dying."

"That's not fair."

Not catching my meaning, she says, "Yes. That is right. It is not fair at all."

The second I agreed to help them, Katya picked up her phone to order clothes for me, American businessman Michael Stevenson. An hour later, a pert bald man showed up at the orphanage with his tape measure. Then Katya had Alyona, who is apparently the resident stylist as well as artist and criminal profiler, cut my hair.

"I resent this," I told Katya, who laughed when I emerged from the room with my dark hair, more gray showing than ever, at a respectable length.

"You look handsome, Stuart," she said. It was more like a mother talking to a boy than the kind of comment you'd want from a beautiful woman your own age.

"Not helpful," I said, and then felt bad when I saw the hurt look on Alyona's face. I had to explain to her that the cut was fantastic.

The next day, I observe my two new suits and a new pimped-out suitcase meticulously packed with two pairs of casual pants; two pairs of dark denim jeans I wouldn't be caught dead in at home; nice button-up shirts—two striped, two white; and European underwear and socks. There's also a pair of loafers and, embarrassingly, cowboy boots tucked back into the boot compartment.

I've been known to wear the same T-shirt and faded holey jeans for days. My post-therapy self knows this is one of the ways I showed Whitney she couldn't polish me up. It drove her nuts when we first married. At some point in our relationship—probably about the time she started to find me passed out drunk on the couch, sleeping all day, and not following through with the little agency work I had—she stopped caring what I wore. She just wanted me to get out and do something. Once she stopped caring, I upgraded my clothes on my own. She really has put up with a lot from me. I owe her, big-time.

Will she forgive me if something goes wrong with our undercover sting operation?

With these strong women in my life, I'm becoming less like myself every day.

I know I should pray, but the hum in my brain is taking over and I can't find any words. The only prayer I really know anyway is the acknowledgment of what God is doing in my life now.

I feel stiff in my clothes, even if they do fit better than anything I've ever owned. The last time I was dressed up like this was at Whitney's mom's funeral, last fall. Her pastor was Reverend Campbell. He was the kind of pastor you'd want your family to hang out with—and he stayed with the family till the last guest left their house. He threw back a cold one and laughed at the stories of all the ways Whitney's brothers terrorized their mom when they were growing up. I could tell he was a man of God. He was stocky, a man's man, like Whitney's brothers and dad, but gentle with a low, reassuring voice. Reverend Campbell had been her pastor for as long as Whitney could remember. I can still hear that voice, the words he read at the church:

"Though I walk through the valley of the shadow death, I shall fear no evil. For Thou art with me."

I can picture these words in my head, like they're chiseled onto a headstone. Perhaps that's the wrong image. Not a headstone. The words are chiseled into some kind of metal. The image is blurry, and then it becomes sharp. A shield. The words are inscribed on a three-pointed medieval shield. If God is angry about anything, it has to be this industry. If He's not with me in this, how can I believe that He's with me in anything?

I'm startled by Vlad's deep voice outside my door. "Ready, comrade?" Had I nodded off?

"Ready," I say. I walk behind his broad frame and put my foot in the size fourteen imprints he leaves on the carpet to meet Katya down the hall; the image of the shield, the inscription, the promise, still fresh in my mind.

As I walk past decor presenting the glimmer and cheer of the holiday season, I feel something like breath on my right, like someone's clothes are brushing against mine, but no one is there.

Katya is talking to me in a fast hushed voice: "Vlad will give you everything you need. Follow his instructions to the letter, Stuart." I feel strange and disconnected from her words. Maybe I did fall asleep.

Katya makes the sign of the cross on my head and then presses her forehead to mine.

"*Bozhe khrani i oberegai tebya.* [God keep and protect you.] We have everyone in the network saying prayers for you. *Ya ne perestanu molitsya, poka ne uslishu.* [I will not stop praying until I hear word.]"

Chapter Thirteen

The next three days were like bliss. I had a warm room to stay in and three meal tickets a day to a buffet where I could eat as much as I wanted. There was a TV in the room, and I watched every episode of Santa Barbara *I could find. I thought, if America really is like what the TV portrays, it's the closest thing to heaven on earth.*

After two days, another girl named Natasha joined me. She got a job with another family in the same city in Israel. We knew it was fate. We would be best friends forever. We would hang out on the beach all day, go to movies, and buy lots of clothes with all of our money.

I felt like the luckiest girl alive. Life didn't get any better than this.

"Do you want to stop and take a break?"

I hear my own voice in the background as Marina pauses to brush a strand of hair from her face. The film editor had thought we should leave my intrusion on her monologue. During the filming and editing process, we decided to keep all the rough cuts between scenes, to keep the film raw and on the edge of disorienting. Not that it needed much more than Marina's words.

"No. Let's keep going," Marina says in a weary voice. "Where were we?"

"Natasha had joined you," I say.
"Okay, yes. Natasha."

Poor Natasha.

I hadn't heard from Alexandra again until the day she came to pick up me and Natasha. We were in the middle of popping popcorn and watching a movie when a knock came on the door. At that point I remember feeling like I didn't want to leave. I wanted to stay in this room and eat popcorn forever.

But I opened the door anyway. Alexandra came rushing in with two other women. Those women never looked at us, never smiled.

"Girls, get ready right now, we must head to the airport," she said.

"But we aren't even ready," I told her.

"There's no time to get ready," she said. "Get your things together and get dressed as fast as you can. I bought some new clothes for you to wear. It's my little going-away present."

The clothes were amazing. I was dressed in a lacy black skirt with a white sweater and Natasha wore a gorgeous black dress. We looked like sisters.

We rushed downstairs and saw a fancy black Mercedes-Benz waiting to pick us up. We felt like royalty sitting in the back of that car. It had leather seats and smelled like heaven. Natasha and I were so excited we grabbed hands, looked into each other's eyes, and screamed happy screams.

Everything went fine at the airport. Alexandra helped check us in *at the ticket counter. Then the nice lady behind the counter said, "Enjoy your trip to Egypt."*

"Egypt?" I said. "We're not going to Egypt; we're going to Israel."

"Yes, of course you are, dear," said Alexandra. "A very good friend of mine is picking you up in Egypt and taking you to Israel. It's much cheaper this way. That's why we can afford to pay you so well." She gave me a reassuring smile and put her arm around me, drawing me close like a mother would.

She even kissed me on the cheek.

I looked at Natasha, and she shrugged.

She handed us our tickets and an envelope, then walked us to the security line.

The instructions she gave us were very specific. I remember every word.

She said, "Now, girls, listen very carefully. The man who is going to pick you up is my cousin Amir. He knows exactly what you look like because I sent him your pictures this morning. I also told him about the outfits I bought for you so he knows how you'll be dressed. Any questions?"

Natasha said nothing. But I was so moved by Alexandra's kindness I had to speak. I thanked her. I told her I could never repay her for such generosity.

She smiled and said, "Alexandra is such a formal name. Why don't you call me Auntie Alex?"

She flashed her warm smile with perfect teeth once again, then gave us both huge hugs. She was like the family member I never had.

"Thanks, Auntie Alex," we both said.

And with a kiss on the tops of our heads she was gone.

Chapter Fourteen

In the hotel's main foyer stand life-size images of Father Frost and Snow Girl, which flank a twenty-foot Christmas tree ringed with white ribbon. Crystal ornaments reflect prisms through white lights. The whole room glistens. In Russia, Father Frost has taken over for Santa Claus. They look the same, except Father Frost wears white boots and never leaves home without his long magical staff or, apparently, his granddaughter, Snow Girl.

"Good afternoon." I put my suitcase down on the white marble floor and straighten my tie. I hardly recognize myself in the mirror behind the desk.

"Welcome to the Metropol Hotel. How can I help you?" The attendant is a young fresh-looking blond, barely twenty years old by my estimation. I detect a slight Russian accent, or else I'd peg her as Norwegian.

"I would like to make a reservation. Michael Stevenson."

"Room for one?" She bats long eyelashes at me. Her eyes and face sparkle with glitter. A perfect match for the hotel bling.

"Uh, yes, just for one. I'll be staying seven nights."

"Would you like one of our suites?"

"No thanks. A standard room will be fine." I hand a Platinum American Express card across the counter. How did they come up with credit cards to go with my passport so fast?

"Very well. Our regular room rate is $420 per night."

I can't help but swallow.

"That will be fine." I drum my fingers on the counter. Katya insisted on a manicure, again compliments of Alyona. What would the guys back home say? At least it gave me some time to think about my wife.

On my thirtieth birthday Whitney bought a massage, pedicure, and manicure for couples. We were still dating at the time and I told her that I appreciated the gift, but it was an insult to my manhood. She told me to deal with it because this was something fun we could do together.

Having someone dig in my cuticles with knives and brush my calloused skin and corns with steel wool was not my idea of fun.

When we were done, Whit turned to me and said, "See, you actually enjoyed it, didn't you? Be honest."

Looking into those hypnotic, gorgeous eyes, there was only one answer to give: "It was *amazing*. Thank you."

Katya and Vlad were adamant that I use this credit card everywhere. Theatres, restaurants, hotels.

Vlad told me it was of utmost importance to leave a trail that a child could follow. Then, he could do a reverse trace to find "them," whoever they are.

"Is there anything else I can do for you tonight, Mr. Stevenson?"

Right on cue, just like I practiced with Vlad, I say, "In fact there is. I understand *The Nutcracker* is playing at the Bolshoi?"

"Why yes!" Her eyes sparkle, like she's just met the rich, cultured American man of her dreams. "It may be sold out, you know, for

Christmas Eve. But I think I could try to secure tickets for you. Would you like that for tonight's performance, Mr. Stevenson?"

"That would be great."

"Is that for two?" Her voice is über-professional, but her eyes, bright pink lips, and seductive smile say differently.

"Just one, thank you."

I break eye contact and take a casual glance around the lobby.

"My pleasure. One moment please." She snaps back into professional mode.

She walks to the back as I slide out Michael Stevenson's new cell phone. I've got to get used to being somebody else. In truth, now that I'm committed, I'm energized by the adrenaline. Like every trip I took into a hot zone to shoot pictures, the lead time would nearly kill me, especially my gut. But once there, I was all business.

I reach for the camera strapped around my neck, but it's not there. My phantom limb.

I am Michael Stevenson.

"Stuart, keep telling yourself who you are, like a tape running through your head," Vlad had said. "Don't veer in your mind. Act like you're in character in a Russian spy film." He cracked himself up with that comment—for Vlad, that meant a chuckle.

So this is how false identity works? I feel more like Val Kilmer in *The Saint.* Instead of a microchip, I'm stealing girls.

"Your instructions," Vlad had said, "are to check into the hotel and buy a ticket to the Bolshoi Theatre for tonight. Sit through to intermission, and then walk outside to the water fountain in the front of the building where you will meet two men."

"Everything is already set up," he told me. "You are here to choose and purchase your first order of ten girls for your nightclubs. Half will be sent to Des Amore, your club in Israel, and the rest to the United States through Seattle."

"Why do I have to sit through half the ballet?" I asked him.

He shook his head as if I'd insulted his mother.

"It's a marvelous theatre, Stuart! Best in the world. And *The Nutcracker Suite* is playing. When will you ever have another chance to enjoy such a show? Really, it's very, how shall I say it, down to the earth, for someone like you. Come on, you can tell your wife and daughter about it."

"I think I'll pass." My mother and I listened to the Tchaikovsky album every Christmas. She used to take me to the ballet every year until I was old enough to think ballet wasn't cool. I can hardly imagine sitting through it just before I have to meet up with the Russian criminal element.

"Well, you can't take a pass. No one ever died from having to watch an opera at the Bolshoi, now did they?"

I was guessing someone in Russian history had, but I decided to let this observation go.

"Okay, okay, whatever you say. But I'm guessing people *have* died trying to infiltrate the sex trade. I'm right about that. Aren't I?"

He looked up, as if he needed to consider this, then back down at me.

"Hundreds of thousands of girls are trafficked every year around the world. It's not like you're stealing millions of dollars from them. You'll be paying for the girls, and then it's over. These girls are just commodities to them."

I couldn't tell if he was being cavalier or trying to put my mind at ease.

"What if something goes wrong?"

"Follow my instructions every step of the way. We'll be watching the entire time. If there's danger, we'll be right there. But even so, never let your guard down."

"Uh huh."

"You are simply buying the girls. That's it. Once you buy them, they're yours, well, ours. And they won't care about you again. That's our plan. That's our hope."

"I *hope* you're right."

"Get to the fountain at exactly 8:15 p.m. The shows run like clockwork, so you will stand at intermission and have time to move out with the crowd. But check your watch anyway. Are you following me?"

"*Da. Da. Ya ponyala.* [Yes. Yes. I've got it.]"

"There will be two men dressed in black overcoats. Stand beside them, like you're waiting for someone. One of them will ask if you would like a real Russian cigarette."

"Okay."

"The main guy's name is Sergei."

"Then what?"

"Then they will make arrangements for you to see some girls."

"Tonight?"

"Yes, tell them you want to make sure they are young. Negotiate the price, just how we rehearsed it, and set a time and place for delivery tomorrow night. They are used to things moving quickly and prefer this. Less chance for mistakes on either side."

"Vlad?"

"Yes?"

"*Mne kazhetsya, menya seichas virvet.* [I think I'm going to puke.]" With a jerk of the wheel, the car flew to the side of the road.

"Don't mess up your shoes," Vlad said, deadpan, from his seat in the car as I stepped out onto the ice. I stood and took deep breaths in the frigid air.

I slid back in, and Vlad gave me a fatherly pat on the back.

He dropped me off just outside Moscow city limits with a driver who was to take me to the hotel, a slender man with a tweed cap and a kind face.

Before he closed the back door of the black town car, Vlad leaned down and said, "We'll be in the shadows. Play your role down to every expression—your very breath, because others will be watching too." He gripped my hand and gave it a good squeeze.

"Oh, and, remember, Mikhail, you don't speak Russian."

Chapter Fifteen

I take a light dinner and drink in my room to steel myself. What would Michael Stevenson drink? Stolichnaya vodka, of course. Straight up, with a twist of lime. This was one time I didn't really want to stop at one Stoli and lime, but that wouldn't be wise given my current circumstances. I try not to think about the girls, only my next step. Another Vladian mantra.

As I eat, I look out the window, which faces the square and the majestic Bolshoi Theatre. Vlad said it would be better to stick to my room until just before the performance, so I heed his instruction, though I'd rather be out walking in the night air. A cold blast of reality would do me good.

Snow falls in cotton-ball flakes, blanketing the city with a fresh coat of white, transforming the landscape. What a scene for the night before Christmas.

'Twas the night before Christmas
And all through the house

Not a creature was stirring
Except for an American posing as a
sicko pedophile who buys prostitutes.

The time has come—maybe a little too quickly. Right at 6:45, I take a deep breath and head out toward the monolithic Bolshoi. The building is a prime example of Moscow architecture, where God is in the details. Eight white pillars guard the entry like sentinels of the tsar. Perched high at the top is the god of the arts, Apollo, in his horse-drawn chariot, triumphantly ruling over Russia's most famous theatre. Each alcove and shape is lined in ornate crown molding to accentuate the building's beauty.

Cars are moving at a snail's pace, some snaking on the ice, trying not to slide across the median.

I recall Vlad's words about being in the shadows, but I feel as alone as if I'd been banished to Siberia. The heavy brown coat provided for Mr. Stevenson, however, is doing an even better job of keeping me warm than my North Face ski jacket.

"God, be my help and protector," I breathe out as I walk, my words becoming smoke in the cold. White lights sparkle off the snow and frozen water like a thousand diamonds. I glance at the frozen fountain as I walk by, imagining the scene that's nearly ready to play out.

Inside the Bolshoi, I feel like I've stepped back in time. The theatre is shaped in a half circle. There are three majestic levels, each intricately decorated with what looks like garlands of white pine around a Christmas tree with a gold clasp at the bottom. Gold accents appear every six inches in the form of swirls and intricate bows. Every few feet, a heavenly golden cherub holds up a beam with his arms. The chairs are decorated in a '60s-style sky blue cloth. I wonder if they're actually *from* the '60s. The most magnificent feature of all is the grandiose red silk curtain decorated with hundreds of gold hammers and sickles with the letters CCCP. I suspect the theatre hasn't changed since communism was alive and well in good ole Russia.

I take my seat, and the lights go out.

The show is brilliant. Ballerinas in white tutus move like nymphs from another world to Tchaikovsky's "Dance of the Sugar Plum Fairy." The costumes are first class. Bursts of color explode from the mechanical dolls, harlequin, and soldiers; even Mr. and Mrs. Stahlbaum are brilliantly outfitted in seventeenth-century traditional Russian outfits. The *Nutcracker* performances I've seen in the United States don't touch the quality of this performance, but I won't give Vlad the satisfaction of knowing I've enjoyed the show. Perhaps I should just skip my meeting and watch the second half. God, I wish it were that simple.

I slip away from the heat of the crowd and step outside right on schedule. I see two average-sized men standing just off to the right side of the fountain in black coats. One is wearing a black skullcap and is a bit overweight, the other sports a Russian-style ushanka. I casually walk over and stand near them, as if I'm getting some air, just as Vlad said. My hands are stuffed in my pockets, my back straight to make me look taller, and my chest is puffed out.

"You like a real cigarette? A Russian cigarette?" says a burly voice with a thick accent. The two of them walk over to me, and the man in the Russian hat sticks out his hand.

"Sergei?"

"Da," he says with no accompanying expression, no movement at all except his lips.

"Hello, Sergei. Good to meet you. I'm Michael." I feel my throat contract.

He points to the comrade on his left. "This is Ivan."

"Hello."

"I have friends who say you want to do a little bit of business together. Is this true?" He methodically pulls a brown cigarette from his pouch, lights it, then hands it my direction.

Against my better judgment, I take the smoke.

"Thanks."

"A fellow smoker, eh? I like you already." Ivan waddles up to Sergei's side, and I realize he is much heavier than I first thought. His belly protrudes like a woman in her eighth month of pregnancy.

"Always loved Russian cigarettes. Good and strong."

"My contact, Oleg, tells me he checked you out thoroughly. That you bring cash and you are a true businessman, yes?"

"That is true. I know what I want, and I will pay top price if you have what I'm looking for."

"He said you have plenty of money," says Ivan. I can't tell if he's asking a question or merely repeating what his buddy just said.

"You drink, yes?" Sergei pulls a silver flask out of the inside of his jacket.

"I do." Both men nod and laugh.

"In Russia, it is customary for Russians to toast to new friends." He holds his canister in the air. "To my good friend Mikhail, from America. May he come to love our country, our women, and most important, here's to us making a lot of money together."

He takes a long drink, then hands it to me. I hold it up in the air, tip it in his direction, and take a swig. Liquid fire explodes in the back of my throat and snakes its way down to my gut.

"Ha, ha, ha," he laughs, slapping me on the back. "Vodka is

good for you, my friend. This is real Russian vodka, not the weak stuff you Americans drink. It's what we call *Samigon* [Moonshine]. Gives you strength in your body and makes you virile." He grins, revealing a gold-capped front tooth.

"Excuse me?"

"Virile, my friend, virile. You're going to need some virility tonight with the girls you'll try out."

"Ah ... I see. Of course. I didn't know ... I mean I nearly forgot I would be trying them out tonight." This was not included in my instructions.

"You will see that Sergei has the best girls in the business. Let's go."

The vodka is keeping the panic from my face since it's already red. Thankfully, he doesn't seem to hear it in my voice.

I can hear music as we head down the stairs into the Teatralnaya stop on the underground Metro. Stationed just inside the tunnel is a five-piece orchestra, college kids playing classical music, Christmas tunes of course, for tips. One of the violin cases is opened and ruble coins and bills are scattered inside. The acoustics rival any music hall. The music is beautiful, but it's the wrong score for this scene.

> God rest you merry, gentlemen,
> Let nothing you dismay,
> Remember Christ our Savior
> Was born on Christmas day,
> To save us all from Satan's pow'r
> When we were gone astray;

O tidings of comfort and joy,

Comfort and joy,

O tidings of comfort and joy.

For Marina's sake, I hope this is true.

"Where are we going?" I ask, trying to be a perfectly composed Michael Stevenson.

"We have a very special night lined up for you, my friend. Some of the most beautiful girls in all of Russia are waiting for you in a flat not far from here. They are anxious to show you what they can do."

"Show me what they can do?" The words fly out of my mouth before I can stop them.

"You will see. It's the best part of the transaction."

A cold chill runs down my spine. What am I walking into?

We turn right down the corridor and get on the escalator. It dives deep into the earth. I feel like I'm descending into a missile silo.

Every head turns into the wind of the approaching train, which screeches to a halt at the platform in front of us. The door opens with a thud.

"After you, friend," Sergei says, and I follow Ivan onto the green line with a few hundred other passengers.

Talking on the Metro doesn't seem to be the appropriate cultural thing to do in Russia, and I'm relieved. The first stop whistles by, and Sergei passes me his flask with a nod. The idea of sharing a bottle with this pig is enough to make me sick, but I swallow another dram of white lightning. I scan the passengers discreetly and wonder if I have any friends onboard. Most of them either look straight ahead into space, read a book, or sleep. Not much different from the New

York subway, minus the occasional beggars or thugs. The only sound is the *thump, thump* of the steel train wheels moving across the tracks.

Two stops later we arrive at Chekhovskaya and get off. I can't help but notice that the very next stop is Pushkinskaya, the place where the young girl was shot yesterday. This area must be a hotbed for prostitution and criminal activity.

"The flat is not far, my friend Mikhail. I know you Americans can't stand to be in the Russian winter for long." He puts his arm around me as if we were old college buddies.

I glance over at Ivan. The guy is creepy. He walks with a slight limp, has beady black eyes, and an oversized nose with black hairs sprouting out of it like a Chia Pet. I turn to see him snort something inside his coat.

Sergei isn't kidding. After a brisk five-minute walk, we arrive at an apartment building. This building is different from most of the apartment buildings you'd see around Moscow. Most are giant gray structures with ten to twenty floors, layer upon layer of flats. Built during the communist era of the 1970s, they're nothing to look at. They were built for one purpose: to house as many people as possible in the smallest possible space.

But this building looks more like a large three-story home, not a mansion by U.S. standards, but for Russia, very nice. The building is walled, and Sergei types in a code on a panel next to a ten-foot-high iron gate. A loud click releases the lock, and we walk into the compound.

Several men are seated at the front, smoking and talking. They're not the most fearsome guards I've ever seen. Their poker game holds more interest than the stranger walking into the compound.

"*Zdrats*," one of them says as we walk up the stairs.

"*Zdrats,* Nicolai. You perverted old goat," Sergei barks. Nothing like the love shared between pimps.

The door is open, and we walk into a small sitting room where we take off our coats and boots. The inside of the building is definitely not as nice as the outside. Ragged, well-used furniture is arranged in haphazard fashion, and the floors and walls are filthy. Dirt is standing on its head in corners and around the baseboards. I notice a lot of lit candles. An attempt, perhaps, to cover up a rancid smell.

Sergei stops outside a narrow, paint-chipped door and says, "Now, my friend, we have a nice surprise for you."

Chapter Sixteen

Natasha and I had never been on an airplane. It was strange sitting so close to so many people. I was nervous as the plane sped down the runway then lurched into the air.

For the first five minutes I held on to Natasha's arm. Everything was swirling around me, and I felt like I might be sick. The man sitting across the aisle handed me an open bag, putting it in front of my mouth. Thanks be to God. The dizziness went away in a short period of time.

It's fascinating to see all the earth from so high above the ground. I remember wishing I had a camera so I could capture this moment forever. The sounds, the people, the food! It was like being on a ride at the amusement park that comes to Kostroma once a year.

The flight was long. Much longer than I had hoped. I was sure that we would land within an hour. About four hours later the tires screeched to a halt on the runway.

We walked off the plane in Cairo where we were assaulted with gusts of boiling, suffocating air. Never had I been to a place so hot and windy. We followed everyone to the place where you pick up your bags. We watched them wait for their luggage that arrived on a squeaky metal snake. Our bags came, and we exited with the other passengers.

Outside, there was a crowd of people waiting for arriving passengers. Everyone greeted each other with kisses, smiles, and hugs. It was like a *whole bunch of family reunions. We stood in the center of the crowd hoping someone would recognize us. Slowly everyone left, and we stood alone like flowers growing between cracks of concrete.*

Finally a short, stout man approached us. He was speaking fluent Russian on his cell phone.

He grunted our names, "Natasha. Marina."

"Yes," we said at the same time. I remember we laughed together at that.

Then he grabbed us harshly by our arms and dragged us out of the airport. He threw us into an old black pickup truck. I was in the front seat, and Natasha was in the back with two other teenage girls from Russia.

The man demanded our passports. I thought it was odd for him to ask, but I was also starting to get a little scared, so I gave him mine. The other girls did too.

I asked the man, "Are you Alexandra's cousin?"

"Cousin?" he said. "Cousin?" He laughed so hard he started to cough. He called her a crafty witch.

Darkness entered the car at that moment and lodged somewhere in the depths of my soul. I panicked.

I mustered all of my confidence and yelled, "Let me out of the car! Now!"

He reached across the cab and slapped me on the face with the back of his hand.

Then he said, "You whores better listen to me now. One wrong move from any of you, and I will kill you. Do you understand me?"

That's when he pulled out a handgun and waved it in the air.

And he kept on screaming at us. "You try to run away, you're dead," he said. "If any of you have family … a mother? Sisters? Brothers? I'll kill them next. I don't play games, and I have a job to do."

All the girls began to cry. For the first time we knew something was desperately wrong. And there was no way of escape. With Cairo fading in the distance, we drove in silence for the next two hours. The more we drove, the more desolate the landscape became. There was nothing as far as the eye could see. No trees, no cacti, no living thing on the horizon. Nothing but sand.

The truck stopped in the middle of the desert where five men huddled together surrounded by three camels.

Amir got out of the truck and spoke in a foreign language to the men. They exchanged something that looked like money and several small packages. Then he came back to the vehicle and yelled at us to get out.

We did as we were told. We stood together like chickens stripped of their feathers. My knees were shaking, and my heart was pounding.

Natasha walked to get her suitcase from the back of the truck, but Amir stopped her. "What do you think you're doing?" he said. "You can't take your luggage. The only thing you own now is what is on your back. Put any clothes on that you want and leave the rest."

We obeyed out of fear of getting beaten. My nose and lips were swollen from the hit I took earlier. We put on a few clothes, then Amir got back in the car and sped off.

The men were dressed in robes with cloth wrapped around their heads. All of them had guns hanging off their shoulders. They tied our hands together and linked us like we were criminals on a chain gang. They got on their camels, and we were dragged behind like animals.

For three days and nights we walked across that desert. We were given little food and water. Once a day they would throw dried figs at us along with chewy brown strips that tasted like meat. We were so hungry we didn't care what it was.

Our feet blistered and our skin broke out in welts and sores from the punishment we were taking under the brutal sun. Each step I took, pain would shoot through my entire body.

There were times we stumbled and the camel would keep going and drag us along the ground. The men would yell at us in Arabic, but we never understood a word they were saying. We didn't know where we were going or what would happen to us when we got there.

Many times I asked God what I had done to deserve this. I didn't understand. I had not lived a very good life, but not a bad one either. How could I, an orphan girl, have done anything different? Maybe I was cursed. Cursed from my birth to be hopelessly punished for the rest of my life.

I wanted to die.

Chapter Seventeen

The door opens into a large parlor. The walls are the color of Pepto-Bismol. I wish I had some to calm my nervous stomach. Someone has plopped a pathetic Christmas tree in the corner and strung it with blinking colored lights. About twenty girls stand on command when we enter, like soldiers at attention when a general enters the room.

They are barely clothed with worn but brightly colored lingerie. Most can't be a day older than seventeen. Drugstore perfume permeates the air, a sick cover for the smell of urine and vomit, like a fraternity on a Friday night. All the girls' faces are overdone with makeup, perhaps to make them look older than they are. It is a garish scene.

They stand in sexy poses, some with their arms draped around each other. One girl, with porcelain skin and bright pink lips, is struggling to keep her composure, her girly, knobby knees trembling. I wonder if she's been drugged. Most are doing as they've been told, cocking their hips and leaning forward in seductive poses.

Marina isn't here.

I recall Vlad's words. "Don't think about the girls, only about your next move."

Sergei snaps his fingers, and three girls walk toward me. They wrap their arms around me; one of them breathes in my ear and kisses my neck. Inside, I can feel the vomit rising in my throat. One girl has deep purple hollows under her eyes, her breath like moldy cheese in my face.

I work to keep my composure.

"Oh, yes, yes, Mikhail. You like one of these? Huh?"

I am Michael Stevenson.

"Beautiful girls, yes. It's true, you have a nice selection, Sergei." I try to sound nonchalant, like this is nothing new for me, like I'm at a livestock auction.

"Which do you like the best?"

I look around the room and sputter, "They're all nice. Very nice."

"Pick one."

"Well, I'm here for ten."

"For now, I mean. Pick one."

I can tell I'm making this too difficult for him.

Ivan walks through the room with a disturbingly crooked smile on his face. He is carrying a fresh bottle of vodka, cradling it like a newborn baby.

I scan and see a blue-eyed blond who looks about fifteen. She reminds me of Marina. "That one." I point to her. "There, with the blond hair." Her face is expressionless, but I detect disdain in her eyes. She doesn't move.

"Good eye, and nice choice, my friend."

Sergei snaps his fingers. "Now."

She obeys and stands in front of me. Sergei lifts his hand to stroke her hair, and she flinches reflexively.

"Yes, a fine selection. Dasha is one of my best girls. More

expensive than the rest, but not too expensive for you. She's been here a very short time and hasn't been used much at all. Go ahead, see what you think. I'll let you do what you want with her for free. A goodwill offering of a long business relationship together."

I don't know what to do. Ivan lowers the bottle from his lips and starts thrusting his hands back and thrusting his hips forward.

"C'mon, Mikhail, she not hurt you," Ivan taunts like a playground bully.

A bald man who rivals Vlad in size walks into the room. He's older, maybe forty-five to fifty years old. He looks like one of those perverts who hangs around the Victoria's Secret boutiques in the States just so he can snag a catalog. Beady eyes, furrowed brow, and walking hunched over like the freak from Notre Dame.

I place my hand on her cheek. She shivers but doesn't make a sound. I grab her arms to see how firm they are, then spin her around to look at her backside.

"She looks good. I think my clients would be pleased with this one." I try to sound more like a frat boy. "Oh yeah, I like her."

"Like her? How do you know if you like her until you take her?" He grabs her by the arm and throws her to the ground in front of me. She lets out a barely perceptible squeak, and I am certain she is muffling what would normally be a piercing scream. She's gritting her teeth.

"Have them all as far as I care. Then take your best ten."

"I really wasn't prepared for this. I didn't even bring a condom." I laugh and slap him on the shoulder and chuckle.

He reaches in his pocket and pulls out a square silver package with a distinct circle in the middle and hands it to me.

"We have all the provision you need."

"Ah, well, in that case—"

"Now, take her. Unless you're a cop or something." This time he looks at me seriously, and no one in the room is laughing.

I know I need to act. Do something, before it's too late.

"Very well," I grab the girl around her waist and place my lips close to her neck. Her hair smells of pungent smoke and cheap hairspray. I grab a handful as if I'm pulling it, but I try not to actually hurt her, to pull too hard.

God forgive me.

"Now that's more like it," Sergei says.

"Where's the bedroom?"

"Bedroom? Why don't you just take care of it here? It's nothing we haven't seen before." He and Ivan laugh. The big guy is sitting on the couch, one girl on his knee, giving me a suspicious eye.

"Sergei, I'm American. That's not my style. I like my privacy. In fact, I want three at once in the bedroom. And they better perform to the highest standard if you expect me to buy them." I exert as much authority as I can manage. "Otherwise, I'll have to take my business elsewhere."

"You'll cheat us out of our entertainment will you, Mikhail? If you insist. Pick the other two girls."

I look around the room and grab a tall skinny brunette and a petite dark brunette, probably a gypsy, standing next to her.

Kids. They're all just kids.

"Now follow me."

He takes me around the corner and points to a room at the end of the hall.

"Take your time," Sergei says. "We will keep ourselves busy with the leftovers."

I swear I just heard the voice of the Devil.

The girls walk in front of me down the hallway and open the door. I turn on the light, close the door, and push in the lock. In one corner of the room sits a small twin bed with grotesquely stained linens; in another corner are a miniature bathtub and rust-stained sink. The toilet is nothing more than a cement hole in the ground framed by two places to put your feet.

The blond, still shirtless, and the tall girl go to the bed, and the small brunette, in festive red lace, grabs the chair in the center of the room. The smell of sewer and body odor seems to seep out of the walls.

It is Christmas Eve.

Chapter Eighteen

In unison, like strange bright birds in a distorted ballet, they begin to remove their clothing.

"Nyet. Nyet." I whisper to the girls and hold my hands up in the air to signal for them to stop.

They freeze, puzzled mannequins.

I put my finger over my lips to signal for them to be quiet. I'm in a room with three half-naked teenagers in a foreign country, not a position I ever pictured myself getting into. This is far from the normal work of a photojournalist. This scene has crazy implications beyond rational or moral belief.

God, help me to know what to do here.

I speak to them in Russian. "*Poslushaitea*," I whisper fiercely, "*Ya zdes, chtobi pomoch vam.* [Look, I'm here to help you.]"

Dead silence. The girls look at me like I've sprouted an alien head.

"*Pozhaluista, odentes.* [Please put your clothes back on.]" They obey with uncertainty, eyes wide open, flinching like abused puppies.

"*Ya vas ne obizhu.* [I'm not going to hurt you.]"

"*Aga, konechno zhe nyet* [Of course you won't]," the blond girl with blue eyes says in disgust.

"Your name is Dasha, right?" I wonder how many times they've heard that and then found themselves subject to unthinkable abuse.

"It makes no matter. Just call me Natasha. That's what they tell us to say."

"Why?"

"We're all Natasha."

"What do you mean?"

She doesn't answer, only waves her hand like she's telling me to go away. The smaller girl looks at me with big dark eyes and slowly slides on her red getup. She appears to be the youngest of the group. She looks petrified, and I realize they are probably more scared now than if we'd had sex.

"What is your name?" I say to her.

"Valya," she replies. Dasha crosses her arms and shoots her a look of irritated disbelief.

"Valya, listen to me. I'm going to buy you from these men to help you get away, but I can't help you if you don't help me."

She looks up and whispers from her chair. "Do you know what they will do to us if they know we didn't have sex? Do you understand?" Her body is crouched, as if she's ready to receive a slap.

"I don't have time to explain, but I have friends in high places in Russia. They have helped—"

We all stop at sounds of a girl screaming in the next room. I hear a thud on the wall and a man's laugh, cruel and base.

"*Pomogitea! Bozhe, pomogi mne!* [Help me! God help me!]" a girl's voice cries out.

"Oh no," says the tall girl. The girls exchange a look of pity.

"What's wrong?"

"There's a new girl," Dasha says.

"*Tss, Dasha. Zatknis i pomalkivay ob etom* [Shush, Dasha. Just shut up about it]," Valya hisses and puts her hands over her ears and head, like she's trying to block out sound and memory.

"What do you mean?" I ask.

"You don't want to know."

I feel anger rising in my body, the same kind that has led me to do things that landed me in jail. I know I've got to pull myself together.

I crouch down and try to make eye contact. Dasha is the only one who will look at me directly. "Girls, listen to me carefully. You must tell these men we had sex, or whatever it is you have to tell them." I feel power in my voice. "Say nothing else. If everything works like I'm hoping it will, I will have you somewhere safe in a day or two. Understand?"

The girls nod, but they are obviously unconvinced. Dasha is the one I need to win over.

"Dasha, I know you have no reason to believe me. Say nothing about this again. Not to each other: nothing. If they find out, your chances for freedom are over."

I don't know if this is getting through.

"Girls, look at me. Do you understand what I'm saying? And do not let them know I speak Russian. I am an American, English-speaking businessman."

They slowly nod their heads.

"We understand, mister," Valya says.

I unlock the door. "Okay, stay here for now, please."

I fly into the living room as if I'm trying to be Superman changing his clothes. My heart is pounding, and my face is red-hot. The girls are huddled together, some with their heads turned away. I stumble in to see Ivan's puffy hand fly across the face of a young girl. Then again. She slams into the corner. He turns her around against the wall, loosens his belt, and begins to move at her.

"Hey! What's going on here?" I yell out in a voice that doesn't sound like my own. I feel like smashing this guy's face till it becomes wet pulp.

Nobody moves or says a thing.

"Get off that girl now!"

Sergei and the big bald guy fly into the room from outside.

I wheel around to face them. "Is this how you do business? You let this pig ruin my property? I don't know what kind of operation you run, but my girls don't get clobbered and used. Do you understand?"

"Now wait a minute...." Sergei is angry, with whom I can't tell. But there's no turning back now. Blood is trickling from the girl's nose. She can barely lift her head as she slides down the wall into a curled-up sitting position. I turn away. The animal has stepped back and buttoned his pants. He's seething mad, his right hand opening and closing.

I take a deep breath and walk up to Sergei. "No, Sergei, you listen to me. My clients pay a lot of money for girls that are clean." My voice is compressed and quiet. I lean toward him, man to man, and nearly whisper, "Do you think I want a girl with a smashed nose? Or a disease? Do you expect to sell me damaged merchandise? Or a girl who is pregnant?"

"Well no. Of course not." He tucks in his shirt and clears his voice.

"I thought we were professionals here. Do I need to have a conversation with Mr. Lishensky, our friend Anton?"

He flinches and steps toward Ivan. I've got him!

"*Bozhe moy, Ivan! Chem ti tolko dumayesh?* [My God, Ivan! What are you thinking?]" Sergei says. "*Zabiray svoyu vodku i smativaisya otsuda, poka ti vsyo ne razvalil. Znaesh, chto sdelaet s nami Anton, esli vsyo provalitsya?* [Take your vodka and get out before you blow this deal. Do you know what Anton will do to us if this falls apart?]"

Ivan spits bullets at me with a lethal look and leaves the room. I put my hand in my pocket and feel the unused condom.

Dasha, Valya, and the other girl must have followed me back into the room, and they stand with the others and stare. I've upset the scales. I've got to play this right.

"*Na chto ustavilis, shlyukhi?* [What are you looking at, you whores?] *Poshli von otsyuda! I zaberitye tu devku s soboy* [Go out of this room—and get that girl out of here]," Sergei says, not aware that I can understand his words. "Wait a minute. You three stay here." He motions toward Dasha, Valya, and the tall girl.

"Did you find them pleasant?" he says to me, changing to his former boy's club tone.

"Your girls were quite satisfactory." I nod in the direction of the three. "Though I barely had time to finish before I was interrupted."

I put a hand on Sergei's shoulder. "Sergei, I apologize for my outburst. But you must understand: It is of utmost importance to me and my boss that the girls are, how shall I say it, as undamaged as possible."

Sergei holds up his hand in an obsequious gesture. "Of course, my friend. Who wouldn't?" Thank God. We're friends again.

"Undamaged girls are important. But you understand that will cost you more?" His eyebrows rise as he licks his lips like the Cheshire cat.

"Then, if we have an understanding, Sergei, I am ready to do business."

Chapter Nineteen

At the end of the fourth day we started to see buildings in the distance. There were barbwire fences and signs with pictures of skulls and crossbones.

The men yelled at us and forced us to lie down, faces in the sand, as military patrols came toward us. Reaching inside the saddlebags draped over the camels, they pulled out several long-barreled guns and pointed them in the direction of the Jeeps.

We made a small camp outside of the barbwire fences that night. It was clear and cool. The stars bounced in the sky like a million snowflakes. Even though I had been kidnapped, there was something about the sky that night that brought me peace. Somehow I knew I wasn't alone.

I fell asleep.

In the middle of the night I woke when one of the men shook me by the shoulders. He had his hands over his mouth signaling for us to be quiet. We left the camels and crawled through the dangerous-looking fence, following him into the darkness.

After walking for what seemed like hours, there was no life left in me. I was dehydrated and hadn't eaten decently in days. Everything started to spin. The last thing I remembered was another group of men pulling up to the side of the road. They spoke Russian too, and I heard one of them say, "Ah, this one is beautiful. I'll have fifty men lining up to pay top dollar for her on the first night."

Then I passed out.

When I woke up, Natasha and I were in a small room with nine other girls. The door was locked, and the room smelled like something had rotted under the carpet. We weren't allowed to shower or eat or use the bathroom. Several of the girls couldn't hold it any longer and went in the corner.

About two hours later the door opened, and we were funneled down the hall and into a large living room. There were six or seven men seated on the couches, and we were herded to the center of the room.

"Take off your clothes," a small man with deep pockmarks on his face ordered. We didn't move.

He stood up and charged at us. "You worthless swine," he yelled. "Take off your clothes now before I beat you within an inch of your life."

Humiliated and scared, we did what he said. We stood there shivering and trying to cover ourselves as the men gawked at us like we were meat in a butcher's shop. One girl, a tiny blond girl no older than fifteen, started to break down, sobbing over and over, then fell to the floor on her knees.

The evil man yelled at her to obey.

She pleaded with him, screamed at him that she just wanted to go home. She told him she would do anything if he would just let her go back home.

He said, "Oh, you want to go home, do you? Well, your new home is hell." I'll never forget those words. The sound coming from his mouth was the sound of evil. "Let me help you get there quicker."

The next scene plays in my head every day. It never goes away. The evil man grabbed her by the hair, dragged her across the room, and threw her out the window. We heard her scream, then a few seconds later, the crunch of her body hitting the ground far below.

He was right. Our new home was hell.

Chapter Twenty

I have never so much as haggled at a flea market. I've been ripped off in every foreign marketplace I've ever visited, so I was not particularly confident about this part of the plan, even though Vlad had given me specific directions about negotiation.

Apparently, he'd been on the selling end of this business at one time.

"This I am not proud of, Stuart," he had said, and I understood the topic was not up for discussion anytime soon. "You won't believe what you are seeing, and it will seem crazy to you. But please, trust what I tell you, and do exactly as I have said. *Mi ponyali droog drooga?* [Are we clear?]"

I have to keep rehearsing what he said. It keeps my head straight.

Now that we are alone in the room, Sergei sits down at the small four-legged wooden table and pours two shot glasses of vodka. I know this is not just standard but customary. Between the smell of the place and the vodka, my stomach lurches.

"Very well, my friend, as you say. Ten you will choose?"

"Ten, that's correct. But I only want the best—and the youngest."

"For you, no problem. But these are my finest girls. They are very expensive, especially if you want the young ones."

"Yes, I can tell by how you treat them." I know I need to watch my tone. The vodka is making me bold. Maybe that's not such a bad thing for a hard-core negotiator. "You told me earlier not too expensive."

"You know as well as I, Mikhail, you need to show these girls who is the boss, as you Americans say. Surely you understand." He puts his face closer in to mine and looks into my eyes.

"Of course I do. I'm always the boss, but I have other ways that are just as persuasive without doing physical damage."

"Your ways are different than mine."

"Apparently. This is not how we treat girls in my clubs."

"You Americans forget the difference between business and charity. These girls don't deserve charity. They are worthless throwaways. Nobody cares about them, nobody wants them. We might as well make money off them."

As much as it pains me, I utter, "You are right, Sergei. Perhaps I have much to learn from you."

He leans back and relaxes his shoulders. This man would cut my throat without a second thought if he discovered the truth. He raises his glass.

"*Nu, za uspekhi v delakh!* [To good business!]" He downs the entire thing in one gulp.

I raise mine to follow suit and slam it down. I know from Vlad that Sergei is about to make his offer.

Right on cue, he says, "Okay, Mikhail: $250,000 for ten. You get to choose the best girls."

I slam my glass down on the table. "This will not work for me," I say. "Too expensive. You said you would offer a good deal. Now give me one." Then I lean back in my chair.

"These are the best girls, I can assure you." He flips out another cheap Russian cigarette that looks like it's been rolled in a brown paper bag. He refills our small glasses. The bottle is only half empty. I have a feeling we're not done until there isn't a drop left.

"Yeah, but your men have been turning them into used goods, lowering the price."

"*Za tibye* [To you]," he toasts and both shots are gulped down like this is a race between frat brothers.

"Your best price. Give me a good deal. Remember, this could be the beginning of a long business relationship."

If I could get every single one of these girls out of this God-forsaken place, I would. How can I help ten and leave the others behind?

"Da, business. *Chorny* business."

Remembering that I'm not supposed to understand Russian, I say, "Excuse me?"

"*Chorny* business, black business. This is black business. What is your offer?"

"$175,000 for all the girls."

He bellows. "Oh, you are funny, Mr. Stevenson. This is far too cheap. These are girls, not sheep. $200,000 for ten. Here, have another drink of vodka."

"I'll wait until we've come to an agreement before I drink again." I fear I may add to the smell of vomit in the house. "Okay, Sergei, $180,000 for ten."

"Tempting, but too cheap. $190,000."

"I'll give you $185,000. My final offer. Take it or leave it."

He strokes his chin with his thumb and index finger, deep in thought.

"I will take it. You have a deal." He pours another shot, and we pound our glasses and drink. The bottle is empty. I haven't had this much to drink in four years. Thank God I ate something earlier.

He picks up his cell phone and says, "We have arrived at a deal. Send the girls back in."

He says, "Now, you choose your ten."

The girls trail back into the room. They are wearing the same lingerie, but I can tell their makeup has been touched up. I look at the three girls I'd "tried out" and see nothing on their faces that would make me think they've given me away.

"Yes, Dasha and her friends, they were good for you?"

"Good enough. Yes, I'll have those three."

I pick the rest, trying to focus on the youngest. I notice my head is starting to get foggy and my body is feeling unsteady.

"That's nine. And number ten?"

I already know.

"Where is the girl who was beaten?"

"Certainly you are joking? She's a wet dog."

"She is young, perfect for my business."

"As you wish." He calls again on his cell phone, and the girl enters within seconds. Her face is caked with blood, her eye swollen.

"I will call tomorrow and make arrangements for payment and drop-off."

"Very good," Sergei says. "American dollars and new bills please, my friend. Then they are all yours." He sweeps his arm out like Bob Barker to a showcase.

I look directly at the three girls who know, who could make or destroy our lives. Dasha gives an almost imperceptible nod.

"One more thing," I say. I realize I'm taking a risk going off-script once again.

"What's that, my friend?"

"Anyone touches my girls between now and then, and I'll kill them."

Chapter Twenty-one

I can't even repeat what happened next. Not just to me, but to all of us. No human being should ever have to endure that kind of torture. To get my mind off the pain, I thought about other people who have suffered. Like the people we studied in school who suffered more than anyone in the world. The Jews.

I thought about the Holocaust. About how those innocent people were taken from their families, beaten, thrown in prisons, and gassed in death chambers. What I went through, what the Jews went through, tells me one thing. It tells me evil is real and so is the Devil.

The next thing I remember, I was in a small room with four other girls. There was a lamp on in the corner. I got up, my body searing with pain, and tried to open the door. It was locked.

There were four plates on the floor, each with one piece of bread sitting in the middle. Dinner. No one was hungry. I looked over at the other girls. One was sleeping—or unconscious. They all looked the same. Bloody noses, swollen eyes, torn clothes. We held each other and wept.

That night I thought about the good things that had happened in my life. I had to focus on something good and pure to overcome the darkness. I could only find one memory from the time before I went to the orphanage. I must have been three years old. I remembered running through a small apartment in the early hours of the morning to crawl in bed between my mom and dad.

They never complained when I climbed up to join them, never told me no. Only smiled. I remembered Dad getting up so many mornings to cook us breakfast. Eggs would sizzle and pop from our small stove, hot water would boil for tea. I would pretend like I was asleep, but I was watching him as I peeked out of the covers.

I note again how Marina transforms as she speaks about her childhood. For the first time in the interview she smiles. She laughs and twirls her hair like a little girl.

He would carefully set out the whole meal, then come and kiss Momma on the forehead, run his fingers through my hair, and tell us it was time to eat. I loved those days. Those were the days before the sorrow.

I thought, If only I could go back in time …

But I couldn't. All I could do—all any of us could do—was wait. Wait for what, nobody knew. But one thing we did know—whatever came through that door would bring more pain than the time before.

Chapter Twenty-two

I must be halfway to the Metro stop by now. Sergei offered to escort me, but I declined. I typically have a good sense of direction once I've taken a route, which has saved me on many an intoxicated night in strange cities where I've worked. Besides, I need some space to breathe.

My head is thumping, a by-product of too much bad Russian vodka and monumental stress. You'd think with all the money they're making, they could buy some of the good stuff.

It's 3:00 a.m., now Christmas Day. I can't fathom what just happened, how those girls are spending their Christmas. I pray they won't be hurt before we can get to them, but I fear they will. I shudder at the thought. This Christmas, the best gift I could give to them is their freedom. I feel suffocated by darkness, like the despair from that place has settled over me, and it occurs to me I'm likely being watched by enemies.

I speed up, as if to outrun them, to outmaneuver the darkness, and push myself to get to the Metro and out of the blinding cold as quickly as possible.

"It's awful what those men are doing to those girls, isn't it?" It's a woman's voice, high and thin. English, but not American. I can't peg the accent.

I flinch at the sound and turn to see a tall woman in a deep purple cloak. "Excuse me?" I slow my pace and turn to look at her. "You startled me. What did you say?"

"I said, it's terrible, yes, what is going on with those girls."

She looks to be about my age, maybe a little older. Her skin is pallid, although I can see she's beautiful. Maybe she's sick. I wonder why she is out on such a frigid night in a thin coat. She's obviously been following me.

"I have no idea what you're talking about." I quicken my pace.

"Oh, you know exactly what I'm taking about. There's no sense in lying to me."

"Is there something I can help you with?"

"The question is, is there something I can help *you* with?"

I feel like a five-year-old in a copycat contest.

"How do you know about those girls?" I wonder if she's with Vlad's people, but I don't want to say too much.

"Oh, I'm privy to what happens in this neighborhood, mmm-hmm, and what goes on with girls like the ones you've just met."

She falls into step with me, but a half stride ahead, with her face turned toward mine, as if she's trying to read something in my eyes under the streetlights.

"What do you mean?"

"I facilitate connections. Among people." She could be a plant, part of Sergei's network.

I stop. "You? You work for those men?" I take care not to give away names. I'm freezing cold, but this woman seems not to notice the icy wind that's just stirred up around us.

"You could say that, and their associates. But we tell *them* what to do. It's how it's always been." Her face is closer to mine than I would like, her breath strong, smelling of anise, but even as she leans in, she keeps her body away.

"You know, most of those girls would be homeless. Mmm-hmm. Out in the cold, like tonight. Imagine that: a chill that would freeze their very souls. At least they have a roof over their heads and hot meals to eat. Yes, they do."

"A roof and hot meals. And a few things they probably aren't all that thrilled about. I suspect some would rather freeze to death than be where they are. But I'm curious … why would you even say that? Isn't there some sort of solidarity pact among all women?"

"Oh, I see how you think, yes," she says, laughing, a hollow sound that could easily be mistaken for an asthmatic wheeze. "I know so, so much more about what happens than you'll ever know."

This woman is a freak, and my head feels like it's about to explode. "Who do you work for?" I start walking, and we walk in step for a block. She looks at me, even as we walk, but doesn't speak. I can't help but wonder if my cover is blown.

Then she says, "You've played a part in this. I can see it in you. Mmm-hmm. Maybe you think you're different now, but you have said yes in the past. Going to clubs to see girls, sleeping with a prostitute, here in Moscow if I remember correctly. I can see it, barely, but I can." It's almost as if she's talking to herself now. "It's people like you who make this happen, you know. Men just like you."

"You don't know me."

She makes a dead stop and says, "Where's your camera?"

I feel like I've hit an invisible steel wall, headfirst. It's got to be fifteen-below outside, but I'm flushed, and the hairs on my body are standing straight in the air.

"My camera? What does a camera have to do with anything?" I'm doing my best to sound peeved, but I'm certain my fear is showing through.

"You contributed to this happening, with the girls. Men like you make it happen." Her voice is thin and taunting.

I can see the Metro entrance, but I stop.

"I've made this happen? I've made this happen to these girls? You are quite misinformed, and our conversation is over now." I start to walk away.

"Here comes your ride, Stuart." The sound of my name stops me again. She steps into the shadow in an alleyway between two buildings. We're the only ones on the street, save a few passing cars.

"Who are you?" I stop and look directly at her eyes, gray and glassy, like a cat's.

"Your plan to save those girls," she spits out these words, "will not work. You can't do it. No, no. Shouldn't even try." She steps out toward me. "This territory is mine, and *I* say what happens to those girls."

She must work for the government. I decide to play dumb.

"I don't know how you know me or what you're even talking about, 'saving these girls.'"

She breathes a deep, tired sigh.

"You can't fool me, Stuart. You can't even fathom the toes you'll be stepping on if you proceed with this plan, or what will come of you. I'm giving you this one warning. Consider it a favor."

"I have friends in high places," I say, then immediately wish I hadn't.

"You and me both." She lets out a wheeze of a laugh, which she clips abruptly, and says, "Don't forget, you have your family to think about. Yes, you do."

In the lights of a coming car, I can see her expression, like a satisfied cat. She's struck a nerve, and she knows it. The gust of wind blows her purple cape.

"Oh yes, here's your man," she says.

"Who are you, and how do you know me?" I say, louder than I wanted.

"Have you ever read Mikhail Bulgakov? Probably not, no, I imagine not. You can learn about us, yes. Our history here in Moscow is deep and rich. There was more truth in that book than people realize." Then I see her eyes get big. Did she say too much? Maybe she's being watched.

"Stuart?" I hear a deep, masculine voice from behind. I turn and see Vlad pushing open the passenger door to his car.

"Come, get in quickly." I turn back to the woman, hoping Vlad will know who she is, but she's disappeared.

"Vlad, did you see that woman?"

"What woman? Come now, get in the car."

I turn back toward the alleyway.

"You were watching me, weren't you? There was a woman who walked the entire way with me then turned down this alley."

"Stuart, I didn't see anyone with you. We had people watching the entire time; we can ask them."

"She knew my name and that I have family. That I am working to get the girls out."

For the first time since I laid eyes on him, Vlad looks alarmed.

Chapter Twenty-three

The one place of solace for me in the entire country of Russia is a wonderful invention of Western ingenuity. It looks like a Starbucks, tastes like a Starbucks, and smells like a Starbucks. If it weren't for all the Russian, I'd bet money I was in Minneapolis.

I'm deeply troubled by my encounter with the pallid woman. It's not just what happened, it's the feeling. Was she some apparition? A projection of my deepest fears? Vlad checked with every agent, and the verdict was the same—nobody saw a woman.

A series of "what if" scenes plays out in my half-conscious mind. The police charging me with identity theft, shoving me into a car after viewing hidden video footage of me stuffing two underage girls in an equipment trunk. And then there's the scene from last night, police or the Federal Security Service breaking through the door in a sting operation and finding me in a bedroom with three half-naked teenagers.

All of them lead to one very unpopular place: prison. Maybe even the infamous Lubyanka.

I resist the urge to tune out what's taken place in the shadows. I am in the middle of a nightmare that's unfolding in a horror I never could have imagined. I need to know where God is in all this. I'm beginning to think I may have heard wrong. I can't keep risking my life every time I go out on assignment. My responsibilities as a father and husband compel me to take fewer risks. If Whitney really knew what was going on right now ... I don't want to think about it.

Then I remember what these girls are going through. If I could rescue even one, it could be the difference between life and death. Even in this darkness, like in Africa, there are places where God's light can break through. Maybe He wants me to be the lightbringer.

I see a large figure approaching. He is wearing a waving black coat, and I realize Vlad reminds me of a sharper Hagrid from Harry Potter. Minus the long locks of hair. For all his finesse, he has the same loafy, lumbering walk—swaying from side to side and shuffling his feet. He had me take a cab from the hotel, driven by one of his men, to the coffee shop. The same cab that brought me from his car to the hotel the previous night. We debriefed last night's events in perfect detail.

"Sorry I'm late, Michael." He's still not taking any chances. "The traffic this morning is terrible."

"No worries. I'm sitting here having a cup of Russia's finest coffee and catching up on the headlines in *USA Today*. Looks like the stock market's dropping again. Can you believe it?" I'm not taking any chances either. My headache is gone, but I have a dull hangover. Today I'm Michael Stevenson in khaki pants and a casual button-up shirt.

"I don't have time for stocks. There are too many cars in Moscow and not enough streets. This is a big problem. Let's go."

We head out onto the busy street. The streets in Moscow are at least four to six lanes wide to manage the inner-city traffic. We walk down the stairs leading to the causeway running under the street, where it's about ten degrees warmer.

We climb the stairs on the other side, step over a chain that is draped around a short-term parking area, and stop in front of a black Mercedes-Benz.

"Cool ride," I say.

"It's left over from my former life." He pushes a button. The doors make a sound like they're being released from a vacuum chamber and open automatically.

"That life must have treated you well. What did you used to do? You've never said anything about it."

He hits the gas, and we dart onto the busy streets.

"That's because I'm not proud of it. I was a different person."

"What did you do?"

"Before communism broke apart, I was an agent for the KGB. As a child it was my dream; it was everyone's dream. I could be somebody. Somebody strong. Powerful. Somebody with a gun. Nobody was strong in our country at that time. Except the KGB."

"I can relate. But instead of the CIA, I opted for photojournalism."

He looks at me like I'm mocking him. "Never mind," I say. "It's an American joke—well, a joke that only Americans would think is funny. Uh, please continue."

"In the KGB I did things I'm not proud of. I hurt people, I killed, I cheated, I ran drugs. I participated in selling and hurting girls. In that part of my life I was a very bad person." It's hard for me to imagine Vlad in that house, doing anything even remotely similar to what I saw last night.

There's little traffic now. We've left the city and are heading toward the country. We're still on four-lane roads, but the buildings have shifted from shopping areas and offices to apartment buildings.

Dozens and dozens of gray ten-story cement buildings. We're whizzing by cars at ninety miles an hour.

"In 1993, when there was no more communism, I was forced to make a choice: Continue down that road or try to make a new life, a clean life. There was an Orthodox nun named Sister Irina who was very close to my mother, God rest my mother's soul. She was a nun at Epiphany Cathedral in Kostroma. You know, she prayed for me every day.

"I chose to stay in the KGB, which of course changed its name to the FSB, until 1999. Then a terrible tragedy happened that changed everything for me."

"What was it?"

He starts to get uncomfortable. His scar bunches together, his arms straighten, and his muscles flex like he's about to brace for something.

"I was abandoned as a young child, and the government took me to the orphanage when I was five. I had a sister, Anastasia."

"Older or younger?"

"Younger. We are still very close. She had a daughter named Nadia who was one of the most beautiful little girls you've ever seen. She looked like an angel. Nadia's father was an alcoholic who was very violent and abusive. One day, he disappeared with Nadia and fled to the far east of Russia."

"That's terrible."

"The man became a drug addict, and when he was at the end of his rope, he sold Nadia to the mafia. He sold her for a small amount of drugs, that's all. I did all I could with my contacts to find her, but when I followed each new lead, I was always a few days too late."

I look out the window and count eight Orthodox churches, their distinct onion domes reflecting color and character against a gray cloudy horizon.

"It's almost impossible for me to live with. Nadia was never seen again, but I found the man who bought her from her father. He was the head of an organized crime gang. I went crazy one night. I found him and three of his gang members and confronted them. We fought, and I killed them all with a knife. That's where I got this scar."

I don't know what to say. Part of me, the side that has always loved a good Clint Eastwood movie, wants to yell, "Whoa, four men with a knife! Way to take out the pig pimps!" The other makes me want to jump from the car while it's still moving. I just sit there with my mouth open.

"At the time, it seemed like the only thing I could do to avenge her death. At the time, it felt good to kill."

"Did you go to jail?"

"No, I was KGB. In Russia, we have a way of keeping these kinds of things in the club. This man had crossed the wrong people in the Russian government, so this was all overlooked."

"Wow, what a country."

"I had to go away for a while, and I knew I had to change my life. What I did wasn't right. I felt compelled at the time to go to Sister Irina. Of course, she took me in and, over time, she taught me about God, how to pray to the Holy Mother, and how to live for something bigger than myself. This is a time when I also learned about forgiveness, that God has forgiven me even after all I had done.

"Don't misunderstand, Stuart. I still have trouble forgiving the men who traffic these girls. But many men play a part in this, including so many 'regular' men who use these young prostitutes and then return to their own lives. Their own families. It's all about supply and demand."

"I get that. It's so sad.... Those girls are just looked at as another product."

"This trade continues to flourish because the tough new laws are not being enforced in most countries, including Russia."

The countryside has changed dramatically since the last time I looked outside. Rolling hills surround us covered in countless trees poking out of the ground like matchsticks. The lamblike snow blankets the ground, reminding me of the sparkling fake snow we used to decorate our Dickens' village back home.

"I want to ask you again about that woman you said you saw last night," Vlad says.

"Yeah. That was, well, unusual."

"Stuart, we are absolutely certain nobody followed you out of Sergei's apartment last night. There's some concern that you may be cracking under pressure. Are you sure you can do this?"

"What? Am I sure I can do it? No, I'm not sure! You're the one who twisted my arm and begged me to get involved, remember?"

"I'm not accusing you of losing your mind. I'm just trying to understand what really happened."

"I wish I could tell you."

Silence fills the car like a sudden fog. Finally I break it.

"She did say some unusual things. One thing in particular that's quite troubling to me."

"Yes?"

"She said I had contributed to what was happening with those girls because I had gone to clubs and a prostitute—I mean, when I was young."

"What would that have to do with anything?"

"I wish I knew."

"Is this true?" He looks surprised.

"It is, and I'm not proud of it. But how could she know what I did in my youth? It's not like anyone keeps a file on these things." I lean my head back and try to replay the conversation. Then it hits me.

"She said something else too. She said 'their' history in Moscow is deep, like she is part of an organization, that I'd step on very big toes if I pursued the plan."

"'Their'? Russia has many old organizations. What else did she say? I know you were clouded last night."

"Yeah, no kidding." Then it hits me—how could I forget this? "She said to read Mikhail Bul-something—to find out about them."

"Bulgakov. Mikhail Bulgakov. Very famous author here. Stuart, have you ever read him?"

"No."

"Are you sure you studied Russian, Stuart? American education.... You should have studied Russian here!" He shakes his head in mock irritation. "*The Master and Margarita?* No? Let me tell you a quote from it: 'The Devil comes to Moscow wearing a fancy suit.'

"You know, the great Russian writers have written about demons in this city since the dawn of time. Sister Irina said she had experienced a number of demonic visitations. I didn't believe her at the

time, thought she was just saying crazy things because she was getting old. She said when she started the rescue center, a woman like
the one you described threatened her."

"What do you mean?"

"The woman told her she was meddling in things that were too
powerful for her. She talked of secret ancient things that controlled
the city. I tried to understand her, but it was confusing. The last thing
she said is that if she didn't stop, it would cost her life."

"You don't think—"

"You can't deny the dark world has a very big hand in the
trafficking industry. Think about it, it's the ultimate desecration—
dehumanizing girls, keeping them from any kind of life, and allowing
men to indulge their most base fantasies. And all in the name of
money. There's no room for light. For God. That's what Sister Irina
would tell me. Now she helps rescue girls. She doesn't care who is
involved—mafia, organized crime, it doesn't matter. If she finds the
girls, she'll get them, and everyone knows: You don't touch her. At
least in the human world. She has alluded to other struggles, not of
the human world, so to speak."

"She sounds like an amazing woman. Not afraid."

"That's where your twins are now, you know, from the first hotel.
She is a saint. If it wasn't for her prayers, I doubt I would be alive."

My head spins with images of the girls, the strange woman, and
Vlad in his past life. I'm not ready to buy into this "powers of darkness" theory.

"This is a lot to think about, Stuart, I know. Katya and I didn't
bring you into this lightly. You might say we believe you were brought
into this, for the right purpose at the right time."

"You mean *God* brought me into this?"

"We can never be certain of this, and I am very careful about how I speak of God's ways. But I do know, in this place where darkness has a grip, I believe God has acted to open the way where light has started."

"I saw that when I was in Africa."

"You said that before. What do you mean exactly?"

"I learned that in some circumstances you can't control things and you can't work alone. In Swaziland, I tried to fight this kind of stuff. Tried to fix things myself and make something happen out of my smarts and strength. If the door wouldn't open when I wanted it to, I'd just kick the sucker down. Yeah, that's how I ended up getting stabbed."

"Stabbed?"

"It's a long story. But now I try to rely on something, Someone, greater than I am." I'm still not comfortable talking about my faith, but the words spill out anyway.

"So we have some things in common: bad temper, knives, scars—and knowing something of the power of God. I wanted to leave my work altogether, get outside the system. Sister Irina encouraged me not to abandon the skills I used in FSB, but to use them: reconnaissance, surveillance, and covert operations. I still have quite a few contacts in my former profession who come in handy."

"Isn't the FSB involved in trafficking these girls?"

"This is not true. The FSB have been involved in some forms of prostitution, but never the trafficking or sale of any kinds of girls."

"I've seen reports that would say otherwise."

"Only in a few cases. And these were not true FSB officials. When they were caught, they were immediately deposed."

"So they're not in cahoots with the mafia?"

"Cahoots?"

"They're not partnering with the mafia?"

"No, they are their enemy."

"Ah, so that's why you're able to get cooperation from your former friends."

"Yes, but the FSB still doesn't like to get involved. They aren't helping as much as I'd like them to. But there are a few reliable friends to help in times of need."

"Those have to come in handy."

He looks at me and grins.

"There's one person in particular who makes a lot happen. But if I told you who it was, I'd have to kill you."

I laugh, happy for a light moment. I sense there won't be many to come.

Chapter Twenty-four

Every day I wanted to die.

Marina looks directly into the camera, eyes blank and reminding me of the first time I met her as an orphaned child.

We all waited with an unspoken terror of what would come through that door.

At first, we tried to fight what was happening. We fought by not eating and by hitting against the men who were on top of us. But we always paid the price. The beatings left us barely able to move. We couldn't keep up the fight. We gave up. I gave up trying to live. I became a cockroach, not worthy of love, or life, or air.

The food shoved under our door always had a strange, bitter taste. At first, we thought it was rancid. But soon afterward, we would start to hallucinate. Our eyes became heavy, and everything was blurry. It was like we were in some kind of dream state. We were drugged and knew the food was laced. We tried not to eat it, but we were starving, so what choice did we have?

She brushes her hair from her eye, gives her head a flick backward and pauses. I can't help but think how beautiful this young girl is. She's someone's daughter, abandoned by man, but not by God. She continues.

Whatever it was, the drug helped us not remember what was

happening. It numbed the pain on the inside and the outside. Over twenty times a day the door opened. Sometimes we were forced to line up in the living room as groups of men decided which one of us they would take.

They poked at our bodies, made us turn around and model for them, laughed and humiliated us.

It was always the same. Oh, some of them were nice in the beginning, so kind. But a few minutes later they would turn violent. I'll never repeat what happened to me in those rooms.

One day a very fat man with a small, round hat on his head appeared at our door. He also wore strange curls on the side of his face that hung down below his chin.

The girl next to me whispered, "That's a yamaka. He's Jewish. A holy man."

For a few brief minutes, hope filled that room and our souls. A holy man? Could he be there to save us?

He picked me out of the group and led me by the hand down the hall. We passed a bunch of men sitting in the living room smoking and playing cards. They never even looked up at us.

It was too good to be true. Could I be leaving this easy? What kind of good fortune found me? I began to cry for joy. Then he led me to the same bedroom as the other men. I was such a fool. He was just as cruel and evil as the others. Even worse.

Every night I prayed and prayed. I knew there was a God. But I didn't know why He let me get into this situation. Often I wondered if I was suffering in this prison for something I had done in my past. Maybe it was just because I was an orphan and I was forever cursed. And yet, I still prayed. It was the only hope I had.

We woke up one morning to the sounds of shouting and an explosion. We heard thud after thud against the wall, like bodies were hitting it. And they were. It sounded like a war. The door burst open, and four men flew inside our room. They were all pointing guns, these men with navy blue uniforms.

"Girls, there's no reason to be afraid," one said. "You're safe now. My name is John. We're here to rescue you."

Chapter Twenty-five

The car grinds to a halt in front of a five-story gray brick building. It looks like another Stalin-era building from the '70s. As drab as the cloudy Moscow sky.

Security around the place is impressive. We pull up to a steel gate. Vlad waves a magnetic card across a keypad, releasing the gate, and we drive through. Inside, two agents carrying automatic rifles guard a second set of gates made out of some kind of thick-looking chain link, topped with razor wire.

Vlad rolls down the window and hands the guard an ID card.

"Zdastvutyie."

"Zdrats. What's the agenda for today, Vlad?"

"Taking our American friend Stuart here to meet Yeshenko."

The guard's eyebrows raise and a look of concern crosses his face. "Ah, Yeshenko, huh? *Dolzhno bit eto vazhno.* [Must be important.]"

"Some things have changed, yes."

The guard then looks at me and gives a nod. I nod back and the gate opens.

We take the elevator to the fifth floor and are seated in a conference room. Rich dark wood paneling surrounds us. Even the ceiling is covered in wood and tiered in layers to make the shape of a cross.

"Take a seat please, Stuart."

I pull the tall burgundy leather chair out from the table and sit down. Several manila folders are neatly stacked at the head of the table. Other than that, there's nothing in the room except for a small bar table, upon which there are crystal canisters filled with amber, brown, and clear liquids.

Within seconds, the glass door opens, and Katya, who is very official-looking in a navy blue skirt, white blouse, and matching jacket, enters and sits across from me. I want to get up and hug her, but I know it wouldn't be appropriate. She smiles and nods, so I do the same.

The second person to enter is a Secret Service poster boy, with his earpiece, shaved head, and tinted sunglasses. He holds the door for the last man, who I judge to be six feet tall, about two hundred pounds. His designer glasses, peppered gray hair, and crew cut make him look more like a recreational sailor than a government official. His features are chiseled. He looks like an Irish boxer who's spent decades in the ring. His frame is solid as a rock.

He takes the chair at the head of the table, folds his hands on the manila folders, and gives a brief but genuine smile.

"Good morning, Stuart, Vlad."

Vlad nods.

"*Dobroye utro.* [Good morning.]"

"My name is Yeshenko. You're probably wondering who I am and what you're doing here, yes?" I like him already. Very matter of fact.

"You've read my mind, Mr. Yeshenko," I say.

"I've been briefed of your activities since arriving in Russia a few days ago. You've been very busy, Mr. Daniels." He takes off his glasses, leans back in the chair, and smiles.

"That I have been, yes."

"I wanted to personally thank you for your sacrifice. You have already helped a number of children who will now be free from this prison of forced prostitution. Russia is grateful."

"I am glad I could be of help," I say and swallow hard.

"Mr. Daniels, you do not know me, but suffice it to say I represent some of the most powerful people in this country. Five of the most powerful to be exact. You will never know their names, and what they do is hidden from the majority of the government and the public at-large. What you do need to know is that all of them are very concerned about Russia's reputation on the world stage and the most difficult issues plaguing our nation."

"Like child prostitution?"

"Exactly. But there's a more personal issue that's come up with one of the gentlemen I represent. From this point, I'll refer to him as 'Mr. M.' Mr. M's father was brigadier general in the navy. At one time, the general was very respected, but the continual tipping of the vodka bottle got the better of him. He changed into a tyrant and an alcoholic, as well as a woman chaser. To make a long story short, fifteen years ago he impregnated a girl in a town called Pokrov about an hour from Moscow."

"Okay. I'm not sure how this all—"

"You will. Mr. M has only found this out recently, and of course, it's deeply disturbed him. You see, Mr. Daniels, this little girl, his *sestra,* his sister, was abducted."

Yeshenko looks around the room. Nothing else needs to be said. We all understand. He opens the folder and hands several photographs around the room.

"He would be very grateful to you for helping us find her. His sister was placed in the Pokrov orphanage when she was two years old. By the time he found out about his sister's existence, she had already been taken from the orphanage. We believe she's been forced into the sex-trade industry. We also believe that the man you met named Sergei Lebedev is responsible for her disappearance."

He hands a few pictures to me. The girl in the pictures is maybe twelve or thirteen. She's gorgeous with blond hair and blue eyes. The picture is obviously a few years old, but there's no doubt in my mind.

"Mr. Yeshenko, *devochku na etoy fotografiyi zovut Dasha* [the girl in this picture, her name is Dasha]."

Chapter Twenty-six

"Stuart, or as your new friend Sergei likes to call you, Mikhail, you're an American businessman purchasing ten girls for your clubs," Vlad says in his official KGB voice. "There is no reason for anyone to be suspicious. It's a simple transaction."

"Then why wouldn't you be doing this all the time?"

"Now that is a very good question! For one, we don't have unlimited money for such things, and two, we can't get into the habit of buying girls. Rescuing, yes. Because of the sensitive nature of Dasha, Yeshenko's client, Mr. M, has given $182,500 in cash, American dollars. You will give them the cash. They will give you the girls. You walk away. It's that simple."

"I hope you're right." I sigh loudly in spite of my desire to look like a force to be reckoned with. Given the present company, I have to do something to look like I fit in, even if it's a bad acting job.

Yeshenko looks me right in the eye with the confidence of a man who's been to battle many times—and won. "We will have service members strategically placed in key positions around the drop-off point. In the unlikely event anything goes wrong, we will have you supported from a number of different angles."

"Well, it sounds like you certainly have your bases covered." I think the baseball analogy may be lost on them and quickly amend

‌

my words before Vlad can give me that quizzical look that reminds me of something Spock might give Captain Kirk. *Illogical, Captain.* "I mean, it sounds like you have everything thought through and in order."

"Ah, yes. We have our bases covered. *Eto nasha rabota.* [It's what we do.]"

And that is the end of our meeting.

I would meet Sergei in front of the Izmailovo market outside the center of Moscow. The press group I traveled with had stayed at the Izmailovo hotel on my last trip to Russia, so I know this area well. The enormous outdoor market is home to thousands of tourists during the weekend who come to buy everything from hand-painted matryoshka dolls and lacquered boxes to pirated computer software and music CDs.

But this is a Tuesday night, and during the holidays the place is usually deserted. The perfect location for a sleazy child prostitution handoff. I'm sure this isn't the first time this particular place was chosen for illegal activity.

The ten girls I picked out would be delivered to this location. I, in turn, would hand Sergei a big briefcase of money. He would count the money, and the girls and I would walk away.

Simple.

Katya had left right after our meeting. Though trying to convey reassurance, her face belied flat worry. I couldn't help but take it on myself. Does she know something I don't?

Vlad leads me to a room in Yeshenko's compound, spare and more Asian in influence than Russian. "A place to get some rest," he says.

An avant-garde table and matching chairs sit next to a wardrobe inspired by traditional Chinese boxes. Light oak floors are decorated with large beige rugs, and a Japanese painting of magical colored boxes hangs on the wall. This is nicer than the hotel.

Someone will check me out of the hotel and collect Michael Stevenson's things while I make the big transaction. These Russians think of everything.

I can't sleep though my body is wrecked. I ache to hug Whitney, to hold Adanna. I told Whit when we spoke last that I'd be out of range the next couple days and couldn't communicate. Either I'm getting better at lying, or her radar has been dimmed due to sleep and general single-mom deprivation, but she didn't seem to detect anything amiss in my voice. I'd rather not answer her questions about how it's going and what I'm doing. I know she wouldn't like the answers.

"I'm proud of the work you're doing, Stuart," she had said. That was a notable improvement from the "I'm glad you're working at all" days.

My current dread puts me in mind of the time when I was a kid, maybe ten years old. I got caught after breaking a convenience-store window to steal cigarettes, and I had to sit in the store and wait for my stepfather, Mike, to come get me. I threw up, I was so upset. When Mike came in and clubbed me on the face, I think the store owner actually felt sorry he called my house. I was too. Man, did I get a beating.

I keep telling myself, "This is going to go like clockwork. No need to worry. These people are professionals." Breathe in, breathe out.

"Okay, Stuart. Are you ready to go?" For once Vlad's scary KGB voice doesn't startle me. I'm actually starting to find it reassuring.

"Ready as I'll ever be." I exhale loudly.

"Then let's go. Remember, you won't see the rest of the agents. But they'll be there. Just walk into this with confidence, and walk out. Understand?"

"I understand."

"Here's the briefcase. All the money is there; we've counted it three times. When Sergei opens it and sees it's real, he'll be as happy as an Orthodox priest on Epiphany. Any questions?"

"How do I get all the girls out? I mean, is there just going to be one car?"

"You'll have a driver, and he'll have a white fifteen-passenger van. Don't worry, we've thought of everything."

"I'm sure you have. Okay, let's go." My heart is beating so fast I can see my shirt move.

"We'll be close behind."

We exit out the compound door. The white van is sitting, just as Vlad said, and the driver, the same tall, kind-looking man who drove me to the hotel the first time, is ready to go.

"No worries. Just relax and be Mr. Michael Stevenson."

I step into the van, just me, the briefcase, and the driver, who doesn't say a word but gives me a knowing nod. Despite all Vlad's assurances, anxiety rises in my throat. I pray all the way.

We make good time through the city and arrive at the drop-off spot next to the front gate of the Izmailovo market. With its flags, onion domes, and castle spires, the entrance looks like a mix of the stately Kremlin and Disneyland. Scenes of the Russian countryside have been carved into the wooden poles on each side of the ticket booth. Cheerful toy bears, rabbits, and chipmunks, along with a plethora of matryoshka dolls, sit on display in store windows just inside the entrance.

A grove of trees makes a perfect pocketed enclosure nobody but those on this tiny road can see. The driver rolls up and turns off the lights. I glance behind to see only a narrow escape route. For this van, it would be tough. We're sitting ducks if something goes wrong.

My stomach is filled with more acid than a pool cleaner's truck. It burns and gurgles as I await to play the role of my lifetime. We sit for what seems like hours. Nothing. I look down at my watch and see it's only been fifteen minutes.

Lights flash in the distance and blink in our direction. Too late to change my mind now.

A car pulls to a stop about a hundred feet from us. The lights go black, then the parking lights come on. The back door opens, and two figures emerge and walk toward the van.

I take the deepest breath since I came out of my mother's womb. *God, give me courage.* I exhale and step out of the van, briefcase in hand. Yes, I'm going with God, and I'm praying there are a few dozen good-guy snipers in the trees and buildings that surround us.

The two men stop in the middle of the road, half the distance between both vehicles. This looks like a shoot-out scene at the O.K. Corral.

I walk up closer and recognize the men.

"Mikhail, my good friend, so good to see you again." Sergei holds out his hand, and I take it. Then he hugs me like we are family members. Ivan stands next to him with a stupid grin on his face.

"Good evening, Sergei, Ivan. Where are my girls?"

"They are coming. First, we need to take care of a few minor formalities." He pulls the too-familiar, tarnished silver flask out of his pocket. It squeaks as he twists off the top. "After all, this is a Russian tradition, is it not? And, it's also the way I like to cap business deals." He holds the canister in the air. "To my good friend Mikhail. May this be the first of many business transactions."

He takes a giant swig, a double gulper, and hands it to me.

"To the first of many." I take a bigger-than-average drink, hoping this will help to calm my nerves.

"Now, the money please. Ivan needs to count it to make sure it's all there. Not that we don't trust you. I'm sure you understand." There's that familiar devilish sneer.

"Of course. I'm quite familiar with this procedure." I smile and gladly hand over the briefcase. The thing has felt like the burden of Frodo's golden ring, though I've had no inclination to keep the cash.

"This should only take a short minute, and then both of us can be on our way." He looks at me inquisitively. "Your hands are shaking, my friend."

"You'll have to excuse me. It's not every day I make this kind of transaction in a dark alley."

"Yes, to that extent I understand. You're alone?"

"Except for the driver in the van, yes. And we are equipped to manage the girls in transit, if you catch my meaning, though I'm sure your tactics have taught them to behave."

I can see Sergei regain confidence in me, now that I'm speaking his language.

"I want to apologize for Ivan's behavior last night. I can assure you, when we do business in the future, he will be on his best behavior. We, too, have insured the girls are prepared to stay in line."

"Not through unnecessary beatings, I hope," I say, trying to remember exactly the sort of tone I took in our previous confrontation.

"Let's just say if they value their families, they won't even blink unless we give them permission."

My anger seethes secretly, which serves somehow to stabilize me. We pass several minutes in awkward silence. I hear the sounds of the night in the distance: car horns, the random yells of people, even a few birds chirping in the trees.

"You like cigarette, Mikhail?" He pulls the white stick out of the red box and carefully lights it with a black Zippo lighter.

"Why not."

He hands me a Russian nonfiltered cancer stick. "Now have another drink. After all, this is a special occasion."

He hands me the tin rectangle, and I have another swig.

"Sergei." Ivan calls from the black Volga a few feet away. "*Vsyo zdes.* [It's all here.]"

"Very good. Mr. Stevenson, thank you for being honest. I knew you were a trustworthy man. This is good for future business."

He takes out an orange cell phone and hits a button.

"Sasha. Da. Da. It's all here. Bring the girls." He hangs up and smiles again at me. "They are just around the corner. It will only take just a few seconds. If you want some more girls, I can make you very special price."

"I'm looking forward to our next deal. Let me get these girls out of the country, and then we will contact you for another deal."

"Just let me know."

Lights snake down the narrow alleyway and head our direction. There are three cars, all similar to the make and model of the car Sergei arrived in. The drivers exit their vehicles and simultaneously open the back doors. The girls step out into the night and shuffle over to us. They are flanked by three other men wearing dark clothes. One of them has his hand on something on his left hip. Security.

The headlights from Sergei's car shine on the girls. They're standing in a circle wearing nothing but underwear. It's got to be ten degrees out here. Scared and humiliated, they shiver and try to cover themselves.

"Take a good look at your product, my friend. They are just as you ordered them."

I pretend to be counting them, good businessman that I am. I see ten. "Thank you, Sergei." I move toward the girls, who have now huddled together to stay warm. They don't even have socks or shoes on. I throw my coat around Dasha. "Girls, move quickly to the van," I say quietly.

They look at each other but obey immediately. The light reflects off the girls' faces revealing fresh cuts and bruises on their faces and bodies. I glare at Ivan, who smiles at me and nods. He might as well be flipping me off.

"Sorry about the clothing, my friend. We only have so many

sizes, and we need these clothes for the next batch of girls. It's a never-ending supply of women coming through our door. I hope you understand."

I look into his beady eyes and nod.

"Mikhail, before you leave, I would like to introduce you to one of my business partners. She will be choosing girls for you in the future. This is Mrs. Ivanova."

A woman walks out of the shadows wearing a brown full-length leather coat. I look into her eyes and detect a flash of familiarity. The tightly wound dark curly hair, heavyset with plump cheeks and large glasses.

It can't be.

"Nice to meet you, Mr. Stevenson." She holds out her hand, and I take it. She looks intently at me and cocks her head side to side. She doesn't let go of my hand.

"Have we met before?"

I firmly pull my hand away from hers and look back toward the van. Almost all of the girls are in. The driver obviously has orders and has wasted no time getting them inside.

"I don't believe so. Nice to meet you. We must go to get ready for the flight." I make no haste in turning around and start moving toward the van.

"*Nyet, eto on!* [No, it's him!]" she screams in Russian. "*Eto on vikral moikh dvukh devochek iz otelya. Zaderzhitea yego!* [He's the man who stole my two girls from the hotel. Stop him!]"

Like a Wild West gunslinger, Ivan pulls a gun from his coat and points it at my head. Before I have time to react, a shot rings out, and I know I'm dead.

But it's Ivan who drops like a wet blanket and falls at my feet, blood running out of the side of his head. I pull Dasha close to me; and as quick as a striking snake, Sergei is behind me, shoving hard metal into my ribs. More shots fire in the distance as everyone scrambles for cover. He fires a shot right behind my right ear into the trees. My ear is ringing so badly I can hardly hear.

"Listen to me," he shouts to the black of the night. "I'll kill him without thinking twice about it. You know that much about me."

He's backing us up toward his car. Dasha is in front of me, exposed to the danger, so I shift her behind me.

"Don't even try it. I need you alive, not her." We're almost to the car, and he shouts again, "Don't come any closer! I'll kill them both!"

Tires screech, and I look up and the van has backed up in a flash. Either no one notices or no one cares, because no shots are fired. It races around the corner and out of sight. Thank God. At least the rest of the girls are safe.

Dasha and I are shoved in the car with incredible force. I fall on her as we tumble inside.

"It's okay, Dasha. God will help us." It's all I know to say.

Her teeth are chattering. She clenches her jaw and says, almost beyond perception, "*Bog umer. Na nas nadezhdi ne ostalos.* [God is dead. There is no hope for us now.]"

"*Seichas uvidim.* [We're about to see.]"

"There's nothing you can do to keep me safe now." I want to comfort her, but we both know she's right.

The door slams behind us, and the tires squeal as we go peeling down the road and into oncoming traffic.

Chapter Twenty-seven

*John was kind. Kinder than any man I ever met. He had brown hair,
hazel eyes, and was an American.*

*He worked for an organization called iEmpathize. Their job is to
rescue girls like us from the slavery we were trapped in. All of the rescuers
had given up their regular jobs to help girls like us. He said he was part
of a special operative team. He spent most of his life as something called a
"seal." When he said that, it was funny to me because all I could picture
was the animal that lives in the water. He explained that he used to serve
in the military and that seals were some of the best of the military and
they had special skills beyond the average military or law-enforcement
police.*

I felt safe. I was in good hands.

*"What's that on your arm?" I asked him. It was a different kind of
tattoo than I had ever seen.*

*"My tattoo?" he said. "It is a labyrinth. There are no dead ends. The
path of the design leads you into the rosetta middle."*

*He put his forearm in front of me and traced the tattoo with his
forefinger.*

*"The rosette represents the Rose of Sharon—Jesus Christ," he said.
"Every time I look at it, I'm reminded of the pilgrimage we're on. You
enter the labyrinth and contemplate what you need from the Lord.*

Things like forgiveness, strength, or faith for the future. You spend as much time in the center as you desire and then you contemplate your freedom in Christ and your future in Him as you exit."

That's what I needed. I told him I wanted one too. So he took out an ink pen and drew one on my arm.

I told him my whole story. What happened when I left the orphanage, meeting Alexandra, the promises they made to us, everything. He said this was all too common. It's how they lure girls away from their homeland into horrible situations.

He told me they would take me home. But I was still scared. I asked, "What if they come for me?"

"We've taken care of them," he said.

I didn't know what he meant exactly, but I was glad. And secretly, I hoped they were all dead.

John took me to the local police station with two warnings: "Don't say a word" and "Don't trust the police, because many of them are corrupt."

I had to sign paper after paper. The police looked at me like I was trash. One of them even said, "Oh, she'll be back prostituting herself again in no time."

He made it sound like it was my fault.

I kept circling the ink tattoo John made for me as I sat alone. What did I need on my pilgrimage? I needed hope and to be safe again. Hope that one day someone would want me after all I had been through.

It took three days for me to get a ticket home. I sat in a jail cell the entire time, but it didn't matter. I would rather have been in that cell for the rest of my life than where I had been living.

John came back on the last day to say good-bye. He turned my arm over and looked at the drawing. He looked up at me and smiled, then handed me a piece of paper with the tattoo on it.

I'll never forget what he told me.

"In your time of need, this will help. Remember where your source of strength comes from. You're going to be all right. I promise."

I asked, "Are you sure?"

"Of course."

And I asked again, "Are you really, really sure?"

He said, "Marina, I've personally made sure that someone will be at the Moscow airport to help you. It's all been checked out. From now on, your life is going to be everything you hoped it would be."

He made me so happy.

Marina bursts out in joyous laughter.

I couldn't help myself. I ran to him and threw my arms around him to hug him as hard as I could.

"You're welcome," he said. "God be with you."

I told him I'd never forget him.

Chapter Twenty-eight

From the backseat all I can see are flickering random flashes of head-lights. We're heading straight into traffic at blinding speed. I think about the chase scene through Moscow in the movie *The Bourne Supremacy*.

Dasha and I brace for a head-on collision with an oncoming car. The driver, a short, stubby Ivan look-alike, barely averts it as he makes a sharp right onto a small cobblestone road. I can hear the screech of the other car's tires on the road, but we keep driving. Dasha inhales and exhales like someone who's just run a 100-meter dash. If only she'd gotten to the van.

Dasha turns and gives me that disgusted "you really screwed it up this time" look that I became accustomed to in the early years of my marriage. Then she turns her back to look out the window. Though there's no reason for anyone to believe she knew about the nature of my business, we both know she's worse off now than before. I don't blame her for hating me. I resist the urge to apologize, to tell her about Mr. M, her brother. I know we're being watched.

We drive for more than an hour through dark forest groves in silence, except for Russian disco music and intermittent American '80s music, sung karaoke style. On a typical day, I might find this funny. Tonight, it's an absurd accompaniment, like Bozo the Clown at a funeral, and I try to tune it out.

I am with you.

I'm not sure if I hear that voice, or if it's just wishful thinking. I pray for my wife, for my daughter, for Dasha and Marina. It seems beyond the point to pray for myself. Instead of fired up or angry at Vlad or Katya for dragging me into this, I feel detached, resigned. I really wish I could believe that.

I think about our options. Do we have any? If the car slows down at a light, we could jump out and make a run for it. If I were alone, I would take that chance. I'd probably try leaping out of the car even at full speed. But with Dasha, I'm just not sure.

I look out the back window to see a car following close behind, headlights shooting beams through the back window with the bumps in the road. I hope the other girls made it away safely. We slow down along a dirt road. We've been off the main roads for about five or six miles, and this is the first time I've seen buildings.

A small guard shack stands inside an old iron gate. I'm guessing we're at an old abandoned military camp. The driver, Ivan II, honks the horn, and a man emerges with a machine gun draped over his shoulder. He looks like he's had at least one bottle of vodka tonight. We drive through and park in front of a large windowless building.

"Mikhail, I'm very disappointed in you. I thought we were friends." Sergei opens the car door and squats down so we're at eye level. He's had plenty of time to think about tonight, to prepare this speech, and he looks much different than before. Something has snapped. It's in his eyes. I'm no longer Mikhail the businessman, I'm his enemy.

"I shared my vodka with you. Now I find out you are nothing more than a common thief." The driver has turned and is looking back at me with a smirk on his face. I've transferred my disdain for Ivan I, now Ivan the dead, onto this guy. I'm sure it's deserved.

"I don't know what you're talking about."

"You're either a common thief, a crusader, or ex-military work-ing for someone else." He holds up a finger for each option. "No matter, we'll find out. We have our ways."

I try to muster up some fight. "I'm a businessman from the States, and I was sent here by my associates to buy girls for our clubs. That crazy woman doesn't know what she's talking about. She's wrong. I can't imagine what she's talking about."

"That crazy woman is my wife, you imbecile. And she never forgets a face."

"She's mistaken me for someone else."

"And now, now Ivan's dead. Ivan! He was my cousin. We grew up together since we were babies, and you took him from me. And you're going to pay." He chokes out the words and knocks me in the head with his gun so hard I fall into Dasha. Blood trickles from my forehead.

Sergei steps back and lets two goons drag me out of the car by my short hair. Dasha is subjected to the same treatment but barely makes a sound as they drag her right out of my coat and toward the building, her nearly naked body exposed to the cold ground. The snow is deeper out here. There's got to be at least twelve inches on the ground. She's guilty by dumb-luck association, and whatever the motive, it's my fault. These men are worse than animals.

"Ah, you brought one of your girls, Sergei. Good, we could use some entertainment tonight. We're lonely," one of the guards says.

"After I'm through with her, you can do to her what you want.

But first we have some business to take care of with my former friend here, Mikhail. Bring him in."

The men put my hands behind my back and bind them together with an oversized plastic tie, then drag me inside the building.

They slam me in a metal chair and tie leather armbands around my wrists. My feet are secured in the same fashion. The chair is cold, made of iron. It's rusting, and I can see random loose bolts.

"Now, let me give you the chance to avoid pain," Sergei says, positioning himself in front of me. "Who are you, and who do you work for?"

"I told you, I don't know what you're talking about. I'm an American who runs clubs. I came here to buy new girls for my clubs. That's it."

"Wrong answer. Men who come to buy girls don't steal girls. It's against our code of ethics."

The two men who look like Neanderthals strip off my shirt. Sergei takes wires with clips on the end and fastens them to my ears, armpits, nose, and chest. As they snap each one shut, I jerk in pain but refuse to cry out.

I will fear no evil, for You are with—

Sergei walks to the side wall, and I brace myself for what's about to happen. He looks at me with a mix of hatred and pleasure in his eyes and flips a switch.

I feel as if I'm being pierced with a thousand needles. My body sizzles, and I hear popping noises in my head. My body, the air around me, is permeated with a putrid smell of burning flesh. *My* burning flesh. My skin and hair have become fire, and my entire body begins to shake and convulse.

God help me.

Then it's over. Everything is blurry. I can hear Dasha yelling in the background, but I can barely see her. Behind her I make out the form of a man in a black robe. Could it be the angel of death?

Every cell and nerve radiates pain. The men shout and curse at me. I feel a blow to my face. The burnt flesh on the right side of my face cracks and crumbles on impact, like a charred piece of wood. Everything is going dark, as if I'm looking through a telescope where light is succumbing to a black hole.

It can't end like this. I have a family, a daughter who needs a father. "God, please. I was just trying to do Your work. Have mercy on me and save me. I beg You."

Something hits me again, and I scream out as shock reverberates through my body. Now I'm soaking wet and surrounded by ice. I'm shivering, freezing to death.

"Mikhail, my patience is running out. I'll only ask once more. Who are you working for?"

"Alexei. Alexei Moshin, he said his name was."

"Who is he?"

"I don't know."

Sergei screams, "Stop playing stupid with me. I've had enough of this."

He sprints back to the switch. This time, the pain is even more agonizing. And then it stops, and I see Sergei, the Devil in a suit, move farther and farther away from me until I see nothing but darkness.

I feel hands under me, carrying me. Every touch, every movement sends pain through my body. I'm placed onto a narrow, hard mattress, and someone forces my eyes open.

A priest is leaning over me, close. He's wearing a large silver crucifix that swings like a heavy pendulum.

"In time, Seryozha. Now, let him rest. There is no value to killing this man in God's house."

"But, Father," Sergei pleads.

"This man will serve a greater purpose with his senses intact, at least for now. Leave him to me."

Chapter Twenty-nine

I'm told it's morning, but I wouldn't know inside this tomb of a building. Which morning it is, I'm not sure. I didn't ask. I'm not even sure I can talk, or if I still have the right half of my face. I don't want to touch it to find out. I shuffle, bent like an old farmer, following the priest down a narrow hall shaped like ancient early-church catacombs. Icons cover the walls. My head is bent, and I'm looking through one eye, the other is stuck shut. My view is veiled, aperture wide and narrow. Every movement sends pain through my entire body.

A sharp turn to the right, and stairs descend revealing another level that's lit by electronic candles posted along the wall. The priest, his robe billowing behind him, never looks back. The largest canvas, right outside a tall arched door, is the same vivid depiction of a knight slaying a dragon I saw at the Lady of Kazan Church. Everything appears soft and blurred. He opens the high narrow door and steps inside, leaving it cracked open. I shuffle the next few feet and finally reach the opening.

"Come in. Come in. Please sit down." He says this like a distracted professor getting ready to teach a class.

I'm surrounded by books, candles hanging from gold chains in each corner, and the distinct sweet smell of sandalwood. Most amazing are hundreds of icons that must have come from all over the world. I strain to focus. I recognize some from my trips to Ethiopia. The choppy colorful renditions are from Spain or maybe even Mexico. On one side of the room is a stone table with the Communion elements and a mammoth Bible.

"Yes, you can see I've an interest in icons. The Holy Mother, of course. She signifies everything pure and good, everything sacred. What every woman should aspire to be, don't you think?"

I nod my head. This sick bastard likes to hear himself talk.

"And the Son, our Lord Jesus Christ, who gave His very body and blood to atone for sin." He crosses his arms.

He points to a five-part depiction, hung in a circle, of the knight slaying the dragon.

"This one," he says, pointing to the largest icon on the wall, "is Saint George the Dragonslayer, one of our most famous icons. Do you know the story?" He sweeps his hand under the icons in a wide circle.

I shake my head, though now that I see the series, I remember it. I figure the more he talks, the better for me.

"This dragon lived in a lake and was worshipped as a deity. Many children were sacrificed to appease this dragon." He amplifies his singsong voice and points to each depiction as he talks, as if he's a curator giving a guided tour.

"The king's daughter was to be one of those sacrificed. But, just before she was to meet her doom, Saint George appeared and, with the words 'In the name of the Father, the Son, and the Holy Spirit' knocked the dragon to the ground. The princess, at Saint George's command, led the dragon through the streets." He stands and studies me, then pulls up a chair and sits directly across from me.

"You know, these girls, they need to be saved."

He leans down, his face close to mine. "And I am saving them."
I can't believe what I'm hearing.

"It's just like the story: Men are like the dragon in this picture,
you see. They have certain desires, carnal needs they will fulfill. If
men can pay to fulfill their longings, and continue to come back,
you've controlled the desires of the flesh. If clubs and houses for girls
didn't exist, men would take more extreme measures to fulfill them.
They would rape, murder, and destroy to get what they want. What
they need."

He strokes his beard pensively.

"But you are still sacrificing the girls to the dragon." My voice is
hoarse, barely a whisper. My mouth tastes like I've eaten the crust of
a burnt marshmallow, bitter ash, and chalk.

"For all sakes and purposes, these girls would end up living on
the streets. They would be dead within a year or two, killed by men
who couldn't have their desires met in a controlled setting." He spits
out the last words.

"Instead, girls are provided a safe place to stay, a roof over their
heads, food, money, nice clothes, and a job to secure their future.
They go to church, take Communion, and come to me for confession. And due penance. I am able to absolve them of their sins. A
much better deal, don't you think?"

I open my mouth to speak, but there are no words.

"And their eternities are still intact."

"It's hell on earth," I finally say. My mouth only moves vertically,
like a puppet's, making it hard to form my words.

The priest takes a pipe out of his desk drawer, he packs it with tobacco, tamps it down with the end of a silver tool, and lights it. The room fills with the aroma of Irish cream as the bowl of the pipe turns to a glowing red. A homey scent in a cozy room that I would find pleasing in any other circumstance.

"That's why you are who you are, whoever you are, and why I am a scholar and a priest. You could not possibly understand these issues." He blows smoke in my face. "I recognize you, you know. You're the one who interrupted my Mass several days ago with your cell phone. No reverence for God in His own house. And now you have interrupted a good transaction and killed a man. Murder, now that's a cardinal sin."

The hot breath of fresh pipe tobacco plunges into my nostrils. I don't move or speak.

He rolls rosary beads in his hand, blue and white with a silver cross dangling from the end.

"Which side are you on, Mr. Stevenson? Are you on the side of good, or evil?"

I summon strength to answer. For a reason I can only think is beyond my humanity, I speak the words: "He Himself bore our sins in His body. By *His* wounds are we healed. For all of us, even you and those girls you torture."

He leans back, as if he's been slapped.

"You quote the holy Scripture to me! You're nothing but a worthless thief." He puts his face close to mine again, his long beard touches my arm. I feel as if I'm being smothered, like my very soul is being pressed to extinction.

"I am Father Alexander Shapov, a Harvard graduate and a respected leader in the holy Orthodox Church! I didn't create this evil. In fact, it was brought into this world by a woman. And women are the reason it exists now. I have been charged to control it."

I see a look in his eyes I've seen before. When I was in Rwanda, right before the genocide broke out, I saw it in the eyes of the Hutu military leaders. I saw it in the eyes of the man who raped and beat an orphan girl in Africa. I captured it when I photographed a man desecrating dead bodies in the Congo. I even saw it in my own eyes once, when I was at the lowest point of my life and doing things I prefer not to remember.

He puts his pipe on his desk and rests on one knee before me. "Now, is there anything you'd like to confess? Tell Father Alexander your sins. I can help you, you know. I know you are not working alone. Now, my son, tell me who sent you." He's back to his sanctuary voice.

I sit, silent.

"Do you know who I am? I control everything in this city. The church, the government, the police. You can't hide from me."

He rises and looks down at me, and I brace for a blow. Instead, he turns and grabs a cloth, a silver tray with hosts, and a chalice from his large desk. He begins saying those familiar words, making a mockery of the most sacred rite.

"Take and eat." He holds a host to my cracked lips and shoves it in. It dissolves in my mouth. I feel my stomach lurch.

He pours a cup full of wine as he continues this sacrilege. "And drink," he says with a sneer on his face, his spit spraying into my face. He forces the wine into my mouth. I swallow some, but most of the red liquid runs down my chin.

He wipes my chin with the cloth, a gesture more unwelcome

to me than if he'd stabbed me in the heart. After replacing the Communion elements, he picks up a clear jar of oil and then leans right into my face, the smell of Communion wine on his breath.

"This, I use for last rites." He runs his hand down the side of my face and leaves it at my chin. I try not to shudder. "Are you sure there is nothing you wish to confess?"

I look directly into his eyes. Everything is becoming blurry, but I can make out the two men who dragged me into this sick place as they walk toward me. I also see the face of the woman I met out on the street with the purple coat. I knew she had to be working with Sergei's people.

"You have failed her, the one you're after, mmm-hmm," she squeaks. "You are a pathetic excuse for a man. *See,* you have no power. And I warned you to stay away from things that do not concern you."

A sense of hopelessness seeps into my soul like poison. I have failed Dasha. Failed Whitney and Adanna, Katya and Marina.

"Yes, that's right," she says. Her face recedes, replaced by an oncoming fist. I've been hit in the mouth. My face goes numb. I reach up, touch my mouth, and see red glimmering liquid on my outstretched hand. The wine, I'm sure it was the wine.

Chapter Thirty

I woke up to the sound of the wheels of the airplane crashing on to the runway in Moscow. At last, I was home.

I remember my prayer that day: "Thank You, God, for sending John. My rescuer."

There was no luggage for me to collect, so I did as I was instructed. Through the customs line, then on through electronic glass doors that opened to the crowd outside.

John said there would be a priest waiting in the lobby, unmistakable in his black robes and dangling silver cross. I was a little unsure about this at first. I remembered the last time I saw a priest—only briefly and from a distance. But he was with those people—the people who sent me away to Egypt. But surely there were good priests too. John, my rescuer, wouldn't put me in danger. I trusted him.

I can still hear the priest's voice. It was so calming.

"There, there, my dear. You are home now, you are safe."

He held his arms open to me, and I hugged him.

"Father Alexander will take charge of you now," he said. "All of your needs will be met."

Outside, a fancy black car was waiting for us with a driver. It was the nicest car I've ever been in. It smelled new. Tan leather seats, blue and red lights leaping off the dashboard, it even had a place to hold cold drinks.

Father Alexander handed me a Coke. With ice. I settled into the chair and took a deep breath. Fate had turned once again for me. I was so hopeful that I wouldn't have to live on the street or be abused—ever again. That was my prayer.

We pulled up to a place called the Tochka. It looked like a restaurant from the outside. There was a guard at the door. Outside was a window that looked like a theatre window where you would buy tickets to a movie.

When we got out of the car, the priest opened his bag and took out a lacy white cloth, like an oversized scarf. He got out of the car and opened my door. When I stepped out, he put it over my head, like a covering, and said, "With this symbol of my love, you are now indebted to me. You belong to me and you will be my very special Natasha."

I told him my name was Marina.

He said I would be called Natasha from now on.

His arm went around my waist, and we walked through the building. Everyone acknowledged him and bowed. "Hello, Father. Good morning, Father." Some even came to him with their hands cupped together and said, "Father, bless." He gave them a blessing. I thought I was in a church.

I followed him down the hall, the strange scarf on my head trailing behind me. He opened a door to a very fancy room. It looked like the inside of a church. Gold accented the ceiling, there were candles everywhere, a bed sat in the far corner, and it smelled like incense. The room was decorated by icons, most of them of Saint George the Dragonslayer.

I thought that very odd.

"This is my room," he said. "My bridal chamber. Only very special people are allowed here."

He picked me up in his arms. "Let me carry you over the threshold, Natasha."

Then he locked the door.

Chapter Thirty-one

"Walk, you stupid American. Up the stairs." It's Sergei's voice. Light pours down through the thick black, so dark I can't see my own aching, blood-speckled hand, and illuminates a set of narrow stairs. I've been holed up in a cement-block room for what I'm guessing is at least a dozen hours. My entire body is soaked in what smells like urine.

My legs wobble, but I am close enough to the stairs to lean into them and pull myself up, leveraging my weight like I'm climbing a rock wall. I take the steps one at a time. It's Father Alexander, not Sergei, who leans down and grabs my hands. I feel like he may pull my arm right off my body. Pain sears through my joints, along my jaw, and into my head. The priest pulls me out into the large room where we first arrived. The room with the chair.

He puts his arm around me, like the Good Samaritan, and leads me into a corner with slow steps. He whispers, "It's too bad you had to spend the day down there. Such a stench! You smell like a sewer." He distances himself, and I falter, my legs stiff from lying in one position and from a few good kicks.

"How long has it been since your last confession?" he asks. A familiar, tired refrain. "I think today would be a perfect time to tell Father Alexander who sent you. I would like to help you, but I'm afraid if you don't cooperate, they will have to resort to more carnal tactics." He nods toward the chair and the men standing in front of it. "Do you have something you want to say to me?"

I'm too dizzy, too weak to say a word.

He takes a glass of water and holds it to my cracked, sore lips. My tongue feels stuck to the top of my mouth, so I know I'm dehydrated, but my body reviles his gesture, and I start to heave.

"Surely, my son, you would like to feel better. Now, sit here with me." He leads me to the makeshift electric chair and helps me to sit. Sergei stands and watches from across the room.

"If you don't tell me who you are working with, heaven help her," he says.

The two men who dragged me out of the priest's room are doing the same to Dasha, pulling her, one brute arm under each shoulder, across the floor. She's apparently also received the priest's sordid Communion, or something stronger, based on her languid, half-closed eyes. She's naked and looks as if she's been beaten, no doubt abused by the pigs in this room.

I hear her say under her breath, "Please, Priest, God, Father, please help me."

I think of my daughter and fight back tears.

Sergei looks at me and then down at Dasha. I know what he's thinking, what he's about to do to her. The other men smirk at me. This abuse is like sneezing to them, a sick reflex.

I don't have the strength to scream, but I shake my head no.

"No," I say to the priest. "God, no."

He grabs the back of my neck and jerks my head toward his. "Tell me who sent you."

"God—" I say. It's more of a prayer, but the priest's eyes get big, his face red. He turns toward Sergei. "I think we have no choice. Do what you have to do."

"You think you're absolved?" I croak out loud enough to stop him cold.

He flips around and fixes his eyes on me with the same look he gave me when I interrupted his Mass.

"You're not a man of God. You're an emissary of the Devil!"

I hear a commotion, and Dasha says, "Oh, God, no." The men are moving toward her. Sergei is egging them on.

I pray, *Please, God in heaven, show up. Surely You didn't send me here for this.*

We turn at the sound of the door slamming open. A short man with a doughy face, a cleric's beard, and a red robe walks in breathing heavily. He turns to look at the men and Dasha and, without so much as a flinch, says, "Father, come quickly. The chief of police is here, and he's demanding to see you immediately."

"Tell him to come back later." He's still glaring at me.

"But, Father," the guy in the red robe lowers his voice, "he said to tell you this: 'You have no choice; you come out or he comes in.'"

"Sergei," he says, "show our American savior who's in charge." Then he storms out after the messenger, his robes swishing behind him.

Sergei comes toward me, licking his lips like a lion going in for the kill. Before he reaches me, the door bursts open again. I expect the priest, but instead I see four men dressed in black, each with a ready gun. I hear three quick pops and watch as the men, including Sergei, drop to the floor.

"Can you walk?" a big guy says to me.

"Not sure," I answer back. I try to walk and buckle.

"We don't have time—grab him." Two guys flank me; their arms swing in under my armpits and sweep me up like parents lifting a child over a curb. The biggest guy has Dasha in his arms. She starts to thrash and fight him, but he says something that stills her.

I realize it's going to be tough for them to help me through the narrow passage. With the fresh adrenaline rush, I'm certain I can make it on my own.

"I can walk," I say. They release me, and I take a second to gain my balance before starting to move forward.

"Follow us. As fast as you can. Do not talk, and we'll explain later."

We pass the icon of Saint George outside the priest's office, and I rip it off the wall. The men look at me, and then look at each other like, "Why not?" Then one of them takes it to lighten my load. Adrenaline must be working overtime, anesthetizing me from what would be painful bumps as I'm being jostled.

We follow down the twists and turns of narrow halls. I stumble but keep moving. My heart pounds when I see a door at the end of a hall. Another man dressed in the same black spy gear says something on a cell phone, then opens the door so we don't even have to break pace to exit. The icy air cuts through me and gives me a sense of exhilaration at the same time.

The environment doesn't look anything like the outside of a church, it's more of an industrial area surrounded by shops and office buildings. We must have taken an underground passageway to get here.

We pile into a waiting black Audi with three of the guards. The others stay behind.

Dasha's head is down. One of the men in black has placed a blanket over her. As the car lurches away from the curb, she turns toward me, and we catch eyes. Hers are glassy, but I can see a glimmer of recognition, a connection between us. I lean my head back and breathe an audible sigh of relief. We're safe.

At least for now.

Chapter Thirty-two

The car speeds down the road through the light snow I've just noticed is falling from the Moscow sky. I am so thankful. Another few minutes and God only knows what would have happened to us.

God only knows.

Yes. He does. He answered my prayer. Looking through the window toward the sky, I mutter, "Thank You."

Three of us sit shoulder to shoulder in the backseat, the big guy with wide shoulders in the middle. It's cramped, no room to move my numb legs. I lean forward and turn my face toward his.

"*Spasibo, chto vitashili nas ottuda.* [Thank you for getting us out of there.]" I'm still having trouble speaking.

This guy is all pro, from his huge cut frame and chiseled face to his shiny shaved head. With his darker skin, he reminds me of Israeli Secret Service.

He keeps his head and eyes straight forward. "*Eto bil prikaz.* [We were following orders.]"

"Who sent you?"

"We've been instructed not to answer questions. All you need to know is that you are safe and with friends. Vlad said to tell you so. You will be briefed on all relevant information when you arrive at your destination."

Just hearing Vlad's name encourages me. That's all I need to know. Vlad to the rescue.

After fighting traffic, we pull up to the same secure office building where we met Yeshenko a few days before. The guards glide through the gates, and we enter an indoor parking garage.

Our rescuers help us to the elevator, flash their identity cards under a scanner, and type in a code. The elevator opens, and we're greeted by a host of friendly faces. Vlad, Katya, Alyona, and Yeshenko are waiting there.

We step off the elevator, and Katya throws her arms around me and cries. "*Prosti menya, Stuart. Prosti menya.* [I'm sorry, Stuart. I'm so sorry.]" I wince with the hug, and she pulls away. She surveys me, her eyes unable to hide the shock when she sees the condition of my face, my body still bent. What on earth do I look like?

Yeshenko's face shows horror at Dasha's appearance. Her eyes are glassy and red and ringed with black makeup. Her white-blond hair is matted, and I can see blood in her hair and traces on her swollen cheek and eye.

"Come, come to my office," he says with concern, and we sit around the table. Katya helps Dasha down the hall. Alyona steps forward, and in a barely perceptible gesture, places a long sweater over Dasha's shoulders.

Vlad sits next to me at the long table. "So things didn't go exactly as planned."

I just shake my head.

"Stuart, I'm very sorry. The girls are safe—and now Dasha is safe. And you are here, thank God."

I notice he doesn't say I'm safe.

"We'll get you medical attention. A doctor is on the way. That's a nasty cut you have on your head."

Katya brings a cold cloth for Dasha, which she takes without acknowledgment and places over half of her face. She looks at me and starts to move toward me, but I wave her off with my hand and mouth, "I'm okay." I'm not. I'm a mess, but I don't want anyone to see just how much pain I'm in. Besides, I've got too much on my mind to think about the pain. I'm still processing my prayer—and God's answer.

Yeshenko turns toward Dasha. "I'm so sorry those animals hurt you. We will make sure you have the best treatment, the best doctors—anything you need." I sip the hot tea that's been poured and ready. Dasha wraps her long slender fingers around her cup.

"Who are you? How do you know my name?" She is back to herself, at least the Dasha I met.

"My name is Yeshenko, and I was hired to help you."

"To help me?" She looks down at her tea and brings it to her lips to drink. Her hands shake so much I'm surprised anything has gotten into her mouth. I suddenly feel as if I'm eavesdropping on a private conversation. Maybe the others feel the same, because no one moves.

"Why would anyone want to help me? Nobody has helped me my entire life."

"There are people who care. We care about you."

She shoots him a suspicious look and picks at her fingernails. I'm sure she's heard that a hundred times—each time a lie.

"Well, thank you. I guess. Can I go now? I'm not feeling well."

"Oh. But please, don't go. We have an apartment all ready for you. All expenses paid. As I said, your needs are taken care of."

"What do you want from me?"

"Nothing, Dasha, nothing at all."

She glares at Yeshenko like he's another john wanting a trick.

"You don't just give somebody something for nothing. I need to go."

She gets up but realizes she has no clothes. The realization causes her to panic. I can see her lip quiver.

"Dear, dear, it's okay. You see, I was hired by your brother."

She stares at him with disbelief cultivated through years of disappointment and abuse.

"What are you talking about?"

"Your brother, Dasha. He only found out about you recently. He went to the orphanage to bring you home, but you were already gone. He's been searching for you ever since. Day and night without ceasing."

Dasha looks down into her tea. After a few moments, she looks up at Yeshenko.

"I have a brother?"

"You do, young lady. He is a high-ranking Russian official."

"I have a brother?"

"Yes. That's why you're here now."

"I have a brother? He came to find me?"

"Yes." Yeshenko speaks in a soft voice.

She cries out, and it's a cry from a place of deep longing.

Yeshenko clears his throat, a nervous gesture from a man who's not comfortable with emotion, but he moves and puts his arm around her.

"There, there. You are with friends now."

I wonder how long it's been since someone—especially a man—has spoken to her with such kindness.

"Darling," Katya says, "you are safe. Soon, you will be home."

Chapter Thirty-three

Dasha cries into Yeshenko's jacket for fifteen minutes. We just stand there watching. This is holy ground. When she finally calms down, he leans over to me and says, "You have done a good thing. Mr. M will be forever grateful."

"You are more than welcome."

The door opens and two people come through the entry carrying black saddlebags. I recognize one of the men immediately, Dr. Kudratseva.

"Finally, the doctors are here," Katya says with a hint of exasperation. Couldn't have been quick enough for her. She immediately barks orders: "Dr. Kudratseva, please take care of Dasha. And, Dr. Alexi, over here with Stuart."

They move quickly, set their bags down, and go to work.

"I'm fine, really. Just a few nicks and scrapes."

"Stuart, just be quiet and let the doctor do his job."

"Yes ma'am."

Dr. Alexi cleans and examines my wounds. He gives me a few optimistic nods as he checks out my face, then he begins assisting Dr. Kudratseva with Dasha.

"Katya," Dr. Kudratseva says from across the room, "she's going to need a few stitches. Is there another room we could use that is a little more private?"

"Of course. Yeshenko, can you help please?"

"Absolutely, follow me."

Katya carefully cradles Dasha's face in her hands and says something only the two can hear. Dasha looks at me and for the first time, gives me a nod and a smile. I take that as thanks.

The rest of the room empties except for Katya and me. I'm dead tired, but more than sleep, I need to get some answers.

"How did you know where to look, Katya? I thought nobody in the world would be able to find us."

"You didn't think we would let you hang out with violent criminals without knowing exactly where you were, did you?" Katya looks at me like I'm a dunce. She has this way of always making me feel like I'm late to the party.

"What do you mean?"

"We embedded GPS tracking devices in your clothing. We knew where you were at all times." Patting down my pants and jacket, I try to find something that doesn't belong in my clothes.

"You'll never find them. If you could find them, so could your kidnappers."

"That's very crafty of you. I don't suppose you could have come a little sooner, could you? Like, say, before I was tortured in an electric chair? I swear my body still has so much electricity in it I could power a small town. And there's going to be a bruise on the side of my face as big as Texas."

"Oh, Stuart, I'm so sorry about that, and we will get you further treatment as soon as we leave here. But we needed cooperation from the chief of police. Mr. M had to call in a favor, and it took more maneuvers than we expected."

"So tell me about this so-called priest. What a sick devil he is."

"Now you know. He's known as Father Alexander, though that's not his real name. He lives a double life, running his church as a pious man, hearing confessions and leading people through the holiest of sacraments. He especially appeals to the older women whose husbands were highly ranked in the old communist system, some of whom still have old money."

"Then there's the other side," I say. "He force-fed me Communion, Katya. Can you believe that? I just can't see how a true man of God could be involved in this. Seriously, what kind of psychotic disorder does he suffer from?"

"Ah, Stuart, the human condition. Man's sexual lust and lust for power and money. Vlad would say the priest is possessed by the Devil."

"And I would agree with him." I don't tell her about seeing the strange woman. I'm not sure if she was even there, or if her appearance was a product of the wine or whatever drugs were placed into the chalice claiming to hold the blood of Christ. Sitting here now, the sacrilege astounds me.

"There is more to the story," Katya continues.

"I'm all ears."

"Father Alexander was once an orphan. I was able to access his records through my connections in Volshky, where he was born. He was placed in the Volshky orphanage when he was twelve years old."

"What happened to his parents?"

"Apparently, he was an only child of a woman whose husband either died or disappeared. He never knew his real father."

Katya and I are drinking tea, and I start to nibble on a biscuit. I know this is a risk for my unstable stomach, but I need to eat. My spirit feels charged, though I feel every ache now that I've relaxed.

"You would think he might try to help orphans, knowing what that was like," I say.

"You would think that, yes. I talked to the orphanage director, who remembers his mother. She came to visit only twice. The director told me she was beautiful, said she looked like an angel, but she had become a prostitute and an alcoholic. Who knows which happened first."

I push up from the table and look out the window at the city of Moscow. From here, I can see miles of the Moscow River that runs like a snake through the center of the city. It's frozen solid.

"Apparently, the boy adored his mother. But she sent him to the orphanage because Alexander had witnessed his mother with a man, a high-ranking official with the communist party. He was violent with her, and Alexander went after the man with a weapon. The official threatened to kill the boy."

"I attacked my stepfather, Mike, with an axe once. If I would have been a little stronger, my swing wouldn't have missed its mark." I pause to think about what Alexander must have witnessed as a child. Things a child should never see.

"Why didn't his mother keep coming to see him? As crazy as my mom was at times, especially with men, she never would have abandoned me."

"She died. Was beaten and found alongside a road."

There are so many blanks in his story. So many things I'd like to fill in. The reporter in me wants the facts. Facts that might help make sense of this madness.

"I can't imagine how he got to Harvard. Or was that just a lie he told me?"

"He did have some good influences in his life. A priest, a holy man named Father Boris, ran a home for orphaned boys. Alexander moved there from the Volshky orphanage. Father Boris took him, and all the boys, under his wing. He saw the boy was brilliant and helped him through his education in Russia."

I turn back from the window, take the seat next to Katya, and prop my feet up on the table. This brings a sudden sharp pain to my calves, so I carefully set my feet back on the ground, noting Katya's half smile at my failed attempt to act as if nothing is wrong.

"So it all boils down to the same thing, doesn't it? No matter what's happened to us in life, we all have a choice. Good or evil."

"Father Boris told me Alexander always thought in different ways from the other boys. He felt he was superior to everyone else, and it isolated him."

"That makes sense. He's a narcissist. Perhaps brilliant, but driven by his oversized ego."

"Yes, he's clearly a genius, but morally and psychologically demented in other ways. Stuart, do you know how mystics have visions from God?"

"Sure, I've read about them."

"Father Alexander believes he is a mystic. He had a vision where he claims the spirit of Saint George descended upon him. You know, the Dragonslayer."

"Ah, now this is starting to make sense."

"What do you mean?"

"I saw depictions of that icon all over his office. In fact ..." I reach into my coat and pull out the icon I lifted from the wall. "I took a souvenir for the trouble he gave me."

Katya covers her mouth and laughs. "Stuart, only you would steal from some of the deadliest people in Russia as you're heading out the door."

"By the time I left, half of those deadly people were just plain dead."

"Yes, well, that is something I didn't hear you say until just now. I can't really know these details, do you understand?"

"Fine with me. Repeating them would just give me nightmares anyway."

I study the gold around the edges, the halo around Saint George, his angelic-looking face. Then the red dragon flat on its back. Fangs reared toward Saint George, forked tongue hissing in the air, and a sword inches from its open mouth.

"So, the priest believes he's like him, identifies with him somehow?"

"No, he believes he *is* him. In the flesh. Reincarnated, you might say. In the same way that people in the Bible thought John the Baptist was Elijah who had come back."

"You've got to be kidding!"

"I'm quite serious. We know for a fact that he's even killed, rather had killed—we don't know him to have murdered anyone himself—a number of people who have interfered. Even Americans. He's afraid of no one."

"So our priest is a killer? How many people are we talking about?"

"We're not exactly sure. Our guess is around thirty."

"Thirty people murdered, girls beaten and sold, and he's still allowed to be the priest of a church and roam freely around the country? The man's a fiend."

"He has many friends in high places. They have a working agreement. He pays them under the table, and he gets to run his brothels."

"How many people is he paying off? Even the police?"

"Police and government officials are on his payroll, yes. We know this is a fact."

"These girls don't stand a chance of getting out of this hell. So even if they're rescued, they end up at the police station, and the police take them back to their pimps."

"Not always, but often. Yes. Now you see why we do what we do, and why we have to jump when the time is right. I just wish Marina had been with those girls."

"So do I, Katya. After seeing what I've seen, I can hardly stand to think about what she's enduring. So, do authorities who aren't corrupt know about Father Alexander's delusion?"

"They know but don't care or aren't able to admit they do. He has a strong following in this country—people who still want to believe in a sacred authority. Because of his position, and all the money he is making, he is allowed to live above the law."

I realize I'm pulling the hair on the top of my head with both hands. A nervous condition I had as a kid. "If I could justify vigilante justice, I'd kill this guy with my bare hands. I don't understand why God doesn't take wicked men like this out. It'll be one of my first questions to Him when I'm dead."

"I don't think God has anything to do with it, Stuart."

"Neither do I."

"Alexander started brothels all over the city of Moscow. Then expanded into Vladimir, Kostroma, Ivanova, everywhere. Nobody knows exactly how many he controls. He's become very rich from his black business."

"I'm sure. The selling of human bodies is the most lucrative business in the world."

"This is a sad reality of the world we live in. He filled all the perverted appetites and needed more girls. Then, his clientele demanded younger girls, so he started abducting them as soon as they left the orphanages and forcing them to be sex slaves. Many are only fifteen or sixteen."

"How could he get away with something so heinous?"

I walk over to the mahogany table and slam my hand into the wood, hard enough to knock over the plastic bottle sitting on it. The pain feels good on my knuckles.

"He convinced the local authorities that it was a good thing. He created a philosophy to support his actions and, for reasons that elude me, they accepted it. He said he was providing a place for these girls to live, feeding them, providing for them."

"Yes, he gave me that same sales talk."

"It's interesting that he would tell you this."

"Yeah, almost as if he needed to justify himself to me."

We sit in silence together. Absorbing all of this is impossible. But the silence does not change the sad reality.

"I still can't wrap my head around this, Katya. The authorities know exactly what's going on, and yet they do nothing?"

"Not all of them. His cover is that the girls are in a convent at the church. A school where they receive their education and learn to be good church girls and productive members of society. That's what most believe."

"Vile," I spit.

"Good church girls by day and sex slaves at night. You saw them yourself. Dressed in the church and looking like they were enrolled in a convent."

"This is one of the craziest things I've ever heard. I just can't believe he has a blank check to do whatever he wants."

"It happens in almost every country."

Picking up the icon in front of me, I notice it is smooth and silky. I look closer at the detail. The dragon has huge teeth and smoke rising out of its nostrils. The figure of Saint George is smiling. Delighted at what he's about to do.

"Stuart, we have the perfect place for you to hide. You have to go somewhere until this is sorted out. It's safe, and even if he finds out you're there, he won't touch you. Nobody would dare touch her; she's too protected."

"Who, Katya?"

"Sister Irina. She runs an orphanage in Kostroma by the Ipatiev Monastery. She helps rehabilitate the girls that are rescued. It's wonderful and beautiful there. You'll love it."

"Vlad mentioned Sister Irina—but what makes her untouchable?"

"For one, many people believe she is *svyataya* [a saint]. Her entire life has been dedicated to helping needy people—*bednim, nadlom-lennim, broshennim* [the poor, the downcast, the throwaway]."

"That's why people won't mess with her?"

"Well, that, and she's also Mr. M's grandmother."

Chapter Thirty-four

We arrive in Kostroma in a black Volga to the protection of Sister Irina. The car stops in front of a white twelve-foot-high wall that encircles the property. Five armed men, compliments of Mr. M, have accompanied Vlad and me from Moscow. They escort us through an impenetrable, four-inch-thick metal door and make sure we are settled before they speed away.

We go directly to a plain, cramped room: two twin beds, a cross on the center wall, and a small desk in the corner with a chair and a Bible. Built for simplicity. Besides the cross, there's only one thing on the white walls—a prayer etched into a wood carving:

> O Salvation of the travelers
> Save me
> And lead me to your Kingdom.
>
> *Hegomen Youssef Assad*

Reading it gives me a sense of comfort. I need someone to save me, not just in the life to come, but in the middle of the life I'm living. Especially now. It's late, and my eyelids feel like they weigh ten pounds apiece.

"Hey, Vlad, I'm so wiped out I think I'll go straight to bed."

"Sleep well. You'll be safe here, and I'm on guard just in case."

"Thanks, man. I can't seem to keep my eyes open...."

For the first time since I arrived in Russia, I fall into a deep, catatonic sleep.

There's something in the room. I have a sixth sense about this. It's something evil.

A strange, thin voice pours into the room like it's coming through the speakers of a shortwave radio.

It hisses, "You are without hope." It's a nightmare.

My eyes open at the sound of the voice. It's a woman's. "They are all lost. There's nothing you can do to save them. There will always be one more." I feel a weight on me, like someone is pinning my shoulders back. I glance over and see Vlad's hulk under the covers in the bed adjacent to mine.

I try to answer, to say something, but my mouth won't open.

I hear the voice again. "I will kill you."

I know that voice. It's the woman from the street. I see her over me for a flash, and then she fades into black, a dark black like when I was in the hole at the priest's place. How did she get in?

I can't move, not even a finger. I feel as if I'm suffocating. Everything presses in, and I try with all my strength to resist it.

The only thing I hear besides her voice is the beating of my heart. "Who are you?" I try to speak, but somehow my words take the form of dry, cracked air. My throat is a desert.

I can see her form now, at the end of my bed.

I want to run at her, attack her, but I'm frozen. I can sense her hate. She despises me.

"I will kill you. I will stop your heart from beating right in your sleep."

My heart races, and my breath is labored. Where is Vlad? We both went to sleep at the same time.

My lips form a V, but nothing comes out. Where is he?

Evil is so present, so strong. I can't speak, but I can say words in my mind.

Yea, though I walk through the valley of the shadow of death, I will fear no evil: for Thou art with me; Thy rod and Thy staff they comfort me.

Then something pops into my mind from my Catholic days:

I exorcise thee, every unclean spirit, in the name of God the Father Almighty, and in the name of Jesus Christ, His Son, our Lord and Judge, and in the power of the Holy Spirit.

"Don't try to recall those stupid thoughts from your childhood, Stuart. They're no good. God doesn't live here."

My mouth still refuses to move.

Thou preparest a table before me in the presence of mine enemies: Thou anointest my head with oil; my cup runneth over.

Her hate fills the room like stale smoke.

"Surely goodness and mercy shall follow me all the days of my life," I manage to whisper for the first time. "Vlad, are you there?"

Barely audible, I hear him. "I can hear you, but I can't move."

What is happening to us?

"I will dwell in the house of the Lord forever," I say, a little louder this time, and I force myself to sit up.

She speaks words into the air, a language that sounds ancient, one I can't peg to any country I've ever visited. She stands in the corner. Her power is waning, though my heart feels like it may actually burst out of my body, and I'm drenched with sweat.

"Vlad, say the Lord's Prayer with me."

He obeys without a question.

"Give us this day—louder Vlad. Say it with me.

"Give us this day our daily bread and forgive us our sins, as we forgive those who sin against us."

I feel a scratch along the side of my face that burns like acid. She isn't with us anymore.

"And lead us not into temptation but deliver us from evil."

Now I'm standing.

"For Thine is the kingdom and the power and the glory forever. Amen."

Vlad and I stare at each other. The first light of dawn peeks through the small curtained window. Vlad takes a towel by his bed and mops his head and face.

"This was my biggest fear."

"What do you mean?" I ask.

"We're fighting against evil powers, Stuart. Powers we can't see with our eyes. Moscow is a city filled with demons. Our whole country is." Then he kneels by his bed, makes the sign of the cross over his large forehead, shoulders, and chest, and begins to pray.

"Most Holy Mother, send thy angels to defend us and to drive the cruel enemy from us." I kneel next to him, like a father next to his child.

"All ye holy angels and archangels, help and defend us. Amen. O good and tender Mother! Thou shalt ever be our love and our hope. Holy angels and archangels, keep and defend us. Amen."

"Amen," I repeat.

Chapter Thirty-five

"Do nuns drink coffee, Vlad?" I stretch my arms up over my head as we walk down the wooden hallway from our tiny room. "Man, I hope so."

Vlad laughs. "Well, my American friend, let's go find out. Knowing Sister Irina, she will find some for you if you say the word."

In spite of the episode with Ms. Beelzebub earlier, I feel at ease walking down this hallway with Vlad. My sleep started so well, but after the strange visitation, I find that I am still tired. I'm dying for caffeine. Coffee caffeine.

Dozens of nuns walk into the cathedral for early-morning prayer, some acknowledging us with a nod. Most walk in silence. All I can hear is the soft scrape of feet on the hard floor. They are dressed in black robes, covered from head to foot. A strip of white cloth hangs under their chins like napkins.

The waft of incense is faint in the corridor where we walk, but it gets stronger with every step. This one has hints of frankincense and myrrh. Of course, it's the Christmas season; that's all they burn leading up to the holy day of Epiphany.

Not only is the aroma sweet in this place, so is the feeling. Peace is thick, like a down jacket you would put on. God is here. There is no doubt.

Interspersed with the nuns are beautiful young girls, their heads covered with the same small embroidered cloths—perfect spiraled spiderweb patterns.

The girls are wearing uniforms of navy blue outer garments over starched white shirts. We must be quite the sight to see. Two grown men standing in a sea of women. But we feel right at home.

One of the nuns motions for us to follow her into the sanctuary.

"That's Sister Irina," Vlad whispers in my ear.

I'm thinking only of coffee and the chance to talk to Vlad about what happened last night.

Sister Irina stands at the entrance and moves her hand in quick scoops for us to follow, like a child who wants to show you something, so we do.

At the door, Vlad crosses himself and bows. I follow his lead. He's suddenly become more pious than I've known him to be. Or maybe this is just the first time he's felt comfortable expressing his faith. The two large wooden doors are open, revealing dozens of flickering candles inside. The wood is carved with ancient biblical scenes I recognize: Jesus raising Lazarus from the dead, the Last Supper, the stone rolled away from the grave, and the resurrection.

We follow Sister Irina, who bows toward the altar and slides down the row. We inch in next to her. She runs this place but doesn't take any position of honor in the sanctuary. My eye catches movement to the right. Two girls wave, one with big motions, the other with a simple roll of her fingers. It's the twins from the hotel. I smile and wave back, feeling like I'm misbehaving. They look beautiful, fresh. Life has returned to their sparkling eyes. It's almost as if they're glowing brighter than the candles.

There are no chairs or pews inside; everyone is standing and facing the front. I look back and scan the room, trying to be discreet, to take in the twenty or so girls who have filed in with the nuns. Their heads look like billowing clouds of cotton. The faces around me are washed in soft light.

Instead of feeling out of place, as I have in nearly every church I've stepped into since I was a child, this room feels welcoming. Sandwiched between the small nun and hulking man, surrounded by sisters and former prostitutes, I know this moment is sacred. I settle into the stillness and turn my eyes toward the altar and my mind toward God. I focus on the center of the altar, on a round candleholder with forty or so candles, flames dancing in front of the icon of Saint Theodore, the *Feodorovskaya*.

The *Feodorovskaya* is important for the Russian people, a "miracle-working icon" they call it. The story fascinated me, so I wrote a paper on it in college. Now, here it is, hundreds of years old.

The icon is linked to the memory of the great martyr Theodore Stratelates, a warrior beheaded for his faith in Jesus Christ in the fourth century. The miracle comes from a war in the twelfth century. When the Tatars approached the city of Kostroma, Russian militia came out to meet them, carrying before them their holy icon of the Mother of God. As the foes faced one another, a mysterious rider appeared and blazed between them. His purple mantle flapped in the breeze, and his golden shield glistened with a blinding light. The Russians recognized him as the holy great martyr Theodore Stratelates. Seized with fear, the Tatars ran from the field of battle, and Kostroma was saved.

We stand together, listening to the chants of a group of girls on the right. This is a matins service, early-morning prayers. They follow a prayer book and every few minutes sing, "In the name of the Father, the Son, and the Holy Spirit." On those words everyone crosses themselves. Some stand, some bow low to the ground.

After an hour the service ends, and Vlad and I quietly shuffle out of the sanctuary. The twins are waiting for us. They look up at me sheepishly, hands folded in front of them and heads tilted slightly to the ground.

I break the silence.

"I'm glad you're safe. Are you okay?"

The taller one speaks first. "We're fine, and we really love it here. The girls are so nice, and Sister Irina is very kind."

The other twin just nods her head and smiles.

"It's so good to see you."

"You, too, Mr. Stuart. We wanted to tell you how thankful we are that you rescued us. You saved our lives."

Vlad stands next to me, smiling like a Japanese game-show host. I'm trying to compose myself as emotion wells up within. I take the girls' hands and look right into their eyes.

"I'm glad I could help. You girls are so beautiful and so special. And I'm really just so happy to see you, I don't know what to say."

They wrap their arms around me and squeeze tight.

"You are like a papa to us. As long as we live, we will never forget your kindness."

Chapter Thirty-six

"Dear child. We've missed you so. And I've missed you greatly. How was your time in Moscow?" Sister Irina addresses Alyona, putting her hand on her shoulder as she speaks in a motherly gesture of affection that seems perfectly natural. She is the Russian version of Mother Teresa, though taller than I expected. She has beautiful deep-set hazel eyes that explode with light as she speaks. Deep crevasses outline her eyes and forehead like a dozen tiny rivers. I can't tell the color of her hair because it's wrapped in a blue habit that curves out from her head, like wings.

"Wonderful, Sister. It was good to spend time with Katya and the other girls."

In her presence, Alyona is pure happiness. Her blond hair reaches down to the middle of her back. Something about this environment brings out the best in her flawless skin. Thick dark lashes outline oval blue eyes that look like pools of water. She's shorter than Irina, but not by much.

"Well, we are all glad you have returned, especially me." She hugs her.

"I'm happy to be back home."

With Alyona at her side, Sister Irina walks down the long corridor, and I follow.

"We will show you around together, Stuart. There's a special room I want you to see that we are all very proud of. Right, Alyona?"

She smiles and blushes.

"This place is a healing place for girls who have been through the sort of trauma we've been discussing. Counselors, psychologists, and social workers are here who help the girls deal with the pain and abuse they've experienced. We utilize the arts to help bring the healing process to fruition, implementing visual arts, music, and dance in every aspect of their lives."

"What a great idea." We stop in the hallway. The murals on the wall remind me of Katya's center. No doubt, the amazing work of Miss Alyona. Instead of Russian fairy tales, though, these seem more American. The looming figure of Mother Goose is the largest figure on the wall. To her right scoots the mouse running up the clock from "Hickory Dickory Dock." And rounding out the triptych is what looks like Old MacDonald and a few of his farm animals: a cow, a sheep, a goat, and a waddling duck.

"It's more than just a good idea. It's based on quite a bit of professional research. The name of the program is *Iskusstvo i Vdokhnovenye* [Art and Muses]. It's become quite popular within the Russian orphanages. Every year, there's a national art competition held in Moscow. Alyona has won that competition for two years in a row."

"Wow. I can tell she's quite the talent. I saw her work at Nadezhda Home. I couldn't stop looking at it."

"Maybe I should paint something for you, Mr. Stuart? I know you have a daughter. What about something for her?"

"That would be lovely. My wife and I would be thrilled to have something so special for our daughter. How about I make a donation to Sister Irina's work in exchange for the painting?"

"Whatever you want to do," Alyona says. She is obviously uncomfortable with the idea of recognition or money for her work.

"Oh," says Sister Irina, "from what I hear, you already have made quite the contribution. Keep your money. Besides, I have been given a vision from God about you, Stuart. Your work is not yet finished." Then she turns, and we continue to walk.

I choose not to ask what she means. Frankly, I'd like to pretend she didn't say it.

We tour the girls' rooms, then visit the dining area. It's arranged more like a big homey kitchen than a sterile cafeteria. Wall tapestries display bright blues, greens, and yellows in paisleys and circles. The gym has a wooden floor, two basketball hoops, and huge mirrors at the ends with ballet bars mounted into the wall. Through the next hall Sister Irina proudly points out the frosty window to the recreational area outside. I can make out monkey bars, three swings, and a merry-go-round. She shows off each of these rooms like she built and designed them with her own sweat and grit. The look on her face reveals not just pride, but evidence that she knows she's leaving a legacy to a host of girls she loves.

"And now for the main event," the tall, graceful nun announces as she steps on her toes in anticipation. She unlocks a door with a set of keys she pulls from beneath her long blue dress and opens the door. "After you, Mr. Daniels."

Stepping inside, my senses are ambushed by a sea of figures, colors, shapes, and flowers woven together on canvas. The beauty is overwhelming.

"These are awards won by our girls."

Blue, red, and yellow ribbons hang everywhere. There are also cases of trophies and plaques neatly displayed in the corners.

"Many of them are Alyona's. This year, she received the highest honor by winning the most prestigious award in all of Russia: the Kandinsky Prize. For that honor, she also received forty thousand euros."

I look at this frail, blond little button and can't believe what I'm hearing. My good friend from the *Chicago Tribune* did a piece on that award. Those who win it go on to be the most famous artists in all of Russia. It's kind of like the musicians in our country who win *American Idol.* There's not a hint of pride in her eyes. Everything in her simply emanates humility.

"What a genius you are, Alyona. Congratulations."

"She donated all of her winnings to the school." Sister Irina looks at Alyona with the pride of a mother and the approval of a spiritual director.

"God rescued me and gave me the talent. The money is His, not mine."

"Alyona, why don't you meet us in your room in just a few moments. I want to show Stuart something."

"Yes, Sister."

Sister Irina takes me by the hand and leads me down the long, narrow hallway. I typically would find this gesture unnatural, but with her it doesn't bother me.

"I want to show you something to underscore the importance of what you are doing. I feel strongly that the direction your life is taking is much more about bringing the kingdom of God to earth than you understand."

"What do you mean?" We walk in silence, except for the clicking of our heels on the concrete.

"I mean that most people who follow God, most Christians, don't understand the meaning of the word *redemption*. You are a Christian, aren't you, Mr. Daniels?"

"Yes." This is perhaps the first season in my life I've actually been able to answer that question with absolute certainty. "I am."

"I knew it from the moment I met you. *Iskuplenye*, redemption, means *vosstanovlenye i obnovlenye togo, chto bilo pokhisheno*, to restore and renew what has been stolen. Most people squeeze their eyes shut and pretend the Devil doesn't exist. You know better, don't you?" She looks directly into my eyes, and I feel as if she can see my soul. "They live their lives as if there were no problems in the world, no hunger, no orphans, no child sex slaves. They don't do what God calls every single one of us to do, to redeem mankind."

"What does that have to do with me?" I ask.

"It's what you're called to do. Pursuing Marina for example. That's about much more than the redemption of one child. It's about you establishing the kingdom of God in a significant way by finding freedom for the captives. All of this is the beginning of a new life for you."

Her words are filled with substance. They hit me right in the chest.

"This journey I've been on started when I went to Africa. On that trip, a little girl I met named Adanna changed the way I saw the world forever. I can't go back to living my life for useless things anymore. A nice car, money, a nice home … they all mean nothing to me compared to helping others. Well, helping children. Though

I admit I still fight against what I believe God requires of me, like going to church."

"We all fight. That's part of the human condition. But it's our actions, our movements through this world, the honest state of the heart, that matters to God. We give ourselves, in spite of what we might prefer and in spite of fear. I know you are afraid." She stops to look directly at me again. "I used to be afraid myself, and I sometimes still struggle against my own nature. None of us can escape this. None of us is good, but God's salvation is perfect. He can do good through people who allow for it."

It's like the woman is reading my mind.

"Stuart, God's salvation is beyond measure. He has made a way for each of us to have freedom in this world. I believe when you make a way for someone else's salvation, physical and spiritual, as you have, this is also beyond measure. It is priceless."

Listening to Sister Irina, I get a taste of what it might be like to walk with Christ. Something about her makes me understand the kingdom of God and my position before God.

"And, Stuart."

"Yes?"

"God wants you to know you're not alone."

We enter another door with the word Director written on the outside. Inside, it's a modest office with icons depicting the Holy Mother hanging on the wall and dozens of books sitting on a bookcase in the corner, many in English. I recognize a few of the titles: *The Practice of the Presence of God* by Brother Lawrence and C. S. Lewis's *Mere Christianity*. There's also a small writing desk with a lamp and two chairs. That's it.

"I want to show you something." She reaches into her desk drawer, rummages through some files, and pulls out a picture.

"Look at this."

The photo is a grotesque image of a young girl who looks to have been severely beaten. The left side of her face is swollen twice its normal size, both of her eyes are black, and blood is running out of her nose and mouth. She looks more like a prizefighter who's been beaten within an inch of his life than a little girl. If it weren't for her eyes being open, she would look dead. But her eyes ... there's a look of absolute fear and horror in them, like she's just seen something so terrible she doesn't want to live.

"What happened to her? Did she live?"

"She did. Don't you recognize her?"

"No."

"This is Alyona."

"Dear God."

"We found her unconscious beside a trash bin. She was in an alley behind a place called the Tochka."

"Left for dead?"

"Either left for dead or thrown there in a fit of rage. Who knows if someone was going to come for her. She had been severely raped and had terrible infections. There were knife wounds on her body, cigarette burns, and contusions."

Sister Irina begins to weep. This is what compassion looks like.

"This is what the Devil does to little girls. Someone has to go into the pit of hell itself to rescue them," she says.

Chapter Thirty-seven

I take a seat on the small chair in front of her desk.

Sister Irina, what is the Tochka?"

"Oh, you know the owner very well. Vlad informed me about your run-in with him. I hear it almost cost you dearly."

"The priest?"

"This man is extremely dangerous, Mr. Daniels. There are very few lines he will not cross. You happen to be standing behind one of them."

"At this point I don't care how dangerous he is. I'll do whatever I can to take him down."

"If you act alone, you could end up dead. It's God who will ensure your success in this matter, make no mistake about it."

"I just can't wrap my mind around the injustice. He uses the name of God."

"We've had a cast of characters throughout our history in Russia who have used the name of God to perpetrate the greatest of evils. Take Rasputin for example. A so-called mystic healer who was responsible for the fall of the Romanov dynasty and eventually the death of the entire Romanov family. This priest is another."

"Why does God allow it?" I say this almost under my breath. It's my greatest struggle.

"We live in the middle of a war, Mr. Daniels. If your experiences the last few days have taught you anything, they should have taught you this: Satan can disguise himself as an angel of light quite easily."

Can she possibly know about the apparitions I've been seeing? Even what happened last night? She just looks at me, glasses low over her nose, a steady gaze.

"He believes he's God's agent to control evil."

"He told me as much. As he was having me tortured."

"In his mind this gives him the right to do whatever he wants when someone crosses the line. He is unbalanced, and perhaps even possessed."

I look down at the picture of Alyona. It doesn't look like the same girl.

"There is one other thing you need to know. Although he has brothels all over the country, one of the biggest is here in Kostroma. It's also called the Tochka, but people call it the Devil's Lair. Vlad will brief you on all the details."

She stops and looks as if she's weighing two thoughts.

"In all likelihood, he won't expect you to be here. You will be safe. But be certain he *is* looking for you."

"I've been told, which is why I'm not yet flying home to my wife and daughter—or completing the assignment I was given to be here in the first place."

"You should contact your wife. I will make sure you can do that while you are here."

"Thank you, Sister."

"And, Stuart, don't worry. It will all work out for you in the end—because God has sent you, and He is with you." She stops, takes my hand in hers, and looks up at me. "Do you believe this?"

"I don't know, but I have to try."

"Good, good enough." She laughs. "Now follow me. I know Alyona wants to show you her room."

We walk back down the hollow corridor and up a pair of stairs. There are doors on each side of the hall, dormitories where the girls live. Some doors are open, and the girls giggle and stare as we pass by.

"There are one hundred and twenty girls currently living with us here. I never told you the name of our facility, did I?"

"No."

"It's called *Zamok Nadezhdi*, Castle of Hope. A fitting title because we want these girls to know they are surrounded by a wall of protection from the evil they have been subject to in their past. Here, they find hope for a good life and prosperous future. Also, we want them to know they are royalty, like our tsars in history. God's royal daughters keeping their eyes on His kingdom."

"A perfect name. It's beautiful."

Through the corner of my eye, I notice a room up ahead to the right that's different than the rest. Bright colors bounce off white walls in the hall, a familiar scene. Alyona's eyes brighten as she sees us enter through the door. She is holding something behind her back, like a small child who can't wait for her parent to choose a hand. I think of all the childhood she's lost.

"Stuart, I want you to have this. For your daughter. It's one of my favorite possessions." She reveals a toy horse with a rainbow collar.

"Ah, no, I couldn't." Sister Irina jabs me in the ribs with her elbow. "I mean, yes, thank you, Alyona. It's such a generous gift. You are so kind. My daughter will love this."

"Her name is Red, which means beautiful in Russian. There's also a note in her collar you can read later."

"I'm honored." I hug her tightly and pray silently that God's hand of favor and protection would always be over her life, just like I do every night for my own daughter.

Downstairs, Vlad stands near the door in his long black leather coat and black fur hat.

"Did you get the grand tour, Stuart?"

"I did. What a place the sister has here. I'm in awe." I put my arm around the nun and give her a gentle squeeze. "And Alyona, what a talent! She's painted portraits that would put the great masters to shame." I wink at Alyona.

"I am well aware of the young lady's talents. I think I've even posed once or twice for her to paint. But I was too ugly, and the paintbrush broke." Sister Irina and Alyona laugh. He makes a rare joke, but I see he's preoccupied.

"Where are you headed, my friend?" I ask. He looks at me with a somber expression, fracturing my joy.

"Why don't you get your coat? There's something I want to show you." I walk to the couch to grab my jacket, wondering if Vlad wants to show me the house he grew up in.

"You'll need this. Don't take it off."

He throws me a large brown mink Russian shapka complete with ear flaps. "You'll look just like any other Russian wearing this."

Sister Irina faces me, her hazel eyes fixed on me, and gives me an "in the know" look, which sends a wave of anxiety through my gut.

"Thank you for your kindness and hospitality." I bow slightly. Though plain in her features, Sister Irina commands a royal presence.

What she says, how she carries herself, and her easy kindness to strangers prove that she understands more about life than anyone I've ever met.

"We're glad to have you for this short visit. Please make yourself at home, and let me know if there's anything we can do to make your stay more pleasant."

"Thank you, Sister."

Vlad and I walk out of the sanctuary and back into the cold world. Where I come from, it's supposed to get warmer during the day. Not so in Mother Russia.

Chapter Thirty-eight

The heat blasting through the vents in the Volga makes me feel like I'm sitting around a campfire, but there's nothing very Kumbaya about this scene. My skin has a needly, prickling sensation. It's hard to believe the cold can penetrate these gloves. They've got to be an inch thick.

"Man, it's freezing out there."

"Weak Westerner. It's only twenty-five below today. Practically a heat wave."

"You know, Vlad, I think you missed your calling. You should have been a weatherman. Russians would appreciate the humor. Or maybe not. Where are we going?"

The car rumbles down the road alongside the frozen Volga River. I've been here in the summer and seen this mighty river flowing. It reminded me of the Mississippi.

"We're going to do a drive-by of the Tochka, the Devil's Lair."

"Drive-by?"

"I want you to see it for a reason."

"It sounds like a hellish place, no pun intended."

"What does that mean?"

"It's a play on words. Devil's Lair, hellish place. Get it?"

"No."

"Anyway, what goes on at the Lair? Or maybe I don't want to know."

"This is one of the biggest one-stop sex shops in all of Russia. You know who runs this place?" Vlad looks at me and raises his thick eyebrows.

"Yeah, the priest. Sister Irina told me. So why are we driving right into the mouth of the lion? I understand this place is crawling with degenerates, and I wouldn't be surprised if some are on the lookout for a man with my description."

"This place, it serves every sex fetish you can imagine, from Americans who come to Russia looking for a so-called Russian bride, to enslaving little girls coming out of the orphanages, and having their way with them."

"Sometimes I am not proud of our gender."

"It's not just men, Stuart. All kinds of women frequent the place as customers too. Along with political figures from the United States, presidents of foreign countries, Jewish rabbis—I even knew of a primary school teacher. Every sort of person you'd imagine, and every sort you couldn't imagine."

"I don't want to imagine."

"Just remember, rescuing even one girl out of this nightmare, like Alyona or Dasha, is worth it. Someone needs to go into the lair of the Devil and confront him head-on."

"Someone?" I get the distinct sense I'm being enlisted again.

"Well, Stuart, let me tell you this: There's another reason we're going."

"I'm listening, sir," I say with a German accent.

"Obviously, we've had this place under surveillance, but one of our men took a photo of a young girl walking outside and luring in customers with some older women. Just yesterday."

He looks at me, brow furrowed, eyes squinting.

"And?"

"It's Marina, Stuart. We're sure of it."

My heart breaks into a million pieces. Could she really be in the same city, nearly under our noses?

"Where is this place?"

"Just across the river. We'll be there in ten minutes."

We turn onto the bridge. The city looms on the horizon, smoke stacks spewing thick dark smoke into the air. On the edge of the river sits an Orthodox church with gold and blue domes. I'm certain you could see the Tochka from its windows.

"She looks worse than she did before, and we're afraid if we don't act now, it may be too late. Katya is beside herself about this. Of course, we can't just walk in and ask for Marina. We have to be stealthier about it."

"Why are you taking me there now?"

"Because I want you to know what's going on, in case you may be able to help us. If we're going to strike, it has to be fast."

"How fast?"

"They move girls in and out of places rapidly. If we get a chance to extract her, it will be tonight."

The car slows down along the city street. I'm glued to the window like the scene in *The Matrix*. It's lined with unimpressive white and gray buildings. People bundled in scarves and full-length fur coats walk quickly along the sidewalk, not wanting to spend an extra second in the bitter cold. Hot breath escapes out of their mouths as if they were readied tea kettles.

Kiosks line the street with a host of items to buy: gum, candy, soft drinks, and vodka. *Gostinitsa* signs poke out with vacancy signs beckoning visitors to enter. I guess this is a hotel hotspot for good reason.

"On the right here, Stuart."

In the middle of the buildings is a sign: The Tochka. The letters are wrapped around a familiar dragon symbol. A sword cuts through the words and ends in the throat of the beast. This guy is really obsessed.

Above the sign is an apartment block that has seven or more floors. There's nobody in front of the place, and the curtains are pulled across the windows.

"Marina was seen right there." Vlad points to a light pole about forty feet from the entrance. "She seemed to be flagging down customers."

I picture the little girl who showed me all of her earthly possessions in the space it would require to hold my laptop, and I bite my lip.

"I suppose the local police don't care what's going on."

"They don't care if it's a vodka factory, furniture store, or sex shop; as long as they're getting paid, they turn a blind eye. It's all about money."

"What this town needs is some good vigilante justice."

"Don't let your emotions overrule a clear head, Stuart. We have a job to do and girls to save. Keep your eyes focused on that. Don't stare. Just take mental notes."

My eyes won't move off the front door. How many lives have been destroyed in that devil's den? How many men have made their way through that door to have their way with underage girls? And what about those coming to Russia under the pretense of looking for a Russian bride?

"We have several men on watch in the area. If Marina shows up, we'll know right away. Stuart! Are you listening to me?"

"Yes, I hear you. Loud and clear."

If it were up to me, I'd put a bullet in this priest's head and it would be the end of this labyrinth of Sauron. I wouldn't even feel guilty. Not for a second. I continue to stare out the window, lost in my raging thoughts.

"We're going to make one more pass and that's it. Stuart! For God's sake, listen to me. This is no game."

"I'm sorry, Vlad. I'm listening now."

"*Spasibo.* [Thank you.] Now, notice every single detail. Our men will be stationed there." He points to a second-story window above a tree that stands alone and naked, nothing but scraggly branches pointing to the sky. "And there, at the magazine store on the corner. These will provide the best views for our agents in case something goes wrong. We don't know what's going to happen, so we need to be prepared for anything. Understand?"

"Yes, I'm with you." My mind is operating in a fog, trying to process the fact that I'm being asked to risk my life once again. For Marina's sake, I'll do it without complaint. But it's a big request, and for a moment I wonder if I'm pushing my luck this time. God taps me on the shoulder as we slow down near the Tochka. *Luck? Really?*

"Are you looking?" Vlad asks.

"Yes."

I study everything, snap frame after frame of the surroundings, and file each image in my mind, every color, every tree, and every sign on the street.

I will be ready.

Chapter Thirty-nine

I'm surprised to find that I am shaking when we return to the monastery. Our little square room has already become a refuge for me. A physical and spiritual barrier protecting me from the real world. I need to absorb all of this. It's been too much, too quick after the last ordeal.

I toss my coat, gloves, and hat onto my bed.

"Stuart, are you okay?"

"I'll be fine. This is just so intense. Emotions and adrenaline are coursing through my veins like fire."

"This business is always intense."

"I can't believe we're this close to Marina. How did you find her?"

"It's strange. We keep pretty tight surveillance on most of the larger trafficking sites like the Tochka. Last night, Marina appeared out of thin air, just like that. We've been looking for months to no avail. Now here she is."

It's not luck. "It's God."

Vlad makes the sign of the cross and whispers, "Father, Son, Holy Spirit. I hope you're right."

He takes off his jacket and tosses it on the chair in the corner. "I'm going to take a shower."

"Think I'll go for a walk. Or go see Sister Irina. Maybe a few of her prayers can help calm my nerves."

I grab my coat and hat, throw them back on, and head out the door.

My mind is still troubled. So many questions. So many whys. If there's one thing I've learned over the past year, it's this: I cannot trust life, but I can trust the One who created it. I look to the sky and hold my hands in the air.

"God, I know You're listening. There are so many things about this I don't understand. I need Your strength to help me save Marina in the face of impossible circumstances. I know You care about her, and I know this evil she's trapped in is not Your will. Set her free. And I need You to bring me home safely to Whitney and Adanna. Amen."

My hands are freezing, and I shove them into my coat pockets to pull out my gloves, but they're gone. This cold front's got to be a Siberian express. If you expose any part of your skin, you pay the price. I've got to retrieve my gloves before my hands fall off.

I jog back and throw open the door. Vlad is standing next to the door of the bathroom in a towel.

"Whoa, sorry. Forgot my gloves."

"Nyet problem."

He turns to go in the bathroom when I spot something on his right arm just below his shoulder. It looks like a brand, the brand of a dragon. Just like the icon of Saint George the Dragonslayer.

He closes the door, and I hear the water turn on in the bathroom.

The cold forces me to change my mind about a stroll in the courtyard. I turn back into the large hallway that leads to the sanctuary. The girls must be in school because the halls are deserted.

It feels good to be alone. I've been with people almost non-stop for days. I decide to walk in the opposite direction of the chapel. The hall bends to the right and about fifty feet in front of me, I see a yellow door. It stands out against the surrounding green walls.

The knob turns and I open it. I flick on the light switch and the light reveals what looks like an art gallery. Dozens of framed pictures hang on the walls. Each one is a picture of a girl, and they're all dressed in their Sunday best.

They are beautiful.

Above one section of the gallery are the words "Home and Safe at Last." Above another, "Longing for Our Sisters to Be Rescued." I walk to that section and notice white papers tacked all along the wall below.

I look back at the door to make sure no one is watching and take a slip of paper off the wall. I open it and read:

> *Olya, dear Olya. Day and night I cry myself to sleep praying for your safety. Return to me, my love. Our Father, watch over Olya. Keep her safe. May Your grace guide her and lead her back to our arms where she is loved. You are not forgotten, my sister. Every morning when I wake up, I stand at the window, look at the entrance to our home, and call you home.*

Heart and soul these girls pour into the lives of their friends. This is what community should be. Loving your neighbor as yourself.

These girls, this family, bring Whitney and Adanna close to my heart. I miss them so much. What if it were my Adanna on that wall? It's too much to even think about.

The door opens behind me, and a stream of girls come into the room. Embarrassed, I feel like I've been caught with my hand in the cookie jar. This is a holy place, and it's not my place to be. They just look at me; some smile.

All of them walk to the front of the room and take a candle, then form a semicircle facing the photos. The humming of prayers begins. The first girl lights her candle, and in a few minutes, I'm surrounded by light. The prayers continue. Some are whispered, some are shouted, and some are sown in tears.

Something wells up deep within my soul. I don't fight it. The time has come, it's right. I fall on my knees, and from the pit of my gut I begin to weep like I've never wept before.

Chapter Forty

Vlad and I sit on our squatty twin beds. Our knees are practically touching as Vlad's warm menthol breath pushes into my face.

"Now listen, Stuart, I don't know what's going to happen tonight," he says in a concerned tone. "Hopefully, we'll find Marina on the street again. Extracting her will be quick and simple. We'll get her into a car and be off before anyone knows what's going on. But we both know things are not always so straightforward."

"So what's plan B?"

"Plan B is … you go into the Dragon's Lair and pretend to be a customer."

"Great." I bite my lip. "Sure, no problem." I think Vlad is surprised by my complaint-free response. I know *I* am.

"We don't know what to expect, that's the problem with a mission like this. What we do know is there's a lot of foot traffic coming through that place. From what we've determined, there are easily more than fifty girls inside, over half of them under the age of sixteen."

Sister Irina's word from earlier floats into my mind: *priceless.* Salvation is priceless. These girls are priceless.

"You'll have to be careful. I cannot stress this enough." He looks at me like he's seeing me for the first time. "Now why did we drag you into this?" He rubs his head.

"Vlad, Katya said I was here at 'just the right time, for just the right purpose.'" I try to say this with sarcasm, but I can't. Sister Irina's words were eerily similar. I have to figure out how to trust God in this. And I have to figure it out fast.

"Okay, then." He gives me a quick pat on the shoulder. "The priest's men inside the building are armed. They will not hesitate to kill you if they discover who you are. In the event you have to go inside, you'll have less than five minutes. Is that clear?"

"What if I can't find her that fast?"

"You're out in five minutes. If it takes longer than that, then we've missed our chance. Perhaps we'll get another one someday. Perhaps not."

I open my mouth to say something smart. Or funny. Or meaningful. But I don't know which words to choose.

"There's one other thing." He turns around, opens his briefcase, and takes out a black leather pouch.

"Here. You need this." I open the case, reach in, and pull out a revolver. "Do you know how to use one of these?"

It's a Makarov PM. I shot one of these on the shooting range in the States with my Russian friend Pasha. For years it was the Soviet Union's standard military sidearm.

"Yes, I know how to use a gun. But I thought some other agents were going to be with me?"

"I'll be with you at all times, and the others will be close. But like I said, this place is extremely dangerous. I want to take every precaution necessary."

I turn the snub-nosed pistol over in my hands. Pulling back the chamber, I look to see a bullet enter from the clip. The safety is on. I release the clip, see that it's full, then pop it back into place. The gun is steely cold and heavy in my hand.

"Not only can you use a gun, you're practically a professional."

"I used to hunt a lot. I know what I'm doing."

"Good. So the plan is simple, yes? You understand?" I can't help but wonder what he'd have done if I didn't know a pistol from my behind.

"Yes. I hope it goes better than the last simple plan."

"Me too. Let's go."

I step outside to the familiar gnawing cold. Within seconds, the skin on my face dries up like onion skin. I put my gloves over my face and breathe into them for warmth. Thankfully we're in the car in less than a minute.

We pull up on the sidewalk in front of a grocery store and stop. Vlad leaves the car running so we don't freeze to death.

"We'll wait here until we hear something."

Only seconds pass before Vlad's phone rings. I can't shake the eerie feeling that someone's watching us right now. My mind drifts back to the tattoo I saw on Vlad's arm. I think about how he "suddenly" found me when I'd been captured by the priest. And how Marina "suddenly" appeared five minutes down the road from where I'm staying.

I pray. *Lord God in heaven, I have no hope in this situation without You. See the intentions of my heart, my desire to help the fatherless. Be with me and save me from danger.*

"Da. Da. We'll be there in a minute," Vlad's voice croaks. I study him and wonder if he could have been playing a role all this time for some ulterior purpose. We start moving again.

"What is it? What did they say?" My concern about Vlad evaporates with the thought of news about Marina.

"She's been spotted in front of the Tochka. Listen, we're going to drive past the place to have a look. The windows here are tinted so you can look out without being recognized."

"Okay." I feel like I did in high school just before a wrestling match.

"We'll swing back around the block and throw her in the car."

"Got it."

"Okay, Stuart, this is the street."

Flashing signs glimmer and twinkle at the hotels. I look up to see life-size figures of Father Frost and Snow Girl hanging from a seventh-story window. Some Christmas trees are visible from the apartments above. Several people have even outlined their windows with multicolored lights, celebrating the season.

Across the street from the Tochka is a huge Christmas tree decorated with silver balls and red bows.

The sidewalks just outside the club teem with men from all walks of life. Fat old men who look like grandfathers, businessmen, even men who look young enough to still be boys. They grope women who've been stationed out in the cold. A man in a long coat like Vlad's throws a young girl up against the wall and kisses her. Another man slaps a girl across the face. No one seems to care. It looks like the videos I've seen of the streets of Bangkok.

Then I spot her, and my heart stops. Marina stands on the edge of the street, waving at men to come in the club. I never would have recognized her if I hadn't seen the recent photo. She looks drugged. Her steps falter, and her body sways on high heels.

I can see her breath as she exhales. It looks like she's smoking a cigarette.

Thick blue eye shadow is caked on her eyes, bright red lipstick lines her adolescent lips, sparkles of glitter reflect off her hair. God, what a sight. She's dressed in a short blue dress—much classier than the rest of the girls. Her shoulders are wrapped in fur. Diamonds flash around her neck.

My hand instinctively goes for the door handle.

"Stuart, not yet!" Vlad yells. "Everything must go according to plan. Once around the block, and we snag her. That simple."

He's on the phone dialing a number. "Marko. Everything clear? Any unusual movement or activity? Okay, good. We're coming back around the block. We'll call her to the car and open the door. You come behind her and force her inside. Mmm. Da. Sixty seconds, we'll be there."

The car engine revs to pick up speed as we come around the block and move toward the club. I can see her still on the curb by the street.

"Everything's good. This will work fine."

My pulse races, and I realize both of us are breathing shallow, loud breaths.

A black Mercedes-Benz pulls up right in front of us, and a man gets out of the car next to Marina.

"Vlad, is that—"

"It's the priest. Stay put, Stuart."

We are just feet away when he grabs her. He drapes a white cloth, a veil, over her head. Two men quickly flank him. He pulls her tight to him and walks in the front door.

"No, no! She's going in. We should have snagged her the first time." Hope bleeds out of my heart, replaced by fear.

"We won't lose her this time." He looks at me, and I can tell he's shifted into professional mode. I need to do the same. "Stuart, we are going in. I'll be right behind you. If anyone stops you, ask for the girl who was just standing on the side of the road."

The car slides to a stop in the slush and snow, and I dart out of the back like ammo out of a cannon. A prostitute steps right in front of me and throws her arms around me. Vlad slips by me and goes through the front door.

"You want good time tonight, big boy? I make you very happy."

"*Nyet, spasibo.* [No, thank you.] Maybe later, ladies." I move her to the side and run through the front door looking for Vlad. The sign on the door is the picture of a red dragon, a perfect match for the brand on Vlad's arm.

It takes my eyes several seconds to adjust to the dimly lit foyer. Disco balls dangle from the ceiling, casting prisms of light around the room. Several girls sit on couches and at tables, and a few lean along the walls. Most are dressed in scant miniskirts, low-cut blouses, and high heels. Some are dressed like children. I see no one wearing a blue dress.

On the right is a check-in counter. It's encased by black metal bars like a cage. Three women stand behind the bars.

I've got five minutes. I finally spot Marina by the light reflecting off her necklace.

"Excuse me. May I help you?" The voice comes from a man at least the size of Vlad. His face is freshly shaven. He smells of cheap cologne.

"Do you need a menu?" he asks.

"A menu?"

"We have the finest selection of women anywhere in the world, any age you choose. Do you like a young girl? Ah, you're American, you probably like to tie girl up, like cowboy, yes?" He laughs and slaps me on the back. "You tell the lady at the counter what you want, pay the fee, and we give you a selection of girls to choose from."

I've wasted sixty seconds listening to this moron.

"Okay, thanks. Yes, I'll order something to my liking." I take the menu and pretend to scan it. When he turns his back, I head down the hall as fast as I can.

"Hey, where are going?" A large hand on my shoulder stops me in my tracks and jerks me around one hundred and eighty degrees.

"You pay there." He points to the counter I've just passed. "Are you trying to cause trouble?" He reaches for something inside his jacket. I slip my hand behind my jacket into the holster and grab the Russian revolver Vlad gave me. One more move by the Russian, and I'm testing my aim.

"I know what I want. A young girl who was just outside flagging down cars. She's wearing a blue dress. I saw her walking down the hall there." My hand doesn't move off the gun. His eyes dart to my hand and then back to my face.

He smiles and says, "Oh, you want Marina, do you? She's very expensive. Probably more money than you want to spend."

"Money is no object. It's her I want."

"Hmm, you seem very anxious. Let me see if she is available now. Wait here."

The ogre walks down the hall, and I'm left alone to watch the scum of the earth satiate their carnal desires. Most of them don't look like typical scum though; they look like respectable men, family men who might help you fix your car or buy a house. Officials who run cities or countries. The money that must run through this place.

Men walk through the door like it's a free cheese line. Most of them seem to have appointments. They're greeted at the door by a lady who asks their name and checks it off a list. Some carry suitcases. If it weren't for the environment, you'd swear they were at an airline counter checking in for a flight. They wait, then a hostess appears to escort them to a back room.

I watch girl after young girl play the forced role of prostitute. For a minute, I fantasize, not about the girls, but about taking the gun out of my belt and unloading it in as many of these pigs as possible.

I don't have enough bullets.

Most disturbing is the faraway, drug-induced look in the eyes of the girls. They don't even look human. My Lord, if Whitney knew where I was.

What I would do to be with her right now. In the comfort of my own home, with my legs propped up by the fire.

"You there! What are you doing?" a voice shouts out.

Is my cover blown?

"Leave him alone, Yuri. He's with me. Marina is ready for you, sir. Right this way." I stand to follow the menu guy down the hall.

Vlad has disappeared.

I hear the words in my mind, *I will fear no evil, for You are with me,* and I repeat them, a mantra to keep me from coming unglued in this dark hallway. I am overcome with a sense of dread. I feel the hate, the same sense I had with the demon, closing on me, but I am on a mission. I will not turn back.

Red lights hang from the ceiling. They seem to sway. I pass a man walking out of a doorway, his shadow flickers against the wallpaper like a nervous demon. I hear another man tell a girl what he wants to do to her, over and over. Their faces are invisible in this light.

I'm led through a maze of winding passages. I'm desperately trying to remember how to get out of here, but there aren't any markers to help me. Just hallways and doors. And then it hits me. They didn't ask me to pay. *Everyone pays first.*

"Here you are, sir. Marina is waiting for you. Enjoy." He opens the door, and with an obsequious bow he waves me in.

Whatever happens now, it's too late to turn back.

The second I step through the door, I know I've entered the belly of hell.

Chapter Forty-one

The room I enter is more like a great room in a mansion than the tacky version of hell I expected. The focal point is a massive stone fireplace against the back wall. I find the flames disconcerting. They seem more like a bonfire than the typical warm glow from a fireplace. The smell of birch wood, along with something electrical, wafts into my nose. And there's that incense smell again. The door slams shut behind me.

"Welcome, Mr. Daniels. That is your name, isn't it?" The priest is seated on an oversize chair that might as well be a throne. He's wearing his traditional black cassock, with the same tarnished Orthodox cross dangling from his neck, looking more to me like a noose than a symbol of redemption. Perched on his lap is Marina, looking pale and emaciated. Her eyes are glassy pools of blue, and her body teeters against the priest's arm, which is wrapped tightly around her waist. She is still wearing the veil.

"Ah, my old friend Alexander. I suppose you saw me coming from miles off. Love what you've done with this place. It's so much more … colorful than your church." I'm feeling fearless now that I'm certain I'll die in this place.

"I knew exactly where you were and that I'd catch up to you eventually. But I am just a little bit surprised to see you here so soon. Perhaps you've come to your senses and want to offer me that confession."

I keep my lips closed tight, I think about the gun I'm carrying, feel the weight of it tucked into my belt. I don't know if I could get to it quickly enough with that big oaf behind me.

I wonder why I wasn't frisked. I am reminded that God is with me.

"I'm not sure what your interest is in Marina, Mr. Daniels. Maybe you have some carnal desires after all?" He raises his eyebrows and looks directly at me. "We could certainly arrange that for the right price."

My first instinct is to rip the beard off his face. Instead, I try the truth.

"I met Marina as a little girl when I was in Russia years ago. She was an orphan, much like you were once." I see him flinch. "Yes, I've done some research of my own."

I maintain eye contact, fully aware I'm looking into the eyes of the Devil. I don't know what will serve me best, but I know showing weakness will not be in my favor. I continue.

"Through a friend, I followed Marina over the years, as she went through school. She was a good student. She's very bright. Then one day, she disappeared—maybe you could shed some light on that?" I look for a light of recognition in Marina's eyes. Nothing.

"The friend who told you about Marina, is this the same friend who sent you tonight?"

Without thinking, I say, "I was sent by Marina's Father." He looks irritated.

"I thought you said this one was an orphan." He places his hand on her head. In another context, it would look like a gesture of blessing. "So who is he, the one who sent you?"

I do not answer. He pushes Marina over, and she falls to the floor like a carcass. The fall seems to knock a little sense into her fog, but she remains on the floor. Behind the priest, I see the woman from the street and from my dream the first night at Sister Irina's. Neither of the men seems to notice her.

The image of the shield and the sword come into my mind. I focus on them, like a prayer. I open my mouth and speak.

"I come in the name of the living God, the Father and authority of every girl in this place."

The priest, his face contorted with a curious mix of disappointment and anger, calls to the man behind me.

I feel the barrel of a gun to the back of my head.

"Go ahead," I say.

He jabs the gun forward and forces me closer to the priest. Marina tries to stand, and the priest jerks her up toward him. He shakes her arm and says, "Every one of these girls is my property. Do you understand? They belong to me—they live and act by my authority."

He walks over to the fireplace.

"*I* am their father. I take care of them, look out for them, make sure they have food to eat and a roof over their heads."

The thug moves me toward the fire pit. It's intensely hot. My head begins to swim.

The priest pulls an iron poker from the fire. I am not surprised to see a dragon-shaped brand on the end. It's glowing red, the color of the coals. And it's the same design I saw on Vlad.

He sets it down and pulls Marina close to the fire. For the first time, I see fear in her eyes, and she starts to resist.

"This is how I make them my own." He throws her down, hard. One of her shoes flies across the room and hits the wall with a thud.

She looks at me, and her eyes widen and blink with a flicker of recognition.

I lunge toward her, but the man grabs both of my arms behind my back, and forces his gun into my kidney. Somehow, he doesn't notice my gun.

"Before Vanya here takes you to the back room and sends you into the next life, I want you to see who's in charge of these girls, of your Marina." He says this in a matter-of-fact tone, but his face is flushed and contorted.

In one motion, he grabs then stabs the raging-hot iron into her skin. It sizzles and boils against her lower back.

Marina's scream rages out from the pit of her being. Even the priest looks surprised at the strength of her reaction. Then she collapses and moans, "*Otyets nebesniy, pomogi mne.* [Father in heaven, help me.]"

I'm nearly in tears, but adrenaline courses through my veins. In one rapid movement I drop to my knees with the ogre on my back and roll—a move that would have made my wrestling coach, Mr. Henderson, proud.

The thug flies over my back and into the fire pit. The coals fly through the air like hundreds of giant sparks from a forest fire.

For a moment, the priest and I are frozen. Nothing moves but our eyes. Then Vanya yells, crawls out of the fire, and starts flipping around on the floor like a bass on the bottom of a boat. Marina has managed to scuttle away from the burning embers.

The scattered coals smolder on the floor, and pungent smoke rises like a hundred smoke bombs. One after another, they ignite the carpet.

The priest grabs Marina by her legs and starts to drag her toward a door in the back of the room. An alarm goes off, and another black-costumed goon flies through the door with his gun raised. Out of the corner of my eye, I see Vanya, still smoldering, reach for his gun too.

I fire first, hitting Vanya in the chest. His gun goes off and the bullet strikes me in the leg. The hot steel burns as he drops to the ground like a bag of dirt.

I turn to shoot at the other guard, but I'm not fast enough. A shot cracks through the air. I'm as good as dead. But I keep turning, I'm not hit. The gun comes up to my sight, and the man's already crumpling to the ground.

I turn at the flash of a large figure. Vlad charges through the room like Ray Lewis and rushes the priest. The priest drops Marina and races across the room. His cross flies, and his robes billow then tangle around him, pulling him to the floor.

Half a dozen little fires have come to life and begin to crawl up the curtains.

"Grab her, Stuart!" Vlad yells. He runs at the priest, who's trying to stand, and clobbers him.

My back is burning from the heat. I look at Vlad. He has his gun pointed at the priest's head. I hear someone, either Vlad or the priest, say, "Blessed are the merciful; for they shall obtain mercy."

"Vlad, help me!" Marina isn't breathing. I pull her up into my arms and start to limp toward the back door.

"Stuart, let me take her!" Vlad runs and scoops her out of my arms like she weighs ten pounds. I follow him to the door, then glance back to see if I can spot the priest. He's not where Vlad left him. Father Alexander has disappeared.

Vlad places his fingers on Marina's neck as we stumble and run down a dark hallway.

"Stuart, we have to hurry. She has no pulse."

Vlad seems to know exactly where he's going. Girls and customers are running out of rooms, pulling up their pants and covering their bodies, fleeing the growing fire. The entire building is already engulfed in flames. Two men run to Vlad. I'm limping, but I ready my gun just in case.

"*Chto zhe nam delat?* [What should we do, Vlad?]"

We're surrounded by chaos. Smoke is pouring into the hallways. People are flooding out of the rooms like ants, covering their mouths and coughing.

He looks at me and then back toward the hallway. "Get as many of those girls out of here as we can. But first ..."

Vlad kicks open a door and we're suddenly outside in the icy air, apparently at the back of the building. He carries Marina to a car across the street, and I follow him, then stop and look back at the open door. All those poor girls. I freeze. I don't know what to do.

A sudden blast at the back door decides for me. Heartsick, I hobble over to the car. Vlad has set Marina on the ground on the other side of the car to protect her from the billowing smoke and the blazing fire. He places two fingers on her neck, looks at me, and shakes his head.

He tries again.

"There's nothing, Stuart."

I throw my coat under her head and start CPR.

"Stuart," Vlad says, "the building is falling apart. It is not safe here. Get her into the car."

Chapter Forty-two

Park City, Utah

On the movie screen before me, I see the familiar type appear in complete silence, except for the typewriter click with each letter: *B e z i m y a n n i y e.* [Nameless.]

The opening credits roll, and I see my name.

But it's what comes next that makes me draw in my breath, though I've seen it now hundreds, maybe thousands of times. Dark eyes, blue like the Russian Sea of Azov, look directly into the camera. "*Menya zovut Marina. Marina Smolchenko. I vot moya istoriya.* [My name is Marina. Marina Smolchenko. And this is my story.]"

The theatre at the Sundance premiere is packed. Though I filmed her story through my camera, I'm still overwhelmed by her directness, her beautiful face on the huge screen before me, before the hundreds sitting around me. Finally free of the drugs she was forced to take when she was working on the street, yet still scarred from abuse, she looks older than her seventeen years.

Alyona cut her scraggly hair and dyed it black when Marina returned from the hospital to Sister Irina's. From death to life. Somehow, Vlad and his associates had pulled twenty-seven other girls out of the Tochka, out of the fire, out of slavery and to the safety of Sister Irina.

I got my story of the rise of HIV/AIDS in Russia, but from a different angle, through a different lens, and with different results than any of us ever expected. Up on the big screen Marina is seated on a chair in the sanctuary of Sister Irina's monastery. Behind her, there are two icons. One is Saint George the Dragonslayer.

In the very last scene, she repeats the line that opens her story, her voice fierce and breaking with emotion:

My name is Marina, and this is my story. And it is also the story of my sisters, and many other girls in this world who are bound in slavery. This is for them.

Girls appear on the screen, one by one, their faces hidden by shadow at first, then revealed as they speak.

My name is Valya …

… Masha …

… Anya …

… Susha …

… Yelena …

… Dasha …

… Alyona …

… Katya …

… Natasha …

The last girl's face fades to black and these words appear in the lingering silence:

27 million people are victims
of human trafficking.

1 million are children under
the age of 18.

The theatre is silent and still, except for sniffles and muffled sobs.

I look down the row. To my right is Vlad, dressed in a tux and not even trying to hide tears. He looks over at me and nods. This is his story too. To my left is Whitney, her long dark hair swept up in a twist. She is holding my hand tight, and holding back sobs. Her left arm is draped around the young girl beside her, our beloved Marina, our unofficially adopted daughter.

She's ours.

Her hair is long, blond, and beautiful. She's wearing an emerald green silk shirt and black pants—recent gifts from *Tetya Katya* [Auntie Katya]—and square-framed designer glasses that cannot hide her bright eyes.

Marina cradles my two-month-old daughter, Anya, in her arms. She's made it through the entire premiere without a sound. Adanna, her wild three-year-old sister, is asleep with her auntie back at the hotel.

So it is my lot, it seems, to be always surrounded by strong, beautiful women. My blessing. My joy.

A Note from the Publisher

Dear reader,

I well remember where I was when I first read the manuscript you now hold in your hand. I was at home, my surroundings were perfect, and I was sipping a nice cup of tea when I suddenly became enraged. I kept reading, but as I read more and more of Marina's story and remembered that this novel reflected real life, I became even angrier. I remember saying to the author, Tom Davis, "This really makes me mad!"

Reading *Priceless* made me realize how inoculated I have become from the tragic, dark evil that is taking place in others' lives. I recently read that one out of every eight schoolgirls in Russia aspires to be a call girl. Whatever happened to wanting to become a teacher or doctor? More than 200,000 women *and* children from Russia and Eastern Europe are forced into prostitution *every year*. Imagine. The statistics are heartrending. I need not go on. While this is a novel, the characters reflect the tragedy of many women in present-day Russia. I am sure you found some scenes troubling and possibly even wanted to skip over them. Sadly, this is life for far too many. I encourage you to check out the resources listed in the back of this book to see how you—in some small way—can play a part in ending this tragedy.

I can't help but think of the cries of God found in Isaiah 43 where He speaks to the errant children of Israel, *"You are priceless to me. I love you and honor you. So I will trade other people for you. I will give up other nations to save your lives. Do not be afraid. I am with you."* This novel is a timely reminder of the incredible worth of a person's life. I pray you were moved as I was.

Thank you for reading—and sharing,

Don Pape

Publisher, David C. Cook

... a little more ...

When a delightful concert comes to an end,

the orchestra might offer an encore.

When a fine meal comes to an end,

it's always nice to savor a bit of dessert.

When a great story comes to an end,

we think you may want to linger.

And so, we offer ...

AfterWords—just a little something more after you

have finished a David C. Cook novel.

We invite you to stay awhile in the story.

Thanks for reading!

Turn the page for ...

Discussion Questions

Use these questions to spark discussion in your reading group. Want to know the author's thoughts on these questions? Check the section that follows.

1. What sorts of emotions did you experience while reading *Priceless*?

2. What surprised you most about the story? About the characters?

3. Stuart decides early on to help Katya with her mission. What was your initial reaction to this decision? Why would this have been an easy decision for Stuart? Why might it have been difficult? What is our responsibility when we encounter evil in the world?

4. In what ways were the characters of Father Alexander and Sister Irina symbols in this story? What did they represent in the spiritual realm?

5. Why (or how) is Sister Irina essentially "protected" against the evil of the bad men in this story?

6. Who or what was the nameless woman who kept appearing to Stuart, beginning with the conversation on the street after he meets with Sergei and Ivan? What is her purpose in the story?

7. What is your reaction to the subterfuge Stuart had to participate in to free the girls? Is this a case of "the end justifies the means"? Explain.

8. What horrified you most about Marina's plight? In what ways does her escape from the slave trade inspire you? In what way does her story inspire you to take action?

9. What roles does art play in the story?

10. Why do you think Father Alexander related so closely with the icon and character of St. George the Dragonslayer? Based on what the novel reveals about St. George, how might Father Alexander have misread St. George's story?

11. We don't get to see Whitney's reaction to Stuart's dangerous adventure. How might she have responded to his decisions?

12. Vlad is portrayed as a man with a shady past, a past that is not that different from the men he ends up fighting against. What turned him away from the dark side? What does this tell us about God's transformative power?

after words

Author's Responses to Discussion Questions

1. What sorts of emotions did you experience while reading Priceless?

Many, many emotions, and they were all over the map. This is not the easiest type of book to read (or in my case, write). Don't get me wrong, books like *Priceless* must be written and read. It's not acceptable to say that issues like sex trafficking are too painful, so I should just avoid them. I can assure you it's much more painful for the girls who are trafficked.

That said, the research was difficult. Quite often, I would have to put books down after reading a few pages. The brutality of this industry is worse than anything you can imagine. Most things I discovered couldn't even be written in a Christian book.

Pain and heartache stand out as the emotions I felt most. Those emotions then turned into anger, hopefully a righteous anger, which motivated me to do something to make a difference. You can too by the way. (Visit www.SheIsPriceless.com for more details.)

I've been to Russia almost fifty times and have heard so many stories about what happens to kids when they get out of orphanages. Of course Marina's story is one of the worst, but it happens to thousands and thousands of children every year. This is an outrage and our voices need be heard on this issue.

As I write this, I'm one month away from taking a trip to Russia and Moldova to visit some of these beautiful girls who have been rescued. The same emotions apply when I sit down with girls like Marina with the addition of one feeling: hope. Hope didn't exist in the lives of girls caught in this industry; but because someone cared and helped be a part of their freedom, hope has become a reality.

2. What surprised you most about the story? About the characters?

Some of these characters are kids I know, or once knew, so I try to put myself in their situations. What would I do if I were booted out of the only home I knew at fifteen to face a cruel world? How would I respond to a kind lady who offered me a job making more money than I could ever imagine? The answers to those questions drove the book. You and I would make many of the same decisions these characters did.

What surprised me most about the story? Sensing God's broken heart for these scenes as they passed each page and understanding that redemption is found no matter how deep the pit. It seemed like I was always asking the question, "How does God feel about this?"

3. Stuart decides early on to help Katya with her mission. What was your initial reaction to this decision? Why would this have been an easy decision for Stuart? Why might it have been difficult? What is our responsibility when we encounter evil in the world?

Well, if you knew Katya in person, you'd help with her mission too. She's quite compelling! Katya's character is taken from a real person who happens to be the national director for Children's HopeChest in

Russia. In fact, if you go to the book's Web site, www.SheIsPriceless.com, you'll find a video interview with Katya.

Stuart is me, in a sense. In fact, he's everyone who has a heart to rescue the oppressed and see the captive set free. I don't know that he could have made any other decision. What was he going to do? Let those girls go back to be tortured and abused when he had the power to rescue them? No way. Not me, not Stuart. This is more than being a cavalier, John Wayne type of character in a story. It's what the kingdom of God is all about. When we have the power to do good or overcome evil and refuse, we've missed the point of following Jesus.

There's a quote that's had a huge impact on me regarding this issue, as well as issues of apathy that creep up in the lives of Christians:

"The only thing necessary for the triumph of evil is for good men to do nothing." —Edmund Burke

To me, that says it all.

4. In what ways were the characters of Father Alexander and Sister Irina symbols in this story? What did they represent in the spiritual realm?

There's a definite play on the idea of the sacred and the profane throughout the book. One reason is because it can be the sad reality of life. We all live in this tension, and we have to choose how to overcome evil with good. Whether we are aware of it or not, we are making those choices by what we do or don't do.

From a spiritual perspective, it is the cosmic battle between good and evil. I'm a firm believer in this as was C. S. Lewis, who said, "Every square inch of this cosmos is at every moment claimed by Satan and counter-claimed by God."

There is a battle going on that we can't see with our physical eyes. It's a battle for the souls of men, the innocence of little girls who come out of orphanages, for millions of people to have adequate food and water and for God's people to rise up and engage themselves in the world and their communities. Those evil forces are responsible for turning men into the animals they become. They are also the same evil forces that keep us apathetic toward others who suffer. I think this is clearly expressed in Lewis's *The Screwtape Letters*. In this allegory of spiritual realities, the Devil is briefing his demon nephew Wormwood on tempting people. The Devil tells him the objective is not to make people wicked but to make them indifferent. He says, "I the devil will always see to it that there are bad people. Your job, my dear Wormwood, is to provide me with people who do not care."

5. Why (or how) is Sister Irina essentially "protected" against the evil of the bad men in this story?

Sister Irina is "untouchable." This is playing on a physical and spiritual reality. Mr. M represents a very powerful man on earth who utilizes his power to see that nobody harms the Sister, lest serious repercussions come screaming down on their head. But this is also a spiritual reality. God takes care of His own. He provides serious heavenly protection to his sons and daughters who do the work of His kingdom on earth.

Evil can scare us, tempt us, and lead us astray, but Jesus came to "destroy the works of the devil" (1 John 3:8). This issue of sexual slavery is certainly a work of the Devil, and it can be destroyed. That's why God sent His Son. But it takes the people of God understanding this truth, believing it, and implementing it.

6. Who or what was the nameless woman who kept appearing to Stuart, beginning with the conversation on the street after he meets with Sergei and Ivan? What is her purpose in the story?

This wraithlike figure represents evil itself. She's in the background pulling the strings so to speak, influencing the hearts of people and causing calamity everywhere she goes.

She showed up in the worst of scenes intentionally. It was my way of bringing this cosmic battle to life. Of course none of us know exactly how this works, but we do have some indications in Scripture of the reality of the battle. Daniel 10 and Ephesians 6 provide good examples.

Stuart is the force of light in these scenes. Whether he knows it or not, because of who Christ is in him, he has more power than the forces of evil. By stepping out for justice and through prayer and faith, Stuart can make a difference and defeat these powers of wickedness. This is why it's so important in the book that he keeps moving, keeps invading the enemy's territory.

Stuart understands this truth: "Greater is He who is in you than he who is in the world" (1 John 4:4). This is our hope.

7. What is your reaction to the subterfuge Stuart had to participate in to free the girls? Is this a case of "the end justifies the means"? Explain.

No doubt. This is how it works in real life many times. The people who actually rescue girls from the sex industry are constantly going undercover. This is a corrupt, seedy business. You have to fight fire with fire so to speak. Some people would disagree with this, but a legitimate response is for them to get out on the front lines and stop talking about it.

These issues put a burr in my saddle. The people who complain and criticize the most do so from the comfort of their living rooms. That's just not right.

"Apathy is the glove into which evil slips its hand." —Bodie Thoene

8. What horrified you most about Marina's plight? In what ways does her escape from the slave trade inspire you? In what way does her story inspire you to take action?

This is a difficult issue for me to swallow, period. When I think about the horror and injustice of it all, it's overwhelming. This is certainly an area where I wish God would intervene and put an end to the sex trade once and for all. Some things we will never know this side of eternity. But we must fight evil in every place we find it.

I feel like David in the Psalms when he says, "How long, O God, will the adversary revile, and the enemy spurn Your name forever? Why do You withdraw Your hand, even Your right hand? From within Your bosom, destroy them!" (Psalm 74:10–11).

Marina's escape inspires me because when a girl like her is rescued, she is brought from death to life. It's a true resurrection story. As far as the kingdom of God is concerned, this is extremely important business. It's at the core of what Jesus said He came to do in Isaiah 61:1–2: "The Spirit of the Lord GOD is upon me, because the LORD has anointed me to bring good news to the afflicted; He has sent me to bind up the brokenhearted, to proclaim liberty to captives and freedom to prisoners; to proclaim the favorable year of the LORD and the day of vengeance of our God; to comfort all who mourn."

This is our privilege as sons and daughters of the Most High God. We *get* to do this! There isn't anything we could give our lives to that would matter more.

9. What roles does art play in the story?

In this story art represents the beauty inside of each and every child. Children have incredible talents and abilities. They are capable of doing amazing things like painting, writing, or becoming a great leader. It doesn't matter if they are an orphan locked away in some rat hole of an orphanage or a little girl kidnapped and forced to be a sex slave. God created each child with purpose. He knew them before they were born, He knitted them in their mothers' wombs, He loves and cares for them; they are His sons and daughters, just like you and I.

I think this is important to understand because many people look at orphans as the trash of society, cursed, or good for nothing except to be thieves or prostitutes. These are common views orphans face when they get out of an orphanage. This is a lie the enemy spreads in the minds of people, because it furthers his ability to subject them to cruelty and torture. The truth is that God loves them and has created them to be special. They just need help. This is why James says, "Pure and undefiled religion is caring for widows and orphans in their distress" (see James 1:27).

10. Why do you think Father Alexander related so closely with the icon and character of St. George the Dragonslayer? Based on what

the novel reveals about St. George, how might Father Alexander have misread St. George's story?

Father Alexander didn't misread the story of St. George; he perverted it. This is what men and women do who follow darkness. They take something beautiful and pure, like the human body, and they twist and pervert it. He saw the story of St. George and was inspired by it like anyone should be. What could be more courageous than a hero on a horse rescuing a damsel in distress and killing the dragon who enslaves her? There's something inside each one of us that longs to see that happen. We were created to be people who stand in the gap for the innocent who are suffering and rescue them.

I'm thoroughly convinced that if every person who followed Christ would intervene in situations of injustice and do something to change the life of one person, we would solve the biggest problems that plague our world. Children wouldn't starve to death every day due to malnutrition, people wouldn't die from drinking dirty water, there would be no orphans because they would all be adopted into Christian homes, and there would be no children in the sex-trade industry.

11. We don't get to see Whitney's reaction to Stuart's dangerous adventure. How might she have responded to his decisions?

Stuart purposely kept the reality of the situation from Whitney. This wasn't deception on his part; it was protection. If she knew what was really going on, the anxiety would have driven her crazy.

Stuart is in a real dilemma at this juncture in his life. On one hand he wants to go home, live in a perfect world, and love on his wife and child. But he's not in a perfect world. His eyes have been opened to something, and he can't just sit around and pretend like these injustices don't exist.

For me, Stuart is a combination of what we all want to be: courageous and filled with faith. He knows he can't rescue these girls by himself. He needs God's power and protection over his life to make anything happen. But his faith is fueled because he knows how important these children are to God. God longs for them to be rescued, and Stuart knows that God will help in this process—he's not alone.

12. Vlad is portrayed as a man with a shady past, a past that is not that different from the men he ends up fighting against. What turned him away from the dark side? What does this tell us about God's transformative power?

This is the story of redemption. "All of us like sheep have gone astray" (Isaiah 53:6). Vlad has done some things in his life that would make most of us cringe, but even in that state, God loves him and desires to see him repent and be set free. There is even hope for Father Alexander if he would ask for it.

I think this is what makes Vlad such a warm character. What makes him so likable is the fact that he's been to the dark places, he's seen the other side, and it didn't satisfy him. He recognized the lie he was caught in and chose something different. He's one of my favorites!

Author Interview

Your first novel, **Scared,** *was inspired by visits to Africa and the plight of children suffering from the HIV/AIDS crisis there.* **Priceless** *introduces readers to a new location, Russia, and a new evil, the sex-slave industry. What real-life experiences prompted this novel?*

Several things. First, Russia was the place where my heart was broken for orphans. In 1997, I took my wife and eight-month-old son to run a camp for 150 orphans in the Vladimir region. I was never the same after that experience. We met a little orphan girl named Anya who was ten. She became our daughter one year later. When I returned to her orphanage to tell her she was going to be our daughter, a hundred other kids were staring at me with empty looks in their eyes. They were longing for something, something I wasn't sure I could give them. Two little girls burst out of the crowd and hugged my legs as they looked into my eyes and said, "Papa. Papa." I knew they wanted a family. That day I made the decision not to turn my back on the rest of those orphans. Instead, I started asking different questions. What could I do to help their lives be different than what the statistics showed?

I couldn't chalk up those times in Russia as merely more experiences in my journey. The orphans I met and the things I saw were just too important. I had to continue changing my life in such a way that Russian orphans were more a part of it. They deserved a better life than the one they were facing, and I could do something to help change their circumstances. That's exactly what I did.

after words

How much of what you wrote in **Priceless** *is based on true events?*

I would say 80 percent. Marina's story is the story for thousands and thousands of girls in our world. They become trapped in predicaments like this because they have absolutely no one to look after them. Nobody loves them; they are forgotten. Can you imagine what it would be like to believe with certainty that there is no other human being who truly loves you? The hopelessness would be overwhelming.

The pattern is the same for girls coming out of orphanages. They have no place to live, they can't find jobs, and they are easy targets for sexual predators. It's easy to see how they get caught up in this industry. I've done a lot of studying in this area, and once girls are in, it's almost impossible for them to get free without some kind of help. They find themselves in foreign countries where they don't speak the language, their passports are taken from them, they have no money, no way to make phone calls, and they don't personally know anyone in their surroundings. Most are scared to death because they are told if they run away they'll be found and killed, or if they have living relatives, their relatives will be killed.

It's also hard to tell the difference between those who are selling sex because they choose to versus those who are being forced. Once they're in, the only future most of them have to look forward to is an early death or the contraction of a crippling sexual disease that will ruin the rest of their lives. This is absolutely heartbreaking.

Here's a sad fact: When it comes to orphans, the truth of this Scripture is overwhelming. "Be of sober spirit, be on the alert. Your adversary, the devil, prowls around like a roaring lion, seeking someone to devour" (1 Peter 5:8).

The enemy rapes, pillages, destroys, and devours the life of every single orphan he can get his hands on. That's the kind of lowlife he is. He takes advantage of the little orphan girl, because she is helpless to protect herself. There is no natural parental covering, no spiritual covering, rarely even a communal covering. They are caught, all alone, in a blizzard of abuse, and they are exposed to all of the elements. So our enemy devours them.

To devour means to destroy something rapidly and completely. I've seen this too many times in places like Russia and Africa. Currently, there are over 2 million children enslaved to forced prostitution—and this number has drastically increased in the last year. An estimated 171 million children are working in hazardous conditions and with dangerous machinery, forced to work as slaves. Hundreds of thousands of children are caught up in armed conflict as combatants, messengers, porters, cooks, and sex slaves for armed groups. In many cases they have been forcibly abducted.

I firmly believe that the orphan is precious to God. He created them in His image, He loves them, and His heart is broken for them. His answer to this tragedy is *you* and me. We have to utilize our influence, our relationships, and our talents to fight this enemy. As long as we sit on our hands, the enemy will continue to unleash hell and savagely kill the innocent. Dare we continue to just watch it happen?

Why did you choose the Orthodox Church as the setting for this story? And why set up the priest as the bad guy?

Orthodoxy is such a rich part of Russian history. You can't go to Russia without being influenced by the Orthodox Church. The majesty and holiness of God are prevalent in every town and every cathedral. Religious festivals and feast days are observed throughout the year. It's quite beautiful.

However, Russia also has a brutal history. Trusted leaders killed millions of their own people. They imprisoned millions more in arctic death camps in Siberia. The secret police force, called the KGB, would knock on doors in the middle of the night, and husbands and mothers would disappear, never to be heard from again.

Because of that kind of past, I thought that an evil leader would fit the story. Here's a guy that is supposed to be a trusted religious leader. He's even called "Father" by those who attend his church. I had to create a character who was the epitome of evil—the kind of character you love to hate. He is representative of this deceptive sex-slave industry. Sometimes the people you trust are the people you should fear the most.

Marina's story is woven throughout the book, and yet her character is absent in the real-time arc of Stuart's adventure until the very end. What led you to structure the novel this way?

I wanted Marina's story to be the resounding voice in the book because her story is so compelling. But, if I wrote the book only from her point of view, I would be limited in showing the bigger picture. I felt like it was important to see the world through Stuart's eyes because he sees the sex-slave industry from a much different perspective. The question was how to do both. I felt like the best way to show Marina's point of view was to have Stuart do a documentary on her story.

This point-of-view issue in stories drives me up a wall at times to be honest. Maybe it's the ADD in me, but I always want two perspectives in the story.

What sort of reactions do you expect from people who read **Priceless***? What do you hope the book accomplishes?*

I want people to be educated, shocked, and motivated to get involved and make a difference. This is a bit harder of an issue to get involved in than, say, children starving or needing clean water. So if reading *Priceless* has disturbed you enough to do something, we've made it easy to get involved.

Go to www.SheIsPriceless.com. We are helping rehabilitate girls who have been rescued by providing safe places for them to live where they are loved and cared for. These are long-term homes run by professional counselors and staff who help these priceless girls rebuild their lives. You can be a part of that. Also on the site is information about projects we have in Russia and Africa that keep girls from becoming victims of the sex trade. Go there to learn more about Ministry Centers, Family Centers, and Independent Living Programs.

You write both fiction and nonfiction on the plight of children around the globe. In what ways are the goals of these two types of books different? In what ways are they the same? Which is easier to write? Explain.

The goals are the same. I want people to feel God's passion for the plight of the orphan, the captive, the widow, the oppressed, and the poor. My hope is that people will see the world differently after reading these books and that they will truly live compassionately. That's easier said than done.

I think most of us would believe we are compassionate people, but the real meaning of the word *compassion* is "to suffer with." There's a different spin when you understand the word that way. To truly live compassionately, we have to get out of the boat of our normal lives and get in the boat with people who are in need. That can be difficult, painful, and time consuming. But God promises that when we obey Him in this area, our lives will be blessed beyond measure.

Nonfiction is a breeze for me compared to fiction. Nonfiction books are linear. I write a chapter, edit, and move on to the next. Many times, I won't even go back to those chapters once they're done. Fiction is a completely different bird. Every word written in the first chapter has to tie in to the rest of the entire book. It's more like a work of art. Writing fiction has taught me how to really pay attention to detail. As I mentioned before, I tend to be a bit ADD, so that doesn't come naturally.

Where do you go next with your fiction?

Right now, the third book in this Novel on the Edge of the World series looks like it will be a book set in Haiti. Stuart decides to take an assignment with the United Nations on the water crisis, because so many people die in that country from water-borne diseases. He is in Port-au-Prince on January 12, 2010, when a devastating earthquake strikes and he's caught in the rubble of his hotel. I can't wait to write this book!

after words

Recommended Charitable Organizations List

For more information on how you can help stop child trafficking, visit these organizations online:

Children's HopeChest — www.HopeChest.org

iEmpathize — www.iEmpathize.org

Not For Sale — www.NotForSaleCampaign.org

International Justice Mission — www.IJM.org

Stop Child Trafficking Now — www.SCTNow.org

help
wanted.

She was promised a glamorous job in another country.
Now, she's enslaved in a child brothel. Raped multiple times a day.
Two million children share this horror.
They need your help. **Stop the Slavery.**

www.SheIsPriceless.com

(the child in the photo is not a victim of sex trafficking)

iEMPATHIZE

CHILD SEX TRAFFICKING The trafficking of persons is **modern-day slavery**, involving victims who are forced, defrauded, or coerced into labor or sexual exploitation. **8.4 million children are in slavery, 1.2 million** children are trafficked yearly. 2 children per minute are trafficked for sexual exploitation. Up to **300,000 prostituted children** live on the streets in the U.S. **Billions of dollars** are generated yearly.

IEMPATHIZE (iE) is an arts and advocacy organization (501c3) whose mission is to bring light to the darkest areas of injustice affecting children while providing individuals, universities, businesses, and communities of faith the opportunity to become a part of the solution. Proceeds from iE advocacy events sustain child protection, rescue, and aftercare solutions throughout Asia, Eastern Europe, Mexico, and the U.S.

RESEARCH We investigate the causes and effects, get to know the victims, and then we identify those organizations having demonstrable success in combating the problem.

PARTNER We create working relationships with frontline organizations who are making significant strides in eliminating the issue.

COMMUNICATE Using a mix of film, photography, sound, and artifacts, we create immersive exhibits and events. These Empathy Experiences help individuals to engage the reality of the issue.

GUIDE We provide pathways for individuals and businesses to put their resources where they will be most effective.

RESOURCE We direct funds to field partners, addressing their needs and aiding in the expansion of successful programs.

EXPLORE AND ENGAGE

1. Educate yourself and others on the issue of human trafficking. Use our "Explore the Issue" Web tool at www.iEmpathize.org to understand the issue.

2. Justice Personality Profile Take the profile at www.iEmpathize.org to find out whether you are a prevention, an intervention, or a restoration personality. Find practical suggestions of how your specific personality might best engage in justice issues.

3. Partner with iE iE has a myriad of innovative events and programs specifically designed to immerse the public in the issue and engage individuals, businesses, universities, and communities of faith. Contact us for more information!

Visit **www.iEmpathize.org** to explore our media, advocacy programs, Web tools, blog, links, and more. You may also sign up for our e-letter, view the calendar, and contribute.

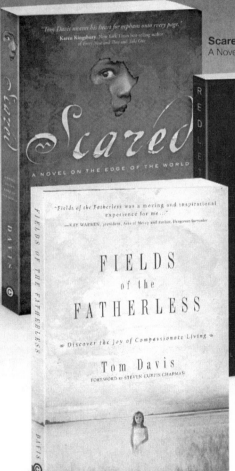